SHADOW'S FATE

SHADOW ISLAND SERIES: BOOK SIXTEEN

MARY STONE

LORI RHODES

MARY
STONE
PUBLISHING

To all the storytellers who have passed down folk tales through the ages, keeping the shadows alive and the things that go bump in the night ever so near. Your tales have woven fear and wonder into the fabric of our imaginations. Thank you for keeping those fires burning.

DESCRIPTION

Death is only the beginning.

Shadow Island is a wreck. Buildings lay in rubble, construction crews swarm the island, and the aftermath of the Yacht Club Massacre has left many dead. But at least Sheriff Rebecca West put an end to the violence against young girls by dismantling the elite men's club.

Or so she thought.

When a teenage girl is found stabbed and half-buried in a makeshift grave at the local cemetery, her arms carved with occult symbols, whispers of dark rituals and black magic spread through the community. The victim's friends insist she died from the legendary witch's curse. But when a second girl is violently murdered, Rebecca fears a far more sinister—and human—threat.

Unfortunately, the witch's curse isn't the only myth refusing to stay buried. And the teen's corpse only scratches the surface of the horrors lurking beneath the cemetery.

Shadow's Fate, the bewitching sixteenth installment of the Shadow Island Series by Mary Stone and Lori Rhodes, is a testament that there are, indeed, fates worse than death.

1

The rhythmic sound of the bike chain grew louder as Whitney Turner neared the Old Witch's Cottage, her pulse quickening with each passing moment. Frigid air whipped at her face as she pedaled through the deserted streets, her breath a misty cloud in the darkness.

In the distance, the ocean's roar rose and fell in accompaniment to the hum of her tires on the cracked pavement.

Navigating the dark streets, Whitney mentally replayed the day. It had started horribly when she'd overslept. Later, when she'd nominated herself to be the leader of the coven, she'd angered some of the members.

If they're willing to meet now, then all must be forgiven, right?

Negative thoughts broke through her hopefulness. As soon as her mom had come home from work, she'd lit into Whitney about her grades. It wasn't fair, really, that her mom could let everything fall through the cracks, but if Whitney's grades dipped even a smidge, there was hell to pay.

Releasing a huge sigh into the frosty air, she feverishly pedaled toward her clandestine meeting, not wanting to be late. She imagined her friends huddled together, sharing confidences under the cover of darkness as they waited for her arrival. A thrill ignited within her chest, warming her from the inside out.

But it was an awfully cold night for a secret meeting. Whitney's fingers grew numb around her handlebars. "Just my luck." The last week of November was usually pretty chilly, but this was ridiculous.

No. Stay positive. Manifest the life you want.

The small-town island landscape stretched before her, its secrets lying hidden beneath the shadowy veil of night. This town held so many buried truths, some of which had only recently come to light. And the secrets of the old witch, the island's original inhabitant, remained shrouded in mystery.

As Whitney's thoughts returned to the fight earlier that day, she wondered if this secret gathering had anything to do with it.

This would be the perfect chance for everyone involved in the coven to come together and talk things out rationally. She recalled other late-night rendezvous where they'd done the same thing.

I guess I'll find out soon enough.

As the Old Witch's Cottage came into view, moonlight draped its weathered exterior in an ethereal glow. Whitney's heart raced with excitement, and something else. She couldn't shake her uneasy feeling, like a whispered warning from the wind itself.

The rustic cottage was familiar, since she and her friends had started meeting there to practice their witchy hobby. Of course, most of the kids on the island knew the place. It was a rite of passage to hang out there or take some lame dare inside.

The hard-packed dirt floor was cool year-round, and a breeze blew through the doorless entry. In the summer, it was a comfortable place to beat the heat. Whitney loved the fireplace, though the mantel was long gone. The cops had taken that after two people literally lost their heads in there.

Whitney dismounted her bike and scanned the area for any sign of her friends. There were no cars or bikes in sight, which wasn't surprising. She and the other local kids knew to hide their rides to avoid getting caught when they hung out at the old structure at night.

After all, the cottage was off-limits, no matter the time of day.

As usual, Whitney laid her bike against one of the nearby trees, hiding it in the wet, thick piles of fallen leaves. But despite her attempts to reassure herself, the place was unnervingly empty.

She checked her phone, the screen reflecting her worried eyes. It was 10:35 p.m. The meeting should've started five minutes ago, yet there was no one in sight. If she'd been able to drive, she might've arrived on time, but her parents wouldn't let her get a car until she went to college.

Guess I'm not the only one running late. Or maybe they're all inside already.

She glanced around once more before approaching the cottage, her footsteps hushed from the damp ground as the wind continued its mournful serenade.

The only barrier keeping her or anyone out was a simple chain stretched tight between two posts in front of the empty doorway. It was the laughingstock of the island.

Like a chain will ever stop anyone.

As she stepped over it, the metal links caught against the rubber sole of her shoe. She stumbled forward into the cottage before catching her balance.

Whitney was very short for her age. The growth spurt her mom promised would come with puberty was still a distant dream. Everything about her figure was childlike, and she hated it. She could deal with being shorter than everyone, but her flat chest and baby face were too much. While all the other girls were turning the boys' heads, Whitney wasn't even on their radar.

Despite the building consisting only of one simple, single room, Whitney couldn't see to the back of the cottage. Though she knew every inch of the cottage very well, the darkness still played tricks on her. Shadows danced across the walls as night clouds raced through the sky overhead.

The men who'd run the town back when the cottage was inhabited had deliberately built the lighthouse to cast a shadow on the witch's cottage after she'd refused to sell her home to them. Natural light rarely made it inside the Old Witch's Cottage after that. As payback, she cursed the island and all those who lived there before she died.

"Anyone who steps foot in the shadow cast on her house will be cursed."

That was how the old legend went, at least.

Whitney shivered.

But it was the legend of the curse that had led to her making new friends and finding a spiritual practice she loved so much. Studying witchcraft on her own had been hard, and now she'd found other girls with similar interests. Even if it required her to sneak out of the house at night to meet up with them.

A breeze gusted through the open doorway at her back, sending her chin-length black hair swirling around her face. Unsettled by the scent of seawater and burned wood carried by the wind, Whitney realized she wanted to go home.

For the first time in this hallowed place, she felt… unwelcome. But her friends had said they would meet her here.

"Hello?" Whitney's voice barely overcame the radio of the

wind. Her breathing was shallow, and the hairs on the back of her neck stood on end.

No response.

"Anyone here?" She took a tentative step forward, her sneaker scuffing the hard-packed earthen floor. There were no floorboards to creak or trip on. Only the silent ground beneath her feet. A flash of anger made her toes tingle, and she kicked the dirt in frustration.

Where the heck is everyone?

Heart pounding in her chest, she ventured farther into the small cottage, the dirt floor deadening each footfall and squelching her hope. Her pulse throbbed in her ears, drowning out all other sounds.

Had her friends come and then left for some reason? Maybe the cops had caught them and sent them on their way.

Whitney ignored the darker thoughts and fears. According to the rumors, there were a lot of reasons to be afraid of the dark on Shadow Island.

The clouds blocking the moonlight cast even more shadows than usual. It played tricks on her eyes, making her see shapes that weren't there.

Or were they?

Maybe they're just pulling a prank. Trying to scare me after the fight earlier. Or maybe they're testing me to see if I have the guts to be the leader. Yeah, I bet that's it.

A leader should be fearless and not just the person who decided to form the group. Blair shouldn't get to boss everyone around. That wasn't what a good leader did anyway.

Whitney walked blindly forward with both hands out in front of her and didn't stop 'til she touched the back wall of the room. Using her hands to guide her, she followed the wall to each corner. No one was there hiding in the dark to watch her or gauge her bravery.

An uneasy feeling settled in her stomach like a stone, growing heavier with each passing second. She checked her phone once again. Five minutes had passed. Maybe one of them was having to drive around to pick up the others? That made the most sense.

"Fine. I'll just wait for them out front." She spoke out loud in an effort to chase away the unnerving silence. "They'll show up eventually."

As she retraced her steps, a sudden movement caught her eye. A figure had stepped out from the shadows of the yard and filled the open doorway. Whitney's heart leaped into her throat until the figure leaned forward and a fleeting bit of moonlight illuminated them.

"Finally!" Whitney laughed, relief washing over her as she recognized the familiar face of her friend. "What took you so long? I've been waiting here for ages."

"Sorry, I got held up."

"Is everyone else already here?" Whitney looked around for any sign of the others.

"Actually, it's just us."

"Us? Nobody rode with you? I didn't hear a car." Whitney bent over and grabbed the chain that spanned the doorway to the cottage, using it for balance. She stepped over, hoping this maneuver would prevent her from falling on her face. She had to twist her body, turning to face the cottage again, as she raised her trailing leg over the nuisance chain.

Before she could set her foot down, pain like a shock of electricity pierced Whitney's back, knocking the breath out of her.

For a tiny moment, Whitney felt embarrassed that she'd somehow managed to hurt herself doing such a simple thing, but then the pain struck again and again, this time lower on her back.

Whitney turned her head, her gaze stopping on a bloody knife in her friend's hand. "Wh-why?" She could barely speak. It felt like there was no air in her lungs, yet her breathing was rapid. Her vision blurred as she grew dizzy and lightheaded. She was suffocating.

As she collapsed, she bounced off the taut chain, landing face down on the dirt floor back inside the cottage after all.

"You were warned. Anyone who crosses the coven must face the witch's wrath."

Darkness closed in around Whitney. The howling wind mocked her as she gasped for air, and the cold, jeering chill of the cottage bore witness to her final moments.

2

Things are looking up on Shadow Island.

Navigating through the familiar streets of Shadow Island, Sheriff Rebecca West could have punched herself in the face. Not ten minutes earlier, she'd been watching the sheriff's station being rebuilt after some assholes had nearly blown it apart. She'd been thrilled that Meg Darby had woken from her coma. Yeah...things *had* been looking up.

That sense of hope hadn't lasted long.

Feeling as if she'd jinxed her small island with her hopeful thoughts, Rebecca tightened her hands on the steering wheel as she drove toward Oceanview Cemetery, where the body of a teenager had been found only minutes earlier.

The destruction left in the wake of recent events still marred the landscape. A couple of buildings awaited repairs, while others were in various stages of reconstruction.

The Yacht Club leaders, knowing their time was up, had one of their assassins plant random pipe bombs around town to cause a distraction. The chaos of the explosions was an attempt to get a shot at their true target, the last survivor of the Yacht Club.

Rebecca had seen through the ruse and managed to rescue one person from what the media had dubbed the Yacht Club Massacre. They'd only had one survivor...but they only needed one to provide testimony on years of misdeeds by the Aqua Mafia.

The Yacht Club was eliminated, but the town was a mess. Construction crews swarmed the area like bees around a hive. At least they weren't reporters. Those vultures had harassed Rebecca and her deputies relentlessly but had finally moved on to fresher stories. Only one straggler had remained, still pestering her only moments before she took the call about the body. She hoped he wouldn't have a reason to stick around.

She couldn't wait for the station to be rebuilt so she could go back to lying low in her office instead of using her cruiser as her place of solitude during business hours.

Since the first explosion—which had taken out one of the walls at the station in a jailbreak that had freed her ex-boyfriend and killed a prisoner on his cot—she and all the deputies under her command had been unofficially using Deputy Trent Locke's house as their makeshift home base. It wasn't ideal, but it served its purpose.

Rebecca parked the cruiser at the entrance to Oceanview Cemetery and surveyed the area. In the distance, her deputy, Jake Coffey, was almost done sectioning off a large area with bright-yellow crime scene tape.

The wind picked up, rattling the leafless twigs on the trees and sending a chill down her spine. Things were about to get complicated. She just knew it.

Grabbing the camera from the glove box, Rebecca climbed out of her cruiser. She stepped through the cemetery gates, gravel crunching beneath her boots as she approached Jake. By the time she caught up with him, he'd completed cordoning off the area and stood solemnly next to a fairly new headstone.

The body of a teenage girl lay face down in front of him, her forearms and hands a bluish gray, which contrasted sharply with the blood on the back of her pink hoodie and the trails down her sides. She wore faded jeans also streaked and smeared with maroon. From the pattern of the dried blood, the girl had been wrapped in something after she'd been killed and then brought here.

The myriad stab wounds covering the girl's back indicated a brutal, merciless attack. And a cowardly one. Stabbing someone in the back was a metaphor for betrayal.

Adding to the horror, the killer had mutilated her body with symbols crudely cut into her arms.

One good thing was that she was fully and correctly clothed. While it wasn't proof the girl hadn't been sexually assaulted, she'd been killed while dressed, at least. Sometimes, the silver linings were microscopic, but that never stopped Rebecca from looking for them.

Reluctant to disturb the hushed silence that hung over the scene, Rebecca spoke quietly. "What have you got so far, Coffey?"

"I don't have a lot to report, honestly. I got here just moments before you. All I've done is call the medical examiner and put up the tape." Jake's pale-blue eyes, which always reminded her of a husky, flicked up before darting down to the disturbed dirt he was standing beside. He looked tired, which made sense.

The beginning of the month had been brutal for everyone. The Yacht Club's reign was finally over, but that triumph did little to alleviate the pain. All of them were still reeling from the death of Deputy Greg Abner, though Hoyt and Trent had taken it hardest.

The loss of another deputy under her supervision layered

more weight on Rebecca's burdened shoulders. She was still trying to come to grips with the fact that her ex-boyfriend had been using their relationship to conspire against her. It would take countless therapy sessions to parse through those complex emotions.

Rebecca shook her head to clear her mind. The last thing she needed was to be distracted when there was another murder case, especially one involving a teenage girl, since they had for so long been targeted by the now-vanquished Yacht Club. Beyond finding justice for the victim, she needed to uncover any lingering connections to the defeated group.

Overcoming Ryker's betrayal couldn't be for nothing.

She ran her gaze up and down the body. "My initial thoughts are that someone who felt compelled to stab another person from behind could be smaller and need the element of surprise to succeed, though the victim herself is small. Or the killer could know the person and was unable to face her while taking her life."

"Or," Jake joined in, "it could be the act of someone who wasn't in their right mind, and they put no thought into the attack at all."

Rebecca couldn't argue with that. Speculation was all they had at this early stage. "In any case, a monster inflicted violence on a young woman."

The rampant violence against teenage girls in the region was supposed to stop after Rebecca and her team dismantled the Yacht Club. At least, that had been her hope.

The girl's body rested next to a partially excavated grave, like someone was planning to dump the teenager into the hole, bury her, and traipse away with no one the wiser. "Looks like they were digging," Rebecca looked at the headstone, "into the grave of…Betsy Taylor?"

"Yeah, I think this is probably a secondary crime scene. There're no blood pools around her body. To me, it looks like a body dump, but," he gestured to the fence within throwing distance, "they either weren't sure what to do, got scared by something, or just gave up and left. Digging graves is hard work."

"But why did they stop?" Rebecca murmured the question more to herself than to Coffey. Crouching, she found no shovels in sight, though there was a mass of churned dirt where the dug-up soil had been deposited next to the girl's corpse. Grave dirt spilled over onto her ankles.

The teen's short black hair was blowing away from her pale profile. Her features were so soft, so young, and her petite frame seemed even more fragile in death. A pang of sadness for the life brutally cut short shot through Rebecca, and she wondered how old the girl was. "Work on sketching the area. I'll take the photos."

"Got it." Jake nodded, turning back to his task. "Dispatch said the M.E. is finishing up another scene, so we have some time before she arrives."

Rebecca retrieved her camera from her belt and began shooting pictures of the body, focusing on close shots of the girl's arms, which stuck forward straight over her head.

The victim looked like she'd been wrapped in something, dragged to this area, unrolled, and dumped here. Though her clothes were twisted on her frame, they were mostly devoid of mud and leaves and other debris, their relative cleanness indicating a somewhat pristine journey to her final resting spot.

Nor did her body get sullied at the grave site. She still must have been wrapped in a blanket when the perpetrator started digging. Otherwise, her body would have picked up some of the dirt that went flying.

The perplexing issue of why the perpetrator had stopped mid-burial made Rebecca's brain itch.

When Rebecca examined the occult-looking symbols

carved into the girl's arms, her stomach churned. Among the symbols, she recognized a pentagram, a five-pointed star often associated with dark rituals and black magic.

"God, I hope we're not dealing with some sick, twisted cult." She tried to suppress the shiver that ran down her spine. "Again." The last cult member she'd hunted down liked to paint messages in blood and feces and flay his victims, and he'd decorated himself with leeches like some kind of living beard. Rebecca still remembered the feel of the leech exploding against her knuckles when she'd fought the guy.

"Me too." Jake had been with the state police for that case and had been the one to record her after-action report, such as it was. He knew firsthand how that case had ended, including that she'd managed to brain herself during the fight, leaving her too concussed to give her statement. "This island has seen enough horror."

Rebecca studied the girl's profile as best she could. It was a small town, and she had sadly spent a lot of work hours looking into the lives of the local teens, but she couldn't decide if she'd seen this one before. "Does she look familiar to you?"

Jake shook his head. "Well, it's harder to tell with her lying face down. But I can't say she does. Then again, I haven't been here as long as you. I still don't know most of the locals."

"Neither do I." Rebecca sighed, frustrated.

With everything that had happened recently, it was hard to focus on socializing. But she needed to remain sharp to bring justice to this young victim and restore peace to their community.

"Strange, isn't it?" She nodded toward the corpse. "No one's reported a missing teen. It's already past noon. Maybe she went missing this morning?"

"It's been at least a few hours. But sometimes it takes a

while to realize someone's missing. Her parents could think she's out with friends or something."

"That tracks. Body's already cold and gray, and her limbs are fairly rigid." Rebecca gingerly tried to lift the girl's arm with gloved hands.

"If she went missing this morning, then it was real early." Jake cast his eyes over the scene. "And I don't see a phone or wallet anywhere. Or a backpack or purse. It was either left wherever she was killed, or the killer took it."

"Could be."

As Rebecca glanced around the cemetery, the cold November wind whipped her hair across the side of her face despite its being pulled back into a ponytail. The desolate landscape seemed to mirror the darkness that had settled over Shadow Island in recent weeks.

She studied the semi-opened grave beside the dead girl. "I wonder why they picked this grave. It's close to the edge but not the closest."

"You think Betsy Taylor might be significant?" Jake gestured to the headstone.

"We can't overlook any detail. Even though a possible connection isn't obvious to us, it's worth exploring."

"Also, did you notice the drag mark?" Jake pointed to the trail on the ground where the grass had been scraped flat. It led from the parking lot to the victim.

"Her positioning suggests she was dragged, maybe in a tarp or blanket." Rebecca gazed down the length of flattened grass. "We should follow the trail and look for fibers."

"That'll be tough in this wind."

Rebecca shrugged. "We'll give it a shot." She turned back toward their victim. "My guess is they unrolled her, and she landed here. But I keep pondering why they stopped digging. Why drag her all the way over here and then just quit?" Stretching, Rebecca stood, pointing toward the fence.

"I suppose they could have been tired. One hundred pounds of dead weight is still a lot."

"True…" When she looked back down at the body, something else captured her attention. She froze, narrowing her eyes.

The digging had stopped only a few feet down. In a cemetery, the only thing that should've been in the soil would be worms, maybe some pebbles. Perhaps a few twigs.

That's not a rock.

Rebecca squatted. Just below the churned-up dirt was the eye socket of a human skull, staring up from its grave, a witness to an unknown horror.

Another dead body.

And one that should not have been there. Bodies were legally required to be buried in a suitable casket. Plus, they were ensconced deep below the earth's surface, not just a few feet down. At least at this cemetery. And yet, she wasn't completely surprised.

This once-hallowed ground held so many secrets. Secrets she'd suspected would get exhumed one day, thanks to the Dwight Stokely case. Stokely had been an assassin who paid off the last caretaker to dispose his victims here.

It looked like this young woman's killer had found one of Stokely's victims. That probably explained why their perpetrator stopped digging. Rebecca would bet money their killer was inexperienced. They took one look at this skull in the middle of the night, its empty sockets staring up at them, and booked it.

Hell, if she hadn't seen so much death, she'd probably run away too.

"Coffey?"

"Yeah, Boss?"

"Did you notice this second body?"

Jake jolted and spun around. "What?"

"There's another resident in this grave. Betsy Taylor has company." Rebecca lifted the camera and started taking pictures of the three-by-three-foot hole, focusing on the little bit of skull she could see. "Because of course nothing is ever simple here."

"Son of a…" Jake dragged a hand down his face.

Rebecca rubbed her temples as she tried to push away the headache that threatened to bloom. This scene was beyond complicated. She had two secondary crimes scenes in the same six-foot area. "We'll have to wait for the M.E. and her team. Could you call Bailey and update her on this new discovery?"

"Will do, Boss. I'm sorry I didn't see that before."

"You got here two whole seconds before me." Rebecca waved him off as she resumed taking pictures of the twice-defiled grave. "I looked at this at least twice before I figured out what I was seeing. Besides, you were securing the crime scene around the grave in a public space."

"I haven't had a chance to check our victim's pockets for any identification. Should we wait for the medical examiner?"

"No, let's see if she has anything on her. I've photographed every inch of her from this angle, so we should be okay." Rebecca carefully reached into the back pockets of the girl's jeans. One was empty, but the other held a crumpled receipt.

"Any luck?"

She smoothed out the paper. "It's from I Scream You Scream. It's dated yesterday."

"Want me to follow up on the I Scream lead?" Jake held out an evidence bag, and Rebecca dropped the paper inside.

"Let me check her other pockets first." Rebecca snaked her hand under the victim and reached into both front pockets. Nothing. "Coffey, does it strike you as odd that a teenage girl would go anywhere without her phone?"

"I'm not well-versed on what teenage girls are up to." He held his hands up. "If I'm honest, I didn't understand them all that well when I was a teenager myself. But if the killer knows her, that'd be a good reason to keep her phone."

"Right. Incriminating text messages and photos. Or it got lost somewhere between wherever she was killed and here." Rebecca surveyed the cemetery as if the answers would present themselves. But she knew it wouldn't be that simple. "Let's find the groundskeeper. We need to know more about this grave."

"We'll follow the drag trail and see if we spot any fibers. However unlikely."

Jake and Rebecca set off on a circuitous route toward the cemetery office. As they walked, Rebecca's thoughts turned inward, her mind a whirlwind of questions and worries. What kind of person would commit such a heinous act, carving up a young woman's lifeless body and leaving it to be discovered in a place meant for quiet reflection and mourning?

"Are you okay, Boss?" The concern was evident in Jake's voice.

"Is anyone these days?" Rebecca gave a wry chuckle, trying to inject some humor into the situation. "But, yes, I'm fine. Just…angry, and tired of seeing things like this."

3

___

Cold wind blew through Oceanview Cemetery, rustling the freshly fallen leaves that blanketed the ground. It quickly became obvious that searching for any fibers would be fruitless.

Rebecca pulled her jacket tighter, the chill seeping into her bones as she and Jake navigated the maze of headstones. Their footsteps crunched on the damp leaves, the only sound in this quiet corner of Shadow Island.

"Great day to meet the caretaker," Rebecca muttered.

"Isn't it?" Jake grimaced at the gray sky overhead. "Let's just hope he's a nicer guy than the last one."

Considering the last caretaker had been paid to illegally dispose of bodies whenever the Yacht Club's assassin needed to hide a victim, Rebecca wondered how the new guy could possibly be worse.

Then she hoped she hadn't jinxed herself.

If there was one thing she'd learned in the last year, things could always get worse. That was a lesson she'd been reminded of just minutes ago, with the discovery of the partially unearthed skull.

Rebecca's gaze roamed over the eclectic mix of tombstones and monuments, wondering what stories they'd tell if they could speak. Hundreds of years were represented in the pockmarked and smooth, the short and tall, the generic and extravagant. If there'd been a plan for the plots when they were laid out, she couldn't see it.

They were here for answers, but the cemetery seemed to only offer more questions. She shook off the chill creeping up her spine and focused on finding the new caretaker, who'd replaced Abe Barclay after his untimely death.

As they rounded a tall monument, Rebecca spotted a man in the distance, raking leaves. His movements were methodical, dragging the rake through the sea of reds, oranges, and yellows surrounding him.

"Looks like we've found our guy." She nodded toward the figure.

"Seems so." Jake squinted at the man.

Rebecca took the lead and approached the caretaker. The man looked up from his raking, and their eyes locked. She noted a flicker of curiosity in his raised eyebrows.

"Hello." Rebecca's voice cut through the crisp autumn air. "We'd like to speak with you for a moment."

The man held his rake in the crook of his arm and wiped his brow with the back of his hand. He walked over, relief and anxiety seeming to war within him. "Oh, thank goodness."

"Hi, there. I'm Sheriff Rebecca West, and this is Deputy Jake Coffey. Are you the person who called about the body?" Rebecca tapped her badge.

"Nice to meet you. I'm Graham Ricky, the new caretaker. Yep, it was me. That poor girl…" The man scratched his beard. "I'm grateful you got here so quickly."

"Thanks, Mr. Ri—"

"Graham is fine."

"The body you found isn't the only thing we want to ask you about, Graham." Rebecca wondered how much this man knew about his predecessor. Gossip traveled fast in small towns, especially when it was about someone well-loved or universally disliked. And she hadn't met anyone who had liked Abe. "I'm assuming you didn't touch the victim."

"Lord, no." Graham whipped his head side to side, clutching the handle of his rake. "I saw her lying there, with her eyes open...she looked so dead, and that's when I took off. That much blood on her clothes, I knew what I was looking at. Didn't even think to call 'til I was out of sight. Maybe that makes me sound weak or bad. I don't know." He ran his hand over his mouth. "But I just couldn't look at that poor kid without feeling sick."

"So you didn't see what was next to her?" Rebecca pushed gently, noticing Graham's skin tone taking on a slightly gray hue as he continued to cling to his rake handle.

"No." He gulped, then gasped, as if he had swallowed down the wrong pipe. "Don't tell me she wasn't dead yet and I could have saved her."

"No, nothing like that. But it appears whoever brought her out here had been trying to bury her in one of the existing graves. And there was another body in that grave."

Graham scrunched up his face in confusion, pushing his lips out slightly. "Bodies are in every grave?" He uptilted the end of his sentence, making it more like a question. "That's what makes them graves instead of holes."

"This was someone buried over the body in the coffin that's supposed to be there. This second body was dumped."

Jake held up his hands, spacing them two feet apart. "Not to mention, this other body was just a couple of feet below the surface."

As Graham's eyes widened in surprise, Rebecca observed

that his shock seemed genuine. "Oh, my...I had no idea. So the stories about that bastard Abe Barclay are true? He was burying murder victims? Dang, I thought that was just a nasty rumor started about him because he was such a jerk to everyone."

It appeared the new caretaker was, in fact, quite up-to-date on the exploits of his predecessor.

"He was doing something like that, yeah. Did you know him? Are you local?" Rebecca was keen to understand more about the man who now tended this troubled ground.

"Wasn't born here, but I've lived here about ten years. I don't think I ever met Abe. Got this job about a week after he was gone. He's not buried here, by the way. I checked." Graham rubbed the back of his neck. "I've done odd jobs around the island, but when this opportunity came up, I jumped at it. Landscaping always brought me peace, and working here...well, it's usually a peaceful place."

"Did you work here yesterday? If so, what time did you leave?" Rebecca watched Graham, looking for any signs of deception.

"I did work, left around five, and I didn't come back until about nine this morning." His voice was still tinged with unease, but his color seemed to be evening out. "I found that poor girl about an hour ago and called it in right away. I was at a bar last night. You can check with the bartender if you need to."

"Thank you for that information." Rebecca made a mental note to follow up on his alibi. "Now, Graham, could you tell us about the grave where the bodies were found?"

"I'd have to look it up. You can follow me." Graham led them to the small, weathered building near the edge of the cemetery. This wasn't the work shed she'd visited before, but an actual little office. Inside, stacks of yellowed papers and dusty binders filled the cramped space. He flipped through a large ledger, running his finger along the lines of text, searching for the answer.

"Here it is." He pointed to an entry. "Betsy Taylor was buried in that spot about a year ago. She was interred in a casket, just like any other burial."

"Are there any records of the grave being disturbed since then?" Jake peered over Graham's shoulder.

"None that I can see. But then, I'm not sure that information would be in these." Graham double-checked the pages. "Everything seems to be in order."

"Does the cemetery have surveillance cameras?" Rebecca had a fleeting hope that some might've been installed after the past issues with Abe.

"Unfortunately, no." Graham sighed.

Rebecca felt a pang of frustration but forced herself to remain focused. "Thank you, Mr. Ricky. Graham." She exited the office, bracing herself against the cold breeze blowing through the trees. "We appreciate your assistance."

"Of course. Happy to assist in any way I can, Sheriff." Graham shook Rebecca's hand firmly, a pleasant change from the misogynistic Abe Barclay.

As they walked away, Rebecca glanced back at the caretaker. He'd resumed working, his shoulders hunched against the cold as he raked up the dead leaves.

"All right, let's try to make sense of all this." She rubbed her arms as the chill autumn air nipped at her exposed skin. "We have two bodies. One freshly murdered girl and an older, coffinless body, buried shallowly."

Jake repeated his first theory. "Seems like someone was trying to dispose of the girl's corpse by burying it here. But when they started digging, they discovered another body already hidden in the grave."

"Sounds about right." Rebecca's eyes narrowed as she considered the possibilities. "But what are the odds of choosing the exact same spot? Unless Dwight Stokely hid way more victims than we thought. We still have no idea how many people he killed."

"We didn't ever figure out how long he'd been killing. It could be one of his. Or maybe someone else who worked for the Yacht Club before him. This could be their usual dumping spot for most of their victims." Jake grimaced. "Other than the ones they simply tossed into the ocean. But that still doesn't explain the girl's murder. It seems unrelated."

"True. But we can't ignore that there might be a connection. This could also be one of the hired assassins the Yacht Club used. Someone who's acting on their own now. But then why would a professional just stop halfway through? It's not like a pro would freak out at the sight of another skull and leave the job half-finished." Rebecca's mind raced with theories and possibilities.

The killer could've been interrupted, meaning the unearthed skull wasn't the cause of their leaving. Regardless, she felt there was something inexperienced about the way the teen girl was left. Her abandonment stood in stark contrast to the mystery body below the surface. Perhaps because she knew Dwight Stokely had used the former groundskeeper to conceal his victims in the cemetery, the placement of the unidentified skull struck her as more organized and strategic.

Though the skull peered at them over the dirt from barely deep enough to avoid detection, even a little erosion from another hurricane wouldn't have unearthed them. Just the necessary amount of work had gone into hiding these remains and not an ounce more.

"Maybe the dump spots are just a wild coincidence?" Jake sounded dubious even as he spoke, but his thoughts clearly echoed her own. "But that seems unlikely. Pardon the pun, but I think we need to dig deeper. Find out if there are any more hidden graves or connections to Barclay and Stokely."

Rebecca smirked at his humor as they circled back to Graham Ricky. The scent of damp earth and decaying foliage hung heavy in the air.

"Graham!" At Rebecca's call, the caretaker paused his chore once more. "We think there might be more hidden graves here in the cemetery. Is there any way for us to find them without digging up the whole place?"

She could think of a few ways to go about this but wanted to see what Graham would suggest. The man would be less likely to protest the cemetery being overrun with law enforcement personnel if he thought the idea was his own. No one liked cops interfering with their jobs.

Graham pondered for a moment before snapping his fingers. "You know, I've heard about a company on the mainland that uses ground-penetrating radar to locate underground objects. Maybe they could help you find any other shallow graves or weirdness."

"Thank you, Graham." Rebecca smiled. "That could be just what we need."

"Of course." A somberness entered Graham's eyes. "I'm just glad I could help." He straightened proudly, and Rebecca gave him a nod before leading Jake back to their crime scene.

"Coffey, go ahead and follow up on the ice-cream-parlor angle while we find out about the radar. See if anyone there can help frame our victim's whereabouts and if she was with anyone before she was murdered." Rebecca pulled her phone from her pocket and called Hoyt.

"Got it." Jake nodded before heading off.

As Rebecca waited for Frost to pick up, her thoughts turned to Viviane. Her rookie deputy was currently preoccupied, taking care of her recuperating mother. Meg insisted she was well enough to handle her new position as chair of the Select Board, even though she'd only recently come out of a week-long coma.

There was always too much work to do in this job and not enough people to do it. Unable to help herself, she turned and stared in the direction of Greg Abner. The freshly filled grave still showed a slight mound of dirt. A temporary marker indicated how recent the burial had been. She turned a little to the right, knowing former sheriff Alden Wallace's grave was just starting to settle with some new grass working to cover the soil.

Too many of her people rested in this cemetery.

4

Heavy clouds hung low in the sky, casting an oppressive gray pallor over Shadow Island. Hoyt Frost sat on the back porch of his modest home, his cup of lukewarm coffee no longer warming his hands. Today he was enjoying a rare extra day off with his accrued comp time.

At his side, Angie, his wife of many years, perched on the edge of a creaky wooden chair. Looking at her warmed him better than any hot beverage. He could top up from the hot carafe in the kitchen, but he preferred to stay with her, mentally saving the tiny detail of her gaze following the thick clouds scuttling overhead.

"Seems like people are finally getting back on their feet after the shitstorm." Hoyt braced against the cold as he watched the wind whip a discarded hamburger wrapper along the mushy stretch of land between the yard and the ocean. "It'll be a while before the island fully recovers, but at least we're making progress."

"True, but it's going to take more than repairing homes and businesses to heal this place." Angie's voice was tinged with concern. "We've got some deep scars to contend with."

"You're right about that. I just hope we can all find the strength to move forward together." Hoyt admired the way Angie always seemed to have her finger on the pulse of the island. "Speaking of moving forward, how's Meg doing now that she's back at work?"

"Ah, Meg…" A knowing smile played on Angie's lips. "She's been itching to make some changes ever since she got back. If there's one thing you can count on with her, it's that she won't let anything hold her back for long."

"Good for her." Hoyt smiled. He had no doubt Meg would make a positive imprint on the island she loved so much. "It's about time someone took charge and shook things up around here."

"Viviane's been keeping a close eye on her, though." Angie's expression grew serious once more. "She's been worried sick about Meg pushing herself too hard, and bless her, she's been there every step of the way, making sure Meg gets around okay."

"Viviane's a good kid." A small surge of pride squeezed Hoyt for the deputy who once played under the dispatch desk as a child. "It's nice to see her stepping up and showing what she's made of."

He took a sip from his cooling coffee, his thoughts drifting to the young deputy who'd proven herself a capable officer, now that she no longer rushed headlong into situations without backup. Viviane Darby was still finding her footing as a law enforcement officer, but her tenacity and drive were undeniable.

"Between Jake, Viviane, and Trent, now that he's pulled his head out of his ass, I think we're building a solid team here." Hoyt set his empty mug down on the porch railing. "Maybe it's time for me to start slowing down myself."

Angie rolled her eyes. "You? Slow down?"

"Hey! It's not impossible. Let's just say I'm considering it."

Hoyt gazed out at the gray horizon, just past the dune grasses that lined their yard. "I love this island and want to see it heal, but maybe there's a better way for me to contribute than wearing the badge."

Angie reached over and placed a hand on his arm. "Whatever you decide, I'll support you."

"Thank you." He put his hand over hers and squeezed. "I'll keep that in mind."

"Remember when our biggest worry was losing tourists to bad weather?" Angie's smile turned wistful.

"Feels like a lifetime ago since—"

Hoyt was cut off as his cell phone rang, shattering the illusion of peace. He glanced at the screen and sighed. "It's Rebecca."

"Go ahead. You know what that's for." Angie leaned back in her chair.

Hoyt considered his wife for a moment before answering his phone. She didn't seem bothered by the idea that their time together today was most likely over. She'd been a cop's wife for most of her life and knew what calls like this meant.

"Hey, Rebecca. What's up?" Hoyt used her first name, hoping this was just a social call despite his wife's pessimism.

"Sorry to bother you on your day off, but I'm gonna need you to come in." Rebecca's tone was grim. "We've got a complicated case here at the cemetery. Well, two, really. We came down for one case and stumbled onto an older corpse already buried. I'm going to work them as two separate cases unless the evidence eventually tells us otherwise."

Hoyt closed his eyes and scrubbed his hand through his hair. "Two cases? Shucks, Boss, and I didn't get you anything at all."

"Your witty repartee is more than enough for me."

Hoyt snorted, picturing his boss's serious expression while she responded to his humor. Though they hadn't worked together long, they made a good team. She played the straight man to his funny man, and it kept them both from getting too discouraged. It also kept up the spirits of those working around them.

If there were two cases in the cemetery, his gallows humor *would* come in handy.

Rebecca continued relaying details. "This morning, the caretaker found a dead teenage girl in the cemetery. When I met Jake out there, we found a second body only partially unearthed that might or might not be a Stokely victim. It's still mostly buried, so we're not sure of the gender or even how long it's been there. I'm need you to take the lead on that case while I work on the one that brought me out here."

"God forbid this island gets a moment of peace." Hoyt clutched the phone tighter. "I'll be there as soon as I can." He ended the call and looked at Angie.

She met his gaze with understanding. "Your day off's coming to an end, huh?"

"Seems so." Still, he hadn't gotten up quite yet. Despite his jokes, an unsettling trouble had taken up deep roots inside him, and he needed to finish unburdening himself. "I barely recognize this island anymore, Ange."

"There's a time for everything, dear. We're in a season of change." Angie took a sip of her coffee, her eyes locked on the sky. "Change isn't bad, but it does cause a ruckus. We just have to get through this."

A season of change. Yeah. He could see that. He hauled himself to his feet and went inside.

As he dressed, Hoyt couldn't help but feel that Shadow Island had changed irrevocably since Rebecca had moved in and expelled the Yacht Club. Despite her success in rooting out crime, the once tight-knit community now felt fractured and suspicious, its idyllic charm replaced by a pervasive sense of unease.

Having followed him inside, Angie watched him from the doorway, her eyes filled with concern. "We got interrupted, but I want you to know how I really feel about you retiring. I'd love to not worry about you anymore, but this is your career. You've dedicated your life to protecting this island."

Hoyt sighed, fastened the last button on his uniform, and adjusted his belt. "I'm getting surer every day. Rebecca, Viviane, Jake, and even Trent are good people. I'd be leaving the island in good hands." He looked at her, both determined and sad. "Besides, I'll still be around if they ever need anything. This island is a good place to retire."

"I support your decision, whatever it is. Just promise me you'll be extra careful." Her brow furrowed. "Abner 'retired,' too, but it didn't save him from the job in the end."

Hoyt closed his eyes a moment, taking a deep breath to ride out the stab of pain to his heart at the memory of his friend's recent death. "The Yacht Club…it all started while I was a deputy, and I feel like I should've done more to stop it. Hell, I closed a trespass case in the cemetery that might've been Stokely when Abe Barclay told me nothing was wrong. I might've caught them red-handed back then if I'd investigated even a little bit."

"You said that was Alden's doing too." Angie's fist clenched at her side. Sheriff Alden Wallace had been a close friend to both of them, so his duplicitousness in covering up Yacht Club activities had hit her just as hard as him.

"True, but he was building his RICO case against the Aqua Mafia. I'm the one who let him pull the wool over my eyes." Hoyt squared his shoulders in determination. "I need to help fix what's broken before I can walk away. Rebecca's a great sheriff. But I need to watch over her, help guide her through all this mess."

He studied his face in the full-length mirror beside the bed. Maybe it was his imagination, but he could swear the wrinkles at the corners of his eyes looked more like cracks than folds in the skin.

"It's not just Rebecca, though." Angie appeared in the mirror at his back, resting her chin on his shoulder as she gazed into the reflection of his face. Wrinkles or not, the sight of her still took Hoyt's breath. "Eventually, you have to let go of this guilt that's been gnawing at you ever since Alden died."

After kissing Angie goodbye, Hoyt stepped outside and called Trent, hunching into his coat against the chill air on the way to his truck.

"Let me guess, there's another crime to solve?" Trent's voice was rough from sleep, annoyance evident in his tone.

"You got it. But we're offering a buy one, get one free sale today. There're actually two crimes. I'm taking lead on the second, and I'd like your help working it."

"Is it gruesome?" Trent sounded as tired as Hoyt, even though he was a decade younger.

"Guess we'll find out. Meet me at the cemetery."

"There's way too many dead bodies there." Trent's bitter irony was not lost on Hoyt.

"Tell me about it." Hoyt ended the call and slid the phone back into his pocket, his gaze drifting toward the horizon where the sea met the sky. The turbulent waves seemed to mirror the turmoil that had gripped Shadow Island, a stark reminder of the fight for justice that lay ahead.

5

Jake pulled up to the I Scream You Scream ice cream parlor, a small establishment nestled among quaint island shops in the middle of town. He'd driven past the place countless times without venturing inside.

The shop was untouched by the recent blasts that had rocked Shadow Island, a stroke of luck amidst the chaos. It wasn't exactly ice cream weather, and the lack of customers reflected that.

His breath fogged up the cruiser window as he stared at the unassuming, sun-bleached pink-and-blue facade. Despite the cold, he was still tempted to get a cup of cotton candy ice cream for himself. Or maybe a Superman sherbet. But today wasn't a cheat day, so he couldn't do that.

Rebecca and Hoyt were always bringing in doughnuts and pastries. He'd put on five pounds since starting this job. With Thanksgiving and the holidays right around the corner, he knew it was only going to get worse.

At thirty-one, Jake had youth and health on his side. Even so, he knew his job as deputy demanded a certain level of fitness. And he didn't need to be slowed down by carrying around extra weight.

Which meant no ice cream today.

Jake opened the door and stepped out into the chilly air. The bell above the entrance jingled as he entered the shop, and he was immediately greeted by the sweet scent of waffle cones and the hum of freezers.

A colorful chalkboard menu hung on the wall behind the counter, proudly displaying the shop's various offerings, with hand-drawn turkeys and holiday wishes along the edges.

In the dim light filtering through the windows, the vibrant colors seemed muted, their cheerfulness subdued. Maybe that was why they'd taken the extra steps to add some holiday cheer. After everything that had happened in this town, he found it reassuring that people were determined to be festive.

"Welcome to I Scream You Scream." A young man in his early twenties greeted him from behind the counter. His name tag read *Paulo Silva* in neat cursive. "What can I get you today?"

One of each, please. Diets fucking suck.

"Actually, I'm here to ask you a few questions, if you don't mind." Jake pulled out his notepad and pen.

Paulo's eyes flicked between the notepad and Jake's face, curiosity mingling with concern. "Sure, what do you need?" His voice wavered somewhat.

Jake took note of the hesitation, filing it away as a potential clue.

"Did you work yesterday around six?" Before Jake got into the real questions, he needed to make sure he was talking to the right person.

"Yeah, that was me." Paulo shifted uneasily. "Did I shortchange a customer or something?"

Jake ignored the question. "Do you remember selling a

pumpkin spice shake to anyone around that time?" His eyes locked on Paulo's face, searching for any signs of deception or unease.

"Um...yeah, to a teen girl. Had black hair." Paulo gestured to his chin, showing how long her hair was. That matched what Jake had seen at the cemetery.

"Is she a regular? Do you know her name?" Jake poised his pen above his notepad.

"Her name's Whitney. She's a regular here, but she seemed more down than usual yesterday." Paulo glanced around nervously, as if worried someone might overhear. "She's usually here with a friend, but yesterday she came alone, finished her shake in silence, and left."

"Do you know her full name?"

"Um, Turner. Pretty sure her name is Whitney Turner." Paulo looked even more worried now.

Jake scribbled down the details. "Have you ever noticed anything unusual about her behavior before?"

"Not that I can think of. I don't really know her, though. She's at least five years younger than me, and the upper grades are in a different building of the school, so I can't say I recall ever seeing her. From what I can tell, she's a lot like most other girls her age." He shrugged awkwardly. "Is something wrong with her? Did she do something?"

"I'm not sure yet." Jake preferred to avoid revealing anything about the case. "Can you remember what time Whitney left yesterday?" He watched as Paulo's eyes scanned the tiled floor for an answer.

"Uh, yeah, she was here for maybe twenty minutes, just long enough to finish her shake, and then she headed out. I guess that would've been around six fifteen or six thirty." Paulo shook his head.

His assessment aligned with the time on the receipt.

"Can you give me a description of the friend she usually comes in with?"

"Sure." Paulo paused, seeming to gather his thoughts. "She's a teen girl. Tanned skin, tall, thin, and I think she has dark eyes. I don't recall ever hearing her name."

Well, that description eliminated the unnamed friend as the victim they'd found. There was no way anyone would call her tall. And Paulo's description already pointed toward Whitney as the unburied body at the cemetery. "Real quick, about how tall do you think Whitney is?"

"Uh." Paulo held up a hand near his armpit. "Really short. Like, sometimes I'd mistake her for a kid 'til she'd turn and I'd see her face."

There might've been numerous girls her age on the island with the same hair and eye color, but far fewer would be that short. As Jake scribbled down the details, he noticed Paulo's expression becoming increasingly worried.

The young man finally broke the silence. "Is everything okay?"

Jake hesitated, torn between reassuring him and acknowledging the gravity of the situation. "I'm not sure yet, Paulo. But your information is very helpful." His words hung in the air, a fragile thread connecting them to the unspoken reality that something much darker might be at play.

"I hope she's okay. I know things have been weird lately." Paulo fussed with his name tag. "I'd hate to think something bad happened to her. She seems really nice."

As if being nice kept bad things from happening.

At least he used the present tense to describe her.

"Thanks for your help." Jake offered a weak smile as he pocketed his notepad.

When he stepped outside, the wind tugged at his jacket. Jake pulled out his phone and searched for Whitney Turner. His fingers were cold and clumsy as they tapped against the screen, but eventually, her name appeared before him. Seventeen years old and living on the island, just as Paulo had said.

He spoke into the his shoulder mic. "Boss, I have a possible ID on the girl from the cemetery. Whitney Turner. She's approximately seventeen years old and lives here on the island. The basic description matches."

There was a pause, and he could almost hear Rebecca processing the information. "Good work, Coffey. Head on back. Locke and Frost are coming in to take over the scene here. You and I will pay her family a visit."

"I'll be right there." Jake released the mic button, staring off into the gray distance a moment before returning to his cruiser.

Notifying next of kin was always hard.

But asking a family member to identify one of their own was a special kind of hell.

6

Hoyt pulled his coat tighter as he stepped out of his truck and onto the cemetery grounds. He spotted Trent, a beefy figure with dark hair and a clean-shaven face, already waiting for him by the entrance.

As Hoyt approached, Trent greeted him with a nod and a weary smile. "Hey." His voice was subdued but still warm.

"Hey."

Hoyt had started getting on with Trent a lot better since he took him out for his long overdue "getting to know you" dinner. He'd created the tradition when he became senior deputy and had managed to dine with everyone else. Recently, he'd finally gotten around to breaking bread with Trent, despite the man's six years on the force at his side.

He'd been the last one to accept Trent, to finally acknowledge that the training he'd received from Abner had stuck. Trent took the job seriously now. His Yacht Club "friends" no longer gained information about cases by picking the brain of the unsuspecting and trusting deputy. The man was one of them now, a true and trusted colleague.

Together, they walked toward the crime scene, where a small group of CSI techs swarmed around two bodies laid out on tarps. Rebecca was hunched over one of the bodies, deep in conversation with Bailey Flynn, the medical examiner.

Hoyt's stomach lurched at the sight of the corpses—one a skeleton the techs were in the process of reassembling and the other covered in flesh, recently deceased. The contrast between them seemed unnatural, even amid the solemnity of the graveyard. He swallowed hard, forcing himself to maintain his composure.

"We're here, Boss." He spoke quietly, his breath shallow as he attempted to not smell anything.

Rebecca looked up from her work, her eyes momentarily searching before landing on him.

"Ah, Frost. Good, you're here." Her gaze flicked to Trent, acknowledging his presence. "Locke, sorry you had to come in early."

"What have we got so far?" Hoyt walked around the women and the bodies, focusing on where the techs were carefully combing through the dead grass.

"Drag mark, a fresh body, and an old one. Body is a teenage girl, currently unidentified." She pointed to a marker set in the grass. "The CSI team found some partial shoe impressions that suggest it could've been more than one person who dragged her body here. Considering they had to carry a shovel, too, it would make sense, but they're not certain yet. The leaves aren't making it easy on them."

"I have a feeling the leaves aren't going to be the only complicating factor." Hoyt shivered. He wished he had a hot cup of coffee to wrap his hands around.

Rebecca jerked her chin toward the brown grass near the victims. "We're still working on getting Body B up. This one will take a bit longer. They've been buried for a while."

"Two killers for Body A, huh?" Hoyt pulled his hat off and dragged a hand through his hair before putting it back on.

Rebecca said she was treating them as two different cases. So now they were likely looking for a third killer for Body B.

Three killers would really complicate the two investigations.

"Maybe." Rebecca's tone was cautious. "We can't be sure until we gather more evidence. But I've already contacted a ground-penetrating radar service, and they're on their way from the mainland. They should be here any minute."

As if on cue, Rebecca's phone buzzed in her pocket, and she fished it out, checking the screen before stepping away to take the call. Hoyt watched her go, his mind racing with thoughts of the grisly scene before him and the possible implications of multiple killers. If two people had killed this young woman, the danger heightened—as did the urgency to solve this case.

Hoyt's gaze lingered on the tombstone. "Betsy Taylor. Jeez, she only just died last year." He glanced back at the pieces of decayed body. "Bailey, any idea on time of death for this skeleton?"

Bailey examined the remains and shook her dark hair. "Hard to say for sure right now, but it was obviously sometime after Betsy was buried. From the looks of the bones and remnants of clothing unearthed so far, I'd say between nine and twelve months."

"Will you be able to identify them?" Hoyt's voice strained.

"Assuming they've got dental records we can match, sure." Bailey picked up the skull that had become detached from the spine and grinned.

As Hoyt watched, a lethargic worm tumbled free from inside the skull and landed with a wet plop on the tarp. He turned away, swallowing down bile, and caught Trent's amused gaze.

"Stokely." Hoyt muttered the name through clenched teeth. "This could be his doing. You know Abe Barclay was working with him and concealing his victims. If this corpse really is a year old, it would line up with when Stokely was active."

Trent nodded. "Yeah, I remember Stokely, that Yacht Club hitter. We all thought that kind of crap was behind us now."

"God, I wish." Hoyt rubbed his temples.

"What do you think would be worse?" Trent cocked his head. "Finding out Dwight Stokely had killed more people than we knew at the Yacht Club's orders, or finding out somebody else entirely has been killing and ditching bodies here?"

The question caught Hoyt off guard, but he mulled it over. "Honestly? I think it'd be worse if it weren't Stokely." He glanced over at the corpses. "Sure, he's dead, and the Aqua Mafia is kaput. Finding out it's someone else would mean another killer's on the loose…" He trailed off, trying to find the right words. "And that would mean we've been letting this happen. Too distracted by the Yacht Club to notice."

Trent nodded in understanding.

Hoyt was surprised by how open he felt admitting this to Trent, but the more they worked together, the more trust was forming between them. They needed that, especially now.

"Yeah, that's how I feel too. They used me to gather information, and I'll never know how much of that information helped them kill someone or transport people while we were looking the other way." Trent swallowed hard enough that Hoyt could see his Adam's apple jerk with the motion. "It still keeps me up at night. How many things could I have prevented if I'd been paying more attention back then?"

"Same, man. Same." He'd never told Trent, or any of the other deputies, about how the Yacht Club had tricked him into having an affair with one of their people to cause havoc with his homelife. And though he wasn't about to admit it now, that dark chapter in his life had been hard to put behind him.

Rebecca approached, cutting off their conversation. "Coffey got a possible name for the newest victim here. I'm going to meet up with him and talk to the parents." She handed Hoyt a roll of crime scene tape. "You're in charge of overseeing the radar situation and establishing any new scenes. They're pulling in now." She pointed over her shoulder to the gate.

"Understood." Hoyt accepted the tape from her.

As Rebecca walked away, the guilt of his past shortcomings pricked his conscience, the consequences of which now rested solely on her shoulders. There was no way he could just retire, leaving this mess for her to dig her way out of.

Rebecca never complained about it. None of this was her fault, but she'd stepped right in, taking over as sheriff, even fighting to keep the job because she knew she was the best candidate.

She'd ripped him a new one about it once. About how his past inaction had allowed the Yacht Club to gain a solid foothold in his community. It had been his best friend, the old sheriff, who'd made a deal with the Yacht Club to look the other way to protect Hoyt and the other deputies. Sheriff Alden Wallace had been determined to take down the Yacht Club on his own, all to shield them from any repercussions. But Wallace hadn't known how.

Rebecca did know how. And she'd done what no one thought possible. Even though it had cost her the man she loved. And she hadn't once shown any signs of throwing in the towel.

I've got Angie. Who does she have to keep her sane and moving forward every day?

"Deputy Frost?"

Hoyt startled, realizing he'd been lost in his thoughts.

Staring at the clouds and reminiscing about the past. I really am an old man.

He turned to find a heavyset man with a big beard walking toward him. "I'm Leonard Blyberg, head of the ground-penetrating radar team."

"Nice to meet you, Mr. Blyberg," Hoyt walked away from the grave site to shake his hand. "And that's Deputy Locke."

Blyberg and Trent exchanged nods.

"Ready to get started?"

No.

A nagging unease settled into Hoyt's gut as he thought about what they might find beneath the cemetery's surface. Bodies that he and Alden never knew about.

"Absolutely." Hoyt pushed a smile onto his face as he watched the team unload a bulky machine on wheels. Ignoring the problem wouldn't make it go away.

And even more compelling, there were families out there who needed answers about what happened to their loved ones. That was the only upside of this. For each victim they found, there was a chance of closing a missing persons case.

His gaze wandered over the gravestones, and an uncomfortable thought bubbled to the surface. What if Alden had known about those deaths? He shook his head, rejecting the idea immediately. He'd been close to Alden—no way would he have let a killer go free if he'd known about it.

"Before we start, I'd like to explain our process." Blyberg tugged at his thick beard thoughtfully. "We've got some cutting-edge technology that'll help us out today."

Hoyt and Trent exchanged glances—Trent's filled with curiosity—before focusing on Blyberg.

Apprehensive, Hoyt nodded. "Go ahead."

Blyberg gestured at the radar equipment, which looked like a bizarre mix between a lawn mower and a vacuum. "We can detect ground disturbances and voids in the dirt where there shouldn't be any. Our new tech allows us to find anomalies around coffins, not just general disturbances in the area. So if there are bodies lying on top of graves, we should be able to pinpoint them." He waved his arm, indicating the entire cemetery. "But we'll need to walk the whole area, so it'll take a while."

"The entire area?" Hoyt peered at the machine, which seemed way too small to cover that much ground.

"That's what your sheriff asked for. The whole cemetery, no stone left unturned, every square inch of ground regardless. She wants us to search the burial area, too, and all along the perimeter. Everything." Blyberg looked back to where his team was rolling a second radar machine out.

"If that's what the sheriff asked for, that's what we'll do. She's in charge." He'd been dreading the day they had to start looking for the rest of Stokely's victims, afraid of how many they'd find below the surface. Hell, he'd hoped either the staties or Feds would come in and deal with it all. "Go ahead and get started. I'll walk with you while Locke stays here with our M.E."

Trent nodded and turned back to where Bailey was digging through mud and squishier things.

"Will do. We'll be mapping the whole area as we go, but you're free to take your own notes if you want." Blyberg nodded to his team. They dispersed, each member taking their position behind a machine as they prepared to scan the area methodically, row by row.

Hoyt fell in line with them. Did the Shadow Island

Sheriff's Office have skeletons in their closet from before Rebecca West ever came to town? They were about to find out.

7

"Coffey." Rebecca broke the silence on the way to the Turner home. "Take a look at those photos of Body A. Hopefully, we won't run through the whole damn alphabet by night's end. See if you can copy some of the symbols from her body onto paper."

He considered her, eyebrows raised. "Why? You think the Turners will recognize them?"

"Maybe. And if this really is Whitney, it'd be better if they don't have to see them carved into their daughter's flesh." Seeing a loved one in crime scene photos was a pain she knew all too well, one she wouldn't wish on anyone.

Blood on the tile.

Blood on the cupboards.

Blood on the pillows.

The broken rattle leaning against Darian Hudson's headstone.

Blood dripping from Meg's face inside her crumpled SUV.

Hoyt trying to keep the blood from pouring out of Greg's chest.

Water splashing up through the hole in Ryker's chest.

Rebecca gripped the steering wheel harder, chasing away

the flashbacks. They'd been getting worse in the last few weeks, her recent losses mixing with the older memories. Maybe it was time to double up on her therapy sessions. She glanced over at Jake to see if he noticed her distress.

Jake had retrieved the camera from the glove box and was focused on copying the symbols from the gory photographs onto a notepad.

At the Turner home, Rebecca eyed the quaint cottage up ahead and parked out front. The picturesque scene was in stark contrast to the grim chore they had ahead of them. "You ready?"

Jake nodded, scribbling faster as he clicked through the rest of the photos. "I think I got them all." He handed the camera to Rebecca. "Ready."

They stepped out together. Rebecca noted a single vehicle in the driveway, an SUV with faded gray paint, but there was room for a second vehicle.

As they walked up to the house, the front door swung open, and a short woman with long black hair walked out holding a garbage bag. She matched the driver's license photo of Whitney's mother, Annabelle Turner, which Rebecca had pulled up to get the address.

"Excuse me, are you Annabelle Turner? Whitney Turner's mother?" Rebecca approached the woman as she tossed the bag into the curbside container.

"I am. Is everything okay?" Annabelle glanced back and forth between her and Jake.

"Can you tell me if Whitney's home? We're trying to clear up a situation and need to know if she's here." Rebecca didn't want to alarm her without cause.

Anabelle shook her head. "It's Thanksgiving break. I figured she'd be out and about. I didn't hear or see her when I got home." She forced a smile, though it didn't reach her eyes. "Let's see if she's in her room with her headphones on, trying to tune out the world." She motioned for them to join her and retreated into the house, Rebecca and Jake close behind.

Jake took off his hat. "Thank you, ma'am."

Once across the threshold, Annabelle began calling to her daughter, moving with some urgency toward the stairs. When she got no response by the time they reached the second floor, she stopped in front of a door and knocked softly. She paused, a sign that she respected her daughter's privacy and agency. "Whitney? Are you in there?"

She turned the knob, and the door creaked open to reveal a room filled with a mix of childhood innocence and teenage rebellion.

Rebecca moved past Annabelle and stepped into the room cautiously, wary of any potentially present evidence. The cemetery was a secondary crime scene. They didn't know where Whitney had been killed yet. Thankfully, there were no signs of violence or that Whitney had been murdered in her room.

The bedroom was a typical teenager's sanctuary, cluttered with clothes, books, and makeup. A distinct aroma of floral perfume hung in the air while popular musicians stared down from posters on the walls.

The farther into the room Rebecca went, the colder the air became.

"Mrs. Turner?" Jake's voice was low and steady as he followed behind Rebecca. "Did Whitney mention anything unusual happening lately?"

Annabelle shook her head, her jaw tight. She was clearly trying to hold it together—a natural response to two officers arriving at her doorstep. "No, nothing out of the ordinary. Her grades took a plunge recently, but that's just part of being a teenager. They get distracted so easily."

"Right." Teenagers weren't the only ones...but Rebecca

kept her mouth shut. A hairbrush rested on the dresser, and Rebecca noted several short black hairs entwined in the bristles. "Mrs. Turner, would you allow us to take Whitney's brush? We'd like to pull her DNA from it."

"Her DNA?" Her chin began to quiver. "Why the hell do you need her DNA?"

"It could help us in the investigation I mentioned." Rebecca had already decided to wait before asking her to identify Whitney via photo for the moment. But she couldn't avoid concerning a mother with her questions.

"Well, Whitney's very particular about how things are in here. But I guess the brush will be okay."

The window curtains swayed as a breeze pushed them inward.

"Of course. Deputy Coffey can just remove the hair from it, and we'll leave the brush here." Rebecca nodded at Jake before continuing. "When was the last time you saw Whitney?" She turned to look at the woman.

Annabelle hesitated, her gaze darting around the room as if searching for the answer. A tear fell.

Rebecca bit her lip, reminding herself not to judge the woman.

Discreetly, Jake slipped on latex gloves, removed the strands of hair from the brush, and deposited them into an evidence bag he'd pulled from his pocket. After sealing the bag, he pulled the gloves off and stuffed them into his jacket.

"Last night," Annabelle finally said, her voice weak and shaky. "We had an argument about her recent grades. After that, she shut herself in her room for the rest of the night. But like I said, school's out. She's probably gone out somewhere."

That vague timeline of the last time her mother had seen Whitney fit with what they knew so far.

A hint of dawning realization and fear flashed across Annabelle's face. "I assumed she wouldn't be here when I got home from work. She rides her bike all over town, meeting her friends, going for ice cream, you know. But I didn't want to start another fight, so I gave her some space. I wanted to give her time to cool off and think about things."

"You say she rides her bike?"

Annabelle nodded.

"Where does she normally park it?"

"Outside." Annabelle pointed to the window, as if the bike would be immediately visible.

The window, hidden behind a set of dark curtains, stood ajar, letting in a cold draft that sent shivers down Rebecca's spine. She stepped forward, pushing the curtain aside to show the open window. She didn't see any sign of a bicycle. She'd look closer in a moment. "And you haven't come in here since your fight with Whitney last night?"

"No…" Annabelle's face turned as pale as the moon as she stared at the open window, her eyes brimming with panic. "Whitney's been caught sneaking out before, but she promised she wouldn't do it again. What is it you think she got involved in?"

Rebecca ignored that question. "Do you have a phone tracking app for Whitney? We'll need a recent photo too."

"A recent photo…?" The weight of the situation seemed to hit Whitney's mother all at once. Annabelle fumbled with her phone, tapping through the screens. "I have both. A photo, I mean. And an app. Let me try…" She entered the necessary information, but her expression crumpled as no results appeared on the screen. "It's not showing anything. Her phone must be off or…or dead. She's always forgetting to charge it."

She held up a picture of a small, dark-haired young

woman, her smile on full display as she gripped the rail of a bridge. That short stature and bobbed hair made Rebecca's stomach sink with the similarity to the corpse discovered that morning.

"Did Whitney have any plans today? Or last night? Friends she might've gone to see?" Jake moved over to the window to examine it more closely.

"I don't think so." Annabelle shook her head. "She didn't mention anything to me, but then again, we haven't been talking much since I started working longer hours. Let me call a few people and see if anyone's seen her."

Rebecca and Jake waited.

With each phone call, Annabelle grew more distressed until tears began to stream down her cheeks. She set down her phone. "Sheriff, where's my daughter?"

"Let's check the yard. Maybe we can find her bike or tracks or something." Rebecca guided Annabelle from the room.

"Her bike. Yes." Annabelle ran for the backyard with Rebecca and Jake following behind her. She stopped at the corner of the house and spun around. "It's not here. So she must've just gone out for a bit. Right?"

Rebecca's mind raced as she considered the missing bicycle and the open window. This wasn't good. Not at all. If Whitney was their murder victim, she could've been killed almost anywhere on the island. But where? And was the spot where her body was left significant, either to Whitney or to the killer?

She placed a hand on Annabelle's shoulder. "Mrs. Turner, let's go back inside for a moment." After they entered through the back door, Rebecca gestured toward one of the kitchen chairs. "Please, have a seat."

"A seat?" She turned in a small, unfocused circle. "I can't sit down. I need to find Whitney."

"Mrs. Turner, we need to talk to you, and I think it would be best if we sat down for a moment."

Reluctantly, Annabelle perched on the front of one of the chairs, though she appeared ready to spring out of it in an instant.

Rebecca sat opposite her, carefully studying her for signs of shock or deception, though the woman's reactions seemed genuine. She located the photo of the unburied victim but didn't show it to the distraught woman yet. First, she needed to explain the situation as delicately as she could.

"Mrs. Turner, as I mentioned earlier, we had a bit of a situation. We discovered a deceased teenage girl out at the cemetery. I'm very sorry, but we have reason to believe this teenager is Whitney." There was no easy way to drop that bombshell.

"Whitney? You know where she is?" Annabelle's gaze flickered between Rebecca and Jake.

The weight of Rebecca's words hadn't dawned on the woman yet, so Rebecca forged ahead.

"I have a photo I'd like to show you. I need you to tell me if the person in this image is Whitney." Rebecca observed the woman seated across from her as her face drained of color. She kept glancing between Rebecca and the camera she was holding. Finally, her resolve won out.

The woman extended her hand. "Let me see."

Rebecca recalled from her own past the desire to know the horrible truth. To witness what she feared was true. She'd burst into her parents' home to see their bodies for herself— but the PTSD and nightmares from those vivid images haunted her to this day. Hell, she'd recalled it all on the drive to this very house less than half an hour ago.

"Before I share this with you, I must let you know that the image might be distressing."

"Waiting to see it is distressing enough, Sheriff. Show

me." Annabelle wiped at more tears, still holding out her other hand.

Jake stood silently off to the side, shifting his weight between his feet, clearly uncomfortable.

Rebecca adjusted the photograph on the camera's screen, so it was zoomed in only on Whitney's face. The gory details of the crime weren't necessary to get the victim identification. If she couldn't shield the woman from grief, Rebecca could at least spare her the image of the bloody sweatshirt replaying in her head. She moved out of her chair and held the camera in front of Annabelle.

"Oh, god. No. No! Not my baby!" Annabelle took the camera from Rebecca and brushed the screen as if touching her daughter's face, but that caused the image to jump to the next crime scene photo. Before the woman could focus on the gore in the image, Rebecca snatched the camera away from her.

"What happened to Whit?" Tears streamed down Annabelle's face as she continued to stare at the camera Rebecca now held with a steady grip.

Noticing the woman's fixation, Rebecca placed the camera in her lap.

"It can't be. It can't be my baby girl…" Annabelle splayed herself across the kitchen table, crying in agony. Rocking her head back and forth, she shook with sobs as she mumbled protest after protest that the girl in the photo wasn't her daughter.

As Rebecca sat with Annabelle, her mind raced through the details of Whitney's case. Somewhere out there, a murderer was roaming free. Rebecca hoped the teen's death was an isolated incident. With the Yacht Club dismantled, things like this weren't supposed to happen anymore.

But if it wasn't isolated, then someone else might be in danger.

Rebecca met gazes with Jake, who was standing quietly in the corner of the kitchen. He looked as heartbroken as she felt.

She needed answers. Answers for the grieving mother seated across from her. Answers for Whitney. And answers for Shadow Island.

8

Rebecca comforted Annabelle until she stopped crying and got her breathing under control. They still had many questions for her, but compassion had won over her sense of duty. Though they had no time to waste, that didn't mean she had to be heartless in her pursuit of justice.

Annabelle had pulled up several digital photo albums, burying herself in memories of her daughter. One album contained a montage they'd done for Whitney's seventeenth birthday. She'd graciously allowed Rebecca to take a printout of one of the photos. In it, a smiling, black-haired girl with light eyes appeared full of warmth and life.

Rebecca swallowed hard as she compared the vibrant image with the mental picture of the pale and mutilated body they'd viewed earlier.

Jake had kept himself busy making hot tea. After setting the cup beside the grief-stricken mother with a kind smile, he took the evidence out to the cruiser to label it and lock it up. When he returned, Rebecca attempted to resume her gentle questioning.

She cleared her throat. "Mrs. Turner, where were you last night?"

"Last night?" Confusion clouded her features. "I went to bed early. It was probably a little after nine. I have to wake up early for work." She glanced at Rebecca, her eyes pleading for understanding. "My job can verify when I arrived this morning, but nobody would've seen me in bed."

"Your husband?" Jake probed further. "Is he home?"

"Out on a business trip." Her voice was ragged from crying. "He left yesterday morning."

"You need to call him. See if he can return early."

Rebecca took a deep breath, making a mental note to verify Annabelle's alibi and track down her husband and his alibi. Trust was a luxury they couldn't afford. Nearly fifteen percent of murders were committed by someone close to the victim who wasn't family, like a friend, boyfriend, or girlfriend.

But family members constituted more than a fourth of all murderers. Rebecca studied Annabelle's distraught face, aware that every question was another jab to her heart. But she needed answers, and she couldn't afford to hold back.

She pulled out Jake's drawing of the symbols found on the victim's body and held it up for Annabelle to see. "Do you recognize any of these symbols?"

"Why?"

"Those symbols were found near the crime scene." By avoiding saying exactly where they'd been, Rebecca could at least try to minimize the horror of Whitney's appearance for her mother. "We're trying to determine if there's any significance to them."

Rebecca watched as myriad emotions flickered across the mother's face, acutely aware of the delicate balance she had to maintain between empathy and professionalism. It was an agonizing dance, one all too familiar to her in this line of work.

The color drained from Annabelle's face as if someone had pulled a plug, leaving her ghostly white and trembling.

"No, I don't know what those are." The words were choked, her voice barely audible. "What was my daughter mixed up in?" She stared at the untouched mug of tea before her.

"I'm sorry, Mrs. Turner, I don't know what Whitney was involved in either. That's what we'd like to find out." Rebecca paused, considering her next question. "We'd like to speak with Whitney's friends. Can you tell us who they are?"

"Her best friend is Sara Porter." Annabelle finally took a sip of her tea, and her color began to return. Her gaze searched the room, as if she'd find answers there about her daughter's death in her dining area. "I can give you Sara's address, but I don't have her phone number."

"Thank you. That'll help us with our investigation." With a final nod of gratitude, Rebecca rose from the table. Jake was by her side as they left the Turner house. Forensic techs would need to go through the whole house more carefully than they'd just done to make sure no evidence was missed.

Once in the Explorer, Rebecca checked the onboard GPS to verify their destination. "The cemetery is on the way to Sara Porter's house. I'm going to drop that hair sample off with the techs there before heading over."

Jake nodded.

Rebecca noted his furrowed brow, revealing his own internal struggle. They drove in silence, both lost in thought.

At the cemetery, Rebecca handed off the hair to one of the CSI techs. "We need DNA confirmation on the victim."

The tech nodded, understanding the urgency of the situation. "Will do, Sheriff." He tucked the bag in with the other evidence bags to be transported back to the Coastal Ridge forensic lab.

She looked across the path to where Trent was meticulously processing the cemetery. Past him, Hoyt was trailing behind the radar team, taking notes as they swept the property.

Both men had their heads down, and she wasn't even sure if they'd noticed her arrival. She felt pulled to work the case of the older corpse, or Body B, but there might be a killer still actively lashing out at teenage girls. And she'd had enough of people doing that.

There was more bad news to hand out to Whitney's best friend. More than one family would be grieving today.

9

Sara's house was a replica of Whitney's. With the same exterior style, the only difference was the color of the shutters and door. The Porters even had barren window boxes, the same as the Turners.

"Let's get this over with." Rebecca nodded, and Jake rapped firmly on the door.

The door swung open, revealing Sara's dad Sam, and beyond him, her mom Kristen, carrying a large, steaming pot in her hands. She stopped, her face etched with concern as she looked over her husband's shoulder and took in the two law enforcement officers on their doorstep.

"Good evening. I'm sorry to interrupt your dinner." Rebecca forced a polite smile. "I'm Sheriff Rebecca West, and this is Deputy Jake Coffey. We're here to talk to your daughter Sara about her friend Whitney Turner."

"Is something wrong?" Sam turned to his wife, who set down the pot and hurried to the door.

"We're afraid there's been an incident." Rebecca spoke cautiously. "We need to speak with Sara about an investigation we're working on. The body of a young woman was found this morning."

Kristen's hand flew to her mouth. Sam wrapped an arm around her, steadying her while he tried to maintain his own composure.

"I'll go get her. Please, come inside." He disappeared into the house.

Rebecca and Jake stepped inside but stayed near the door. She couldn't help but think about how much Sara's world was about to change. Trust would be shattered, innocence lost, and friendships put to the ultimate test. She'd seen it too many times before, and each time, the pain weighed heavily on her heart.

Kristen was collapsing into a kitchen chair when she heard Sara's voice from down the hall, asking her dad what was wrong. The woman quickly wiped her eyes and straightened her spine, preparing herself to be the rock her daughter would need.

Rebecca was impressed and grateful this girl would have a strong mother to help her.

The voices got louder as Sam reappeared, guiding a trembling Sara into the room. Her eyes darted back and forth between Rebecca and her mom. Rebecca tried to soften her expression, hoping to reassure the young girl.

"Sara, we're so sorry to have to talk to you about this." Rebecca kept her tone gentle. "Have you seen or heard from your friend Whitney today?"

Sara shook her head, her voice barely audible. "No...I texted her this morning, but she didn't answer."

"We have some bad news." Jake kept his voice steady but compassionate. "Whitney is dead."

Sara's eyes widened, and she wrapped her arms around herself in a protective embrace. She looked on the verge of tears. Kristen stepped up behind her, resting a reassuring hand on her shoulder. Sara grabbed it without looking, clutching tightly.

"Wh-what happened?"

Jake was somber. "We don't know the details yet."

Rebecca tried to keep her voice neutral, despite the grim circumstances. "That's why we need your help. You might be able to give us some information that could lead us to whoever did this. I know this is hard, but we need you to answer some questions. Do you think you can do that?" Rebecca turned the protective parents. "We'd like to speak with Sara alone."

"Absolutely not." The words were barely out of Andrea's mouth before Sam also cut Rebecca's hopes short. "If you want to talk to her, we insist on being present."

Fighting back the sigh she felt bubbling to the surface, Rebecca nodded instead. "Sara, are you up for answering our questions with your parents here?"

"Y-yeah," Sara choked out, wiping her eyes with the back of her hand before grabbing her father's hand as well. Braced by both parents, she nodded. "I'll try."

"Thank you, that's very brave of you." Jake offered a small, understanding smile. A bright flush of red crept over Sara's collar at the compliment.

"When did you last speak to Whitney?" Rebecca asked.

"Yesterday afternoon." Sara's words came out as a trembling whisper.

"Where were you last night?"

"Here, with my parents, all night. We were watching movies. I went to bed around ten." She glanced at her parents for reassurance, and they both nodded in confirmation.

"Did Whitney get into any fights recently? Or have any enemies or anyone being mean to her? Had she been threatened at all?"

Sara shook her head, tears streaming down her cheeks.

"No, nothing like that. She finally seemed to be coming out of her shell. She's kind of an introvert but was trying to get out more."

Rebecca wondered if the distraction of social obligations had anything to do with her drop in grades. Or if something had happened that no one knew about, which caused both changes in Whitney's life. "What other friends do you two hang out with?"

"Nobody. We only hang out with each other."

Her parents chimed in, confirming they hadn't had any other girls over in quite some time. "We're quite busy, and Sara knows not to have guests over unsupervised. That rather limits visitors." Sam put a protective arm around Sara.

Rebecca furrowed her brow, taking note of this detail. She knew better than to assume teenagers would always be forthcoming about their social lives, but it seemed Sara genuinely had no one else to turn to during this crisis than a pair of perhaps overprotective parents.

"Sara, I'm sorry to keep asking you questions, but we need to know if you recognize something."

Jake held up the paper with the symbols he'd drawn, and they both watched Sara's face closely for any sign of recognition.

Sara looked at the paper, confusion clouding her already tear-stained features. Glancing among each of the four symbols and back again, her pupils dilated, and her mouth dropped open. She quickly snapped it shut, though, and narrowed her eyes.

Was she angry? Confused? Rebecca thought she recognized both expressions crossing Sara's face.

After a moment, Sara lifted her chin almost defiantly and shook her head, her tears no longer flowing. "I don't know what those symbols mean."

Rebecca didn't believe her. Although the girl seemed

genuinely distraught, there was something more. She glanced at Jake, who raised an eyebrow, indicating she wasn't alone in her suspicions.

"Please," Kristen interjected, her eyes pleading, "she's been through enough already. Can you give her some space?"

Rebecca grimaced. "Mrs. Porter, I assure you that, if this wasn't necessary, we wouldn't be here. But if we're going to find out what happened to Whitney, we need to talk to the people who knew her best. And that's your daughter."

Kristen shifted uneasily. "I know. It's just…" She trailed off and stared at her daughter with pain-filled eyes.

"It's okay, Kristen." Sam squeezed his wife's hand. "The sheriff needs us. Whitney needs us."

Rebecca tried to strike a balance between empathy and getting the answers as quickly as she could. "Are you absolutely sure Whitney didn't have anyone else she might sneak out to meet? It's important for us to understand the people she spent time with. You said she was coming out of her shell. Does that mean she made more friends?"

Sara leaned heavily against her dad. "No. Like, she was trying to go out more often. Not just hanging out online all day. She'd take walks, get ice cream, do the trails. You know, better her physical and mental health instead of being cooped up all the time." Sara's voice was shaky as she clung to her father. "It's just…just us. She's my best friend."

Rebecca chewed on her bottom lip, her instincts telling her they were missing something. "What about online friends? Did she talk about anyone like that?" She hadn't seen a computer in Whitney's room. Surely, the girl had one, or some piece of technology to connect her to the world. Everyone did these days, especially students.

"Whitney's mom wouldn't replace her laptop after she broke the last one. She's been using one from school, and it doesn't allow any social media. I think she even left it in her locker for the Thanksgiving break." Sara rolled her lips together and wiped away more tears, but her gaze fell on the paper with the symbols that Jake still held. "You could check her phone, but she didn't tell me about anyone."

That would be useful if they had Whitney's phone. Too bad they didn't. If they were going to get any closer to solving this case, they needed to explore all possible avenues, and that included the girls' social lives at school.

Rebecca decided to bring up the symbols again. She took the page from Jake and held up it in front of Sara.

She recoiled like they might bite her.

"Are you sure you don't recognize these?"

"N-no, I'm sorry."

"Sheriff, please." A plaintive tone entered Sam's words. "She already told you they mean nothing to her."

"Sorry. We're trying to chase every lead." Rebecca noted Sara's recoiling, however. The girl was sad, but there was something else going on. "Sara, do you think your teachers would know more about Whitney's relationships with her classmates?" She pressed gently to see if there'd be any pushback. "Do you and Whitney share any classes?"

Sara nodded. "Yes, Ms. Wells. She's our homeroom teacher."

"Thank you." Rebecca remembered Cynthia Wells from an earlier case involving the tragic death of a retired schoolteacher. She really needed to find better ways to interact with her neighbors. "We'll be in touch if we have any further questions. And, please, call the station if you think of anything that might be useful."

After handing them her card, Rebecca turned away. Jake followed her to the cruiser, and neither spoke until they were safely inside.

"Did you notice?" Jake's voice was soft with a heavy tinge of sadness.

Rebecca nodded. "She said 'is her best friend.'"

"And 'is an introvert.' The poor kid. It hasn't hit her yet that her best friend is gone." Jake pulled his seat belt on.

Rebecca stared at the house where she was certain no one would be sitting down with an appetite tonight. "That wasn't the only thing I noticed, though. What did you think of her reaction to the symbols you drew?"

"I wasn't sure what to think of her reaction, honestly." He twisted in his seat to look at her. "At first, I thought she looked confused. And that made sense to me. But then, all of that seemed to fall away and was replaced with anger. Who knows?" He shrugged one shoulder and faced forward again. "I've never pretended to understand teenage girls."

"Ha, yeah. They are their own breed. But she did seem almost outraged by the symbols. Yet she claimed not to recognize them."

"Yeah, I'm not buying that."

"As for her speaking in the present tense about a dead girl, that pushes her down our persons of interest list. But that's not saying much, since we don't have any names to put before hers." Rebecca started the engine. They needed to speak to as many people as possible. Someone on this island knew something about Whitney Turner's death, and she was going to find them.

10

Cynthia Wells lived in an old Victorian with a fresh coat of paint around a green front door and newly replaced wood boards on the stairs. It was clear she took pride in her home, preserving its character.

The woman was seated on her large front porch, wrapped in a thick shawl, nursing a steaming mug of something.

Rebecca and Jake climbed out of the cruiser and approached the house, footsteps echoing on the wooden steps.

Cynthia's eyes narrowed as she took in the sight of the two officers.

"Evening, Cynthia." Rebecca lifted a hand. "Good to see you again. Have you met our new deputy, Jake Coffey?"

"Nice to see you again, Sheriff West." Cynthia turned to Jake. "I haven't had the pleasure. What brings you two to my humble abode?"

Rebecca considered how best to approach their questions, knowing that trust would be vital in getting the information they needed. This wasn't going to be an easy conversation.

"Actually, we're here to ask about one of your students, Whitney Turner."

Cynthia chewed her lip, clearly troubled by the news. "Whitney?"

Rebecca nodded.

"She's a good student, you know. Though she's been struggling lately, according to her math teacher. All of us teachers have been paying extra attention to the students and how they're coping with recent events. We that grades can slip when external factors weigh on them. Whitney's no different."

Rebecca exchanged a glance with Jake. "I'm afraid it's more serious than that. We found a body this morning that we believe is Whitney. We're investigating it as a homicide."

The color drained from Cynthia's face, and her hands shook as she struggled to hold the mug. "Oh, no, that poor girl. Why does this kind of thing keep happening? First Amy and Seb, and now…"

"We're working on finding that out." Rebecca pulled out her notepad, trying not to wince at the reminder of the past case she'd work with Cynthia. No matter how many perpetrators she caught, those killed during the investigation always remained with her. "Can you tell us anything about her relationships with other classmates? Was she dating anyone? Who she spent time with, or if there was anyone she didn't get along with?"

Cynthia set down her mug, took a deep breath, and tried to steady herself. "Well, she was close friends with Sara Porter. They were always together, you know. Recently, though, I've noticed her and Sara hanging out with three other girls."

Rebecca had forgotten how Cynthia seemed to use "you know" to end every sentence when she was talking. It made her want to smile. But this new information contradicted what Sara Porter and Annabelle Turner had said, raising new questions. She exchanged a glance with Jake. A mother might not know, but why would Sara lie about these other girls?

"Do you happen to know those three girls' names?" Another lead would be great.

"Um, yes." The teacher's forehead wrinkled in concentration. "Abigail Miller, Marie Allman, and Carrie Dugan."

"Thank you." Rebecca jotted down the names in her notepad, sensing the urgency of uncovering the truth behind these relationships. She turned to Jake, who pulled out a folded sheet of paper from his pocket.

"Can you take a look at these symbols, Ms. Wells? Do you recognize any of them?" Jake carefully unfolded the paper and presented it to her.

Cynthia squinted at the unfamiliar markings, her face displaying a mix of curiosity and unease. "You know, I think I've seen some of these before…but I'm not sure what they mean."

"Where did you see them?" Rebecca pressed.

"Actually, I found a paper with similar symbols in my classroom the other day. Someone must've been doodling them during class." Cynthia's voice was tinged with apprehension. "I didn't think much of it at the time, but they gave me an uneasy feeling. They seem occult or pagan in nature, you know."

"Would you happen to know if Whitney or Sara are into that kind of stuff?" Rebecca tried to determine if either girl might be linked to the mysterious symbols.

"I can't say for sure about Whitney, but I never got the impression she was into that kind of thing. I really don't know about Sara." Cynthia shook her head. "As for the symbols, I only recognize the pentagram. It's often associated with satanism, but I couldn't tell you more than that, you know."

Rebecca did, in fact, know that she was trying to hide her annoyance with the woman's verbal tics.

"You know," Cynthia sat up straighter, "there's a shop that opened not long ago called Archive Arcana. Some of the students talk about it as a sort of 'witchy' store. You might find answers there."

"Thanks, Ms. Wells. That's very helpful." Jake nodded with a small smile as he folded the paper back up and pocketed it.

"Of course. If that's all, it's getting cold out, and I think I'm going to call it an early night." With a subtle sniffle, Cynthia offered them a stiff nod and retreated into her house, leaving Rebecca and Jake standing on the porch.

As they walked back to their cruiser, Rebecca pondered the change in Cynthia's demeanor. She'd met the woman first while investigating the death of a retiring teacher and more recently while campaigning for sheriff, and she'd always been warm and friendly. But today, her usual kindness seemed to have evaporated.

Rebecca knew that cases involving young victims and occult practices tended to stir up intense emotions. She couldn't forget the Satanic Panic that had gripped America in the eighties and nineties. The parents and adults she was dealing with now were old enough to remember those terrifying times, so it was no surprise they'd be on edge.

She only hoped a similarly disturbing trend wasn't trying to gain a foothold on Shadow Island.

11

The door to Archive Arcana jingled with bells as Rebecca and Jake entered, revealing a dimly lit space laden with occult gifts. Incense wafted through the air, tendrils of smoke dancing around them.

"Welcome to Archive Arcana," a melodic voice called out, snapping Rebecca from her observations. A woman in her early thirties, with dark hair cascading over her shoulders and a flowy dress that touched the floor, emerged from behind a display case. Her eyes sparkled like jewels. "I'm Morningstar."

Of course you are.

"I'm Sheriff Rebecca West, and this is Deputy Jake Coffey." Rebecca extended her hand.

Morningstar shook her hand, her grip firm and warm.

Jake acknowledged the woman with a nod before continuing to peer at the trinkets, his eyes narrowing as if he were assessing each object for clues.

"How can I help you? Perhaps a protection amulet or a crystal for clear sight?"

"Thanks for the offer, but we're actually here on police business."

"Is there something specific you need help with?" Morningstar's tone shifted to one of concern.

Rebecca hesitated, knowing she needed to tread carefully, not wanting to spook the shop owner or reveal too much about their ongoing investigation. With no real viable suspects, there was always the possibility this woman was behind Whitney Turner's death. Not long ago, their suspect in a different case had sold her shop's fancy lingerie to her victims, her identity as a shop owner and practiced concern making her easy to overlook.

"Actually," Jake scanned the shelves filled with peculiar trinkets and books, their covers adorned with mystic symbols, "can you tell us a bit about your store and what made you decide to open it on Shadow Island?"

Morningstar's eyes glowed bright as she recounted her story. "Oh, sure! I've always been interested in the occult. It's intricate and complicated, a metaphor for our world, really. So I saved up and moved to the island about six months ago. The plan was to attract tourists interested in the old witch legend."

Given the amount of kitschy beach themes Rebecca had witnessed since moving to the island, she could appreciate anyone who tried to weigh in on a different Shadow Island theme. Any different theme.

Closing the back of a display case and latching it, Morningstar sighed. "Back in July, I saw a small uptick in business when that poor guy held hostages in the lighthouse. Everyone was talking about the old witch. After that, some people from the Lovecraft symposium came by, but none of them bought anything. My merchandise doesn't really align with that genre."

And vice versa. Despite the many times she'd scoured the

symposium looking for the killer leaving beheaded victims at the Old Witch's Cottage, Rebecca hadn't noticed a booth for Archive Arcana there. The merchandise in here would've stuck out like a sore thumb.

Morningstar's smile was tinged with resignation as she surveyed her empty shop. "I'm hoping business picks up around the holidays."

"Ah, yes, those were…unsettling events." Rebecca agreed. She'd also thought she could improve her life by coming to the island to decompress for a few months.

Catching Rebecca's gaze, Morningstar reached out to give Rebecca's hand a gentle squeeze.

"I've heard about you. Is it true you came here to take a summer vacation and ended up getting pushed into the position when the old sheriff died? That must've been so hard."

"Uh, yeah." Rebecca didn't doubt the woman had read up on her. She'd been featured in several newspaper articles by now, none of which she appreciated. "That about sums it up. And I've been working here ever since. And made it my home."

"Thank you, by the way, for cleaning up that mess with those Aqua Mafia pervs. It feels good to get those degenerates out of the community." Morningstar gave her hand a final squeeze and offered a grim smile before releasing it.

Rebecca nodded, feeling a twinge of pride as she refocused on the task before her. "We're actually here because we're investigating the death of a teenage girl."

Morningstar's expression darkened, her discomfort evident.

Rebecca couldn't blame her. The whole town was on edge. "Coffey, show her the drawings."

Jake pulled out the crumpled sheet from his pocket,

revealing rudimentary sketches of the occult symbols. "Can you tell us anything about these?" He handed the paper to Morningstar, whose fingers traced the lines.

Morningstar's brow furrowed as she studied the paper. "This looks like a hodgepodge of random symbols." Her voice was perplexed. "There's an ankh, a hexagram, a solar symbol, and a pentagram. All from different historical and cultural sources. There is some crossover with most of these having at least one meaning related to the sun or stars."

Rebecca leaned in closer, intrigued by Morningstar's expertise.

The store owner laid the paper flat on the counter and continued her explanation. "The ankh is an Egyptian hieroglyph symbolizing eternal life, male and female, the rising sun, death, and even the afterlife. But it's been used by other neo-pagan groups. The solar symbol represents the sun, but it also represents immortality, purity, fire, and a relation to the alchemical symbol for gold. The hexagram, which most people recognize as the Star of David, is an ancient symbol that has been used by all the world's major faith traditions. Traditionally, it is said to represent the sun, the star, and gold."

Nodding, Rebecca jotted down notes. "This is very helpful."

Morningstar waited 'til she was caught up before continuing. "The inverted pentagram has a rich history I could talk about at length. The symbol represents power and wisdom, but it's been misunderstood through the ages. Now, when it's flipped upside-down, it has come to be associated with Baphomet, and by extension, satanism, with the five points representing the five wounds of Christ.

The hair on the back of Rebecca's neck stood up.

Again, she paused while Rebecca wrote. "As far as I know, there's no religious or spiritual group in history that's used all of these together, although as I said, they do share some symbolism."

Rebecca's mind raced, trying to piece together the implications of this information. While she hadn't known the name for the ankh, she knew it was Egyptian. The stars and sun throughline seemed tenuous, since the symbols each carried multiple meanings. Were they simply used to throw off the investigation? Was the occult angle just a red herring? Maybe a copycat of the Cthulhu case?

She showed Morningstar the photo of Whitney they'd gotten from Annabelle Turner. "Do you recognize her? Her name is Whitney Turner."

Morningstar looked at the picture and nodded. "Yes, she's come in quite a few times buying different pieces of merchandise. She seems like a nice girl."

Rebecca caught a flicker of sympathy in Morningstar's eyes. "Did Whitney ever come in here with other girls?"

"Sure, but there's always groups of teenagers who like to come in and wander around." With a flourish, she gestured to the space. "This is the teenage version of a candy store."

Rebecca gestured to Jake, and he pulled out his phone, bringing up screenshots he'd captured from the girls' social media profiles on the way over. For now, these were the only images they had of the girls Cynthia Wells had mentioned earlier—Marie Allman, Carrie Dugan, and Abigail Miller, as well as Sara Porter. He showed the screenshots to Morningstar, who pinched her lips and nodded.

"A few of them look familiar. They always just seemed like they were having fun and enjoying the witchy merchandise. I never got a bad impression, but I haven't talked to them much. Some kids ask me questions, but they never did."

Rebecca mulled over Morningstar's information. Sara had stated Whitney had no other friends. Was she lying, or did she not consider the other girls friends of Whitney's? And was she right in that assumption? Either was possible.

"Did you ever overhear any conversations they had?" Jake chimed in as he studied Morningstar.

"Nothing unusual." Morningstar paused to think. "They discussed the old witch of the island a few times, but that's to be expected in my store. Anyone interested in my merchandise is likely interested in the old witch too. As I said earlier, that's sort of what I was counting on when I opened the shop here."

If the girls had only recently started hanging out as part of Whitney's attempts to go out more, that could explain why Sara wouldn't consider them real friends.

"You said a few of them looked familiar. Did this one come in?" Rebecca expanded Sara's image until her face filled the screen.

Morningstar considered the picture for a moment, finally shaking her head.

If Sara didn't come in with Whitney, then it seemed the besties weren't as close as they could be. Though Sara's parents didn't seem the type to let their daughter out of the house much.

Rebecca closed out Sara's photo. "Any idea when was the last time you saw any of these girls?"

"About a week ago, I think." Morningstar's expression grew somber.

"Any chance you have surveillance cameras?"

"Sorry. Even if curious shoppers aren't adherents to a witchy life, they tend to be turned away by cameras." The corner of her mouth curved up. "I guess coming here is a dirty little secret for some people."

Well, that was something to consider.

"But it's just me. I don't have any employees, if that helps."

"Thank you, Morningstar. Your assistance has been

invaluable." Determination to find the pieces that would complete this puzzle surged through Rebecca.

"Of course. I hope you find the answers you're looking for." Morningstar accompanied them to the door.

Rebecca followed Jake onto the sidewalk outside the store. Archive Arcana's dimly lit interior gave way to the all-encompassing darkness of night. The chill in the air was sharper now, and she shivered involuntarily, pulling her coat tighter around herself. Shadows played tricks on her eyes as they darted across the street.

"Damn." She glanced at her watch. "I almost forgot about Frost and the others at the cemetery." She grabbed her radio. "Frost, you got your ears on?

"Hey, Boss, I'm here," Hoyt answered immediately. "Did you learn anything useful? Got the bad guys yet?"

"I learned a bunch. Whitney was a bit of a loner but was working to change that recently." Her breath frosted in the cold air. "We found out Whitney and some other girls were hanging out together at Archive Arcana."

"The new woo-woo spooky shop that opened this spring?"

Rebecca could always rely on Hoyt to be aware of the changes happening on the island. "I'll tell the owner you'll be stopping by on your day off."

"Like that'll ever happen…a real day off."

Rebecca grinned to herself. "We're going to follow up with those girls tomorrow. Any updates on your end?"

"Radar team's been at it all day. They haven't confirmed anything yet, but it looks like they've found some graves worth investigating. We set up some lights so they could keep working. I appreciate how dedicated they are. They'll have more information for us tomorrow morning."

"Sounds like we both have a long way to go still."

"Yeah." Hoyt laughed. "But we're all used to it at this point."

That was sad but true. Rebecca's shift had ended hours ago, but she was still working. Jake was in the same boat. Hoyt wasn't even supposed to be on the schedule today. But as always, when they were needed, everyone showed up to get the job done and support each other.

She smiled, thinking that was what friends did, and climbed into the cruiser. "I'll make sure to grab some doughnuts for everyone tomorrow."

Beside her, for some reason, Jake sighed heavily before stretching the seat belt across his waist and fastening it.

12

My pulse pounded so hard I could feel it in my ears, like I had two more hearts up there instead of eardrums. I scanned my surroundings to make sure no one was around. Hiding in my backyard wasn't my best move—I was freezing my tits off —but it was better than hiding in my room.

And right now, I needed as much privacy as I could get. Pressing the button on my phone, I watched it buzz, waiting for the video call to connect.

The black screen flickered to life. Cordelia, Sapphire, and Minerva were each huddled outside somewhere, their eyes darting around nervously. They looked like they were about to crap their pants. I swallowed hard, telling myself to keep my shit together. "Ladies, I know the cops are nosing around. Sapphire, did you stick to the story I gave you? How'd it go?"

"Fuck! That's how it went, Blair." Sapphire was a hot mess. Typical.

Cordelia's hands must've been shaking, because her video was bouncing all over.

"The sheriff was asking all kinds of questions," Sapphire went on. "Her and some hot deputy guy."

Cordelia, suddenly calm, blinked at Sapphire. "Hot? How hot?"

"Dude, so hot."

For a second, things seemed normal. I took a breath, thinking I had my bitches back under control.

And then Sapphire went apeshit. "What the hell happened, Blair? You guys said you could do this. I thought you were going to bury her so people blamed it on those Aqua Mafia assholes or thought she ran off or something."

"Yeah. The cops are looking into everything!" Cordelia's voice had risen to a kind of whispering shriek. "What the hell are we supposed to do?"

"Shut up!" I glanced around the yard, making sure I was still alone. It was dark, but all the houses in the neighborhood had lights shining through their windows. Each lawn was lit up at least a little.

"And why aren't we together right now? If we're all supposed to be sticking together?" Minerva's tone suggested I had betrayed them all. As if I wasn't just a few blocks over.

"I told you, we have to vary our patterns so no one will get suspicious. Look, everything is still fine. It's just that there was a complication with the body."

"The grave we were going to use was already taken," Cordelia added.

"*All* graves are already taken!" Minerva's red hair framed her freckled face like a fiery halo.

I rolled my eyes. "Not inside the coffin, fuck-wit. We only got a few feet down when we found a bone. A skull. Outside the coffin." The clunk of the shovel hitting that bone had been haunting me all day. Digging graves was no joke. "And we didn't have time to start all over in a new spot. The sun was coming up."

"Great, just great." Sapphire's violet eyes filled with dread. "So what did you do with Willow's body, then?"

I ignored Sapphire's question. "Don't call her Willow. She doesn't deserve that name. She's just Whitney now that the witch curse took her down, and she's no longer part of the coven."

The best lies were always partly true. My mom wasn't good for much, but that was her one piece of advice that made sense.

"What matters is that I took care of it after that, like I said I would. I stand by my word. Listen, we have to stick together. The sheriff might figure out we knew Whitney, but it doesn't matter. Think about it. A lot of people knew *of* her, but no one really knew her because she was such a loner. All we have to do is follow the plan."

"I knew her…" Minerva was on the verge of tears.

"I knew her too!" Sapphire's gritted teeth creaked through the video call.

"Just shut up." I didn't have time for Sapphire's drama.

"So the plan is," Cordelia's voice wavered now too, "we just keep on pretending to be devastated?"

"Exactly. You're 'so sorry, I wish I could help, but I don't know anything.' Don't forget to cry randomly even when no one's looking." I scanned the faces of my coven sisters. "Practice your tears, ladies. That way, you'll have puffy eyes, and people will think you're really sad. Just like the three of you look now. It's perfect."

They *looked* uneasy. Sapphire and Minerva checked their faces in their phones.

Now that they were scared and distracted, it was time to build them back up.

"Remember, we're a sisterhood. We're in this together, no matter what." I studied each of my sisters. They were mine, to protect or punish as I saw fit. "Whitney had to go. You all know why, and the witch agreed. But you're all loyal, which means I'm duty bound to keep you safe. Promise me you'll do what I ask so we're all protected."

This was the moment of truth.

Sapphire bit her lip, hesitating before nodding firmly. "I promise, Blair. I'm with you."

"Good." Then Sapphire the Hot Mess was in.

"Excellent." Cordelia sounded sure. Maybe she'd just been shaking from the cold.

"And you, Minerva?"

Minerva's eyes met mine with a steely determination that surprised me. Out of everyone, I thought she'd be the weakest. "I promise. That witch-bitch will have to come through me. I won't let anything happen to us."

"Then it's settled." I gave them my sweetest smile. "We'll stick to the plan and get through this together."

"Are you sure this is going to work?" Cordelia darted a glance over her shoulders.

"Trust me. We just have to wait for this all to blow over. And in the meantime, cry on cue. How hard is that? Now go back to your families."

They all nodded and signed off with whispered goodnights.

I hung up and shoved the phone in my pocket before heading inside. It was a good thing they all trusted me. Because I really did have a contingency plan if any of them were disloyal.

Just ask Whitney.

13

Sunlight peeked through the dense canopy of trees, casting eerie shadows on the freshly disturbed earth as Hoyt met back up with the radar team.

Trent had been waiting for him in the parking lot, and they walked out to where they'd left off their search yesterday. The radar team had stayed past sunset last night to finish up the first half of the cemetery. Working under the large lights he and Trent had secured, the dedicated technicians kept combing the grounds. So Frost was shocked to see them back at it again already. And on the day before Thanksgiving, no less.

"Morning, Deputy." Leonard Blyberg offered him a tired smile as he walked along behind one of the machines. "We've got some interesting findings for you. I wanted to verify some of the information before we shared it."

Hoyt pulled his hat from his head and raked his hair back. "Already? Let's hear it."

"Twenty-three burial sites flagged." Blyberg tapped the screen of his tablet. "Now, that doesn't mean every single one of them has a John or Jane Doe…but we can be reasonably sure many do. I wanted to verify some of the data, just to be certain."

Trent's gaze swept over the marked locations, his face betraying a mix of shock and horror as his jaw hung wide open.

Hoyt clenched his teeth, suppressing the urge to voice his outrage at the sheer number of potential victims.

"Exhumation is the only way to confirm." Blyberg waited for their instructions.

"Any chance those could be animal burials?" Hoyt hoped against hope for a less sinister explanation.

"Possible, but unlikely." Blyberg smiled grimly and shook his head. "I ran all the anomalies we'd recorded yesterday through our software at the office. These are the ones that are left. The size and density of most of these are consistent with human remains. We went ahead and marked them all." He handed over a printout of the cemetery speckled with dots on one half of the map.

"Damn," Trent muttered, scanning over Hoyt's shoulder.

Hoyt's stomach turned, his mind filling with questions, each darker than the last, as he looked at the map. Who were these people? How long had they been buried here, hidden beneath the soil like discarded secrets? And how many more would their team find before this nightmare ended?

"Good work, Blyberg." He bobbed his head at the leader of the ground-penetration radar team. "Keep us updated on your progress." It was probably useless to hope they wouldn't find any more, but he hoped anyway.

"Will do." Blyberg nodded back before resuming his search.

As the team returned to their painstaking plotting of the bodies, Trent finally got his slack jaw under control. "Twenty-three?" He stopped to shudder. "Damn. How the hell are we going to deal with so many?"

"I don't have a fucking clue. I'd better call the boss and let her know about this. I don't think she was expecting it to get this bad." Hoyt grabbed his radio. "Hey, Sheriff, you on yet?"

"For the last hour or so, Frost. What's up?" Rebecca sounded caffeinated. Hopefully that meant she would know how to handle this.

"The ground radar team has flagged twenty-three potential bodies. I just wanted to give you a heads-up."

"Twenty-three? Did I hear that right?" He detected her fingers tapping away on a keyboard and realized she was most likely in her cruiser, sending messages and emails using the onboard laptop while talking to him on the radio. It had been serving as her mobile office ever since the station had been bombed.

"Yeah, Boss. Two three. Twenty-three possible bodies. That's in addition to Body B."

"Okay."

There was a long pause. Trent's eyebrows crept higher with every passing second.

More tapping came from her end before she spoke again. "I just let Bailey know. She's going to get you as many hands as she can for the extractions. I'm updating Lettinger, as well, to see if she can wrangle some additional medical examiners. We can't just dump all this in Bailey's lap."

"Uh, wow. Thanks, Boss. That didn't take long." Hoyt was pleasantly surprised.

"I can talk, type, and listen at the same time. You got anything else for me?"

"Only that the radar team is still working, so they might find more today."

"They're not finished with the cemetery and already found that many?" For the first time, Rebecca sounded flustered.

"Yes, ma'am." Hoyt watched Blyberg stop to plant another little flag to be double-checked.

"Okay, then I'll tell Bailey and Rhonda you're working this case, and they can coordinate directly with you."

"Aw, Boss, does that mean you're not going to do all my work for me?" Hoyt shared a silent chuckle with Trent.

"I think I've done enough of your work for you just now. You should know the boss's job is delegation. This is all on you. But I'll give you a tiny bit of advice."

"What's that, Boss?"

"Get ready for a media storm." Rebecca's joking tone suddenly turned grave. "Keep me updated. Both of you."

"Will do." He ended the call.

Trent crossed his arms. "Ya know, there's a reason she made it into the FBI and we didn't."

"Because *I* didn't apply." Hoyt shoved the map into Trent's hands and snorted. Before Trent could counter, Hoyt's phone rang, and he held up a finger to tell him to hold on. The name on the screen read, *Bailey Flynn*. "Bailey?" His heart pounded in his chest. "Tell me you have some good news."

"Depends on your definition of 'good,' I guess." Her voice was steady despite the weight of her words. "I've identified that body from yesterday. I see by a note Rebecca added to the file that this is officially Body B. Dental records matched him to a Randall Krull, reported missing eleven months ago. No cause of death for him. That'll require a specialist. I'm not going to even try since he's only bones."

"Randall Krull." Hoyt reached for the pen and notepad in his pocket. "Thanks, Bailey. You're doing great work."

"Happy to help. And I wanted to give you something to do instead of just standing around waiting for me to show up. I hear you've got your hands full out there."

"I'm surprised you're not already on your way," Hoyt

admitted. "It's going to be a long day. You might want to get a move on."

Bailey blew a raspberry into the phone hard enough it left his ear feeling wet. "First things first. I'm getting my assistants, equipment, and vehicles all put together. It takes more time to do a job poorly than it does to plan properly in the first place. But don't worry, we'll be out there as soon as we can."

Then she hung up before Hoyt could come up with an answer.

He pocketed his phone and turned back to Trent, who had been watching him with concern etched into his features. "We've got a name for our fleshless John Doe. Randall Krull. He disappeared a year ago."

"Dang." Trent rubbed the back of his neck. "Well, at least we have answers for one of them. You think we'll have as much luck with the others?"

"Only time will tell." Hoyt turned and walked back to his cruiser. "Let's focus on the name we have."

Dropping into the driver's seat, he whipped the computer around and pulled up Randall Krull's past. Beside him, Trent rested against the open door.

Silence settled over them like a shroud before Hoyt spoke. "Found something interesting. Krull was a private investigator before he went missing."

"Really?" Trent had to lean over to see the screen. "What kind of cases did he work on?"

"Seems like a mix of infidelity and fraud, mostly." Hoyt scrolled through Krull's archived website. "But there are some more serious ones here…kidnapping, missing persons. Makes me wonder if he got too close to something…or someone."

"Could be. Those all sound like something the Yacht Club would do. He might've learned something they didn't want revealed, so they had Stokely make him disappear. We should let Special Agent Lettinger know what we found. She might have some insight."

"Good idea." Hoyt picked up his phone and dialed Rhonda Lettinger's number. Rhonda worked with the general investigation section of the state police and was privy to all missing persons cases in the state.

She answered on the first ring. "Lettinger."

Hoyt wondered if she'd been waiting for his call. Rebecca had said she'd given her a heads-up. "Rhonda, it's Senior Deputy Hoyt Frost down here in Shadow Island. Not sure if you've heard yet, but it looks like we've found Randall Krull, who went missing last year."

"Interesting. His name rings a bell. But it's been a while, so I'll have to review the details. I do recall that the Virginia State Police never managed to find any leads on his disappearance from the Tidewater area. This is the first break in the case. I'll dig into it and get back to you."

"Sheriff West already told you we've got twenty-three and counting, right? Twenty-four, including Krull?" Hoyt still couldn't believe how many there were, despite saying it several times now.

"She did. And I'm ready to send you guys help as soon as you need it. I'm putting together a roster now."

"Thanks. We haven't started digging any of them up yet. Once we do, we'll check for identification to see if we can find any connections between Krull, Dwight Stokely, anyone from the Yacht Club, and our other victims."

"Holler if you need anything."

"Will do." He ended the call and stared at his phone for a moment. "Rhonda's going to review Krull's case and let us know. Let's get back to work."

Trent moved out of the way as Hoyt got out of the cruiser.

"Deputy Frost!" a voice called out, stopping him in his tracks. He turned to find an unfamiliar man approaching, his face creased with concern. This wasn't a face he'd seen around here before, and that made him wary.

"Can I help you?" Hoyt kept his tone guarded.

"What's going on with the radar team? They've been crawling all over this place." The man eyed the technicians working in the distance.

"Law enforcement business," Hoyt replied curtly, already turning away. "Nothing for you to worry about."

"Wait!" Desperation crept into the stranger's voice. "Is this about the girl they found yesterday morning? My niece went missing last year, and—"

"I can't discuss ongoing investigations." Hoyt tried to keep his impatience in check. He understood the man's fear, but there were too many questions still unanswered for him to share any information. He needed to focus on finding those answers before more lives were lost.

"Please," the man pleaded, his voice breaking. "I just need to know if she's…if she's…"

"Listen." Hoyt forced himself to meet the man's gaze. "I understand and sympathize with what you're going through, but right now, we're still working on exhuming the remains, and it'll take a while for identification."

"But—"

"If we find anything that could help you, we'll be sure to let you know."

The man stared at him for a moment before Trent walked past him, snapping a picture of the man's face.

"What the hell?" The man's tear-filled eyes dried up as they filled with heated anger.

Trent tapped away on his phone. "You said your niece is missing, right? I'm taking a picture of you so I can make sure to contact you once we have information to share."

"Oh." The man blinked a few times while Hoyt frowned at them both.

Flipping his phone around, Trent showed Hoyt the screen before addressing the man again. "Are you allowed to get calls at work? You're still a reporter for the *Suffolk Star*, right, Stan? Google's reverse image search is an amazing tool. It linked me to you right away."

Impressed, Hoyt read the screen where Trent had pulled up the newspaper's website and the list of their reporters. Right there was a professional headshot of the "poor grieving uncle," Stan Lubbock. His jaw clenched, and he raised his eyes to glare at the reporter. "Do you even have a niece?"

Stan rolled his eyes at Trent. Without bothering to answer Hoyt's question, he turned and walked off.

"The sheriff warned me this would happen," Trent said.

Hoyt tapped Trent's phone. "Good thinking on the reverse search." He glared at the reporter's back. "We start digging up bodies, and the vultures will start circling. I never thought they'd resort to impersonating grieving family members, though."

Now that it had happened, he understood why Rebecca had warned him. If this was the level reporters were willing to stoop to, it was going to be a hellish investigation.

14

Parked on the edge of the road, Rebecca pinched the bridge of her nose, dropping her head back to land on the headrest of her cruiser. When Hoyt had radioed in, she'd pulled over so she could multitask. And once she'd learned how many bodies they'd located, she was glad she had. Twenty-three additional burial sites. She couldn't believe it.

They were going to require a small army to exhume all those bodies. And they still needed to interview three of the teenage friends of the stabbing victim. There was so much to do and too little time.

Her phone rang again. This time, it was Bailey Flynn. "Hey, Rebecca, I'm going to cut to the chase because we both have a lot going on. Whitney Turner's DNA test came back positive. I've already called her parents and let them know as well. I'm typing up her autopsy now. If you want to come take a look, it might save you some time waiting for my report."

The autopsy results would most likely give her better insight into what happened to Whitney, which would help her ask better questions.

"All right. I'll be there shortly."

Driving two blocks, Rebecca stopped to pick up Jake, who was waiting in front of Trent's house—his front room their temporary bullpen, his driveway and curb their parking lot.

"Morning, Boss. Who are we talking to first?" Jake climbed in the vehicle and slapped his seat belt home.

"Dr. Bailey Flynn." Rebecca grinned.

As she pulled into traffic, he shot her a questioning look.

"She called a few minutes ago. The DNA results came in early, and our victim is confirmed to be Whitney Turner. Let's see what the autopsy can tell us. It might reveal something that'll help when we talk to Abigail Miller, Carrie Dugan, and Marie Allman."

"Sounds like a plan." Jake leaned back and crossed his arms over his chest. "That means I can get a nap in."

Rebecca glanced over at him. He already had his eyes closed, and she was certain he was already falling asleep. Jake was former military police. If there was one thing the Army was especially good at, it was teaching every soldier how to nap at the drop of a hat.

Dull-gray skies and a dark, angry-looking ocean escorted them all the way to the mainland.

Jake stayed asleep the whole ride, waking up as Rebecca parked at Coastal Ridge Hospital. One quick breath and a look around, and he was ready to go. It would be worth enduring three months of boot camp if she could be assured she'd learn how to nap like that.

Rebecca snatched her travel mug—a new one to replace the sentimental loaned mug from Ryker all those months ago —and its beloved contents from the holder and marched inside. They entered the lower level through the back entrance behind the building and were almost immediately greeted by the cold, sterile environment of the morgue.

Rebecca slowly opened the door, not sure if Bailey was in there or her office.

"Ah, Sheriff, right on time." Bailey was standing near the back wall. She was glove-free as she tucked her phone back into her pocket. "I was just taking a quick break to make sure my husband had gotten everything we need for tomorrow's Thanksgiving feast. Let me show you what I learned about Whitney Turner."

Donning a face mask and gloves, Rebecca approached the examination table where Whitney's body lay face down, covered by a white sheet from the hips to knees. Despite having seen countless victims before, Rebecca always felt uneasy when the victims were young.

It was even more disconcerting up close. In addition to the symbols carved into Whitney's arms from her hands to her elbows, there were brownish-yellow splotches on the back of her left arm, plus a similarly colored line along her right shoulder and arm. The discolorations indicated postmortem lividity and blanching of the skin. Whitney's small back was covered in stab wounds, and Rebecca noticed the slightest hint of marble-like effect just under the skin.

Jake joined them at the table, clad in his own protective gear.

Bailey gave an approving tilt of her head toward Jake as she pulled on gloves. "Good to see someone who hasn't been influenced by Frost's weak stomach."

"I've been at too many DUI scenes to have something this clean bother me anymore, ma'am." Jake bobbed his head respectfully at the medical examiner.

"All right, Bailey, what have you got for us?" Rebecca wanted to know more about the discoloration on Whitney's arms and what Bailey had learned from that.

"Eight stab wounds in the back. No defensive wounds, as you'd expect from a knife in the back. The first strike to her back punctured the left posterior upper lobe of her lung, causing her to begin to suffocate. Blood would have begun to fill the punctured lung, and she'd have found it increasingly difficult to catch her breath."

"Poor kid," Jake murmured.

She surveyed the body before continuing. "Even more damning, I could tell from the intercostal tissues, the muscles that connect the ribs, that she was bent over with her back arched slightly. This poor girl was literally stabbed in the back while in a defenseless posture."

"Any idea what the murder weapon was?" Jake's tone displayed an unexpected level of nonchalance, considering the troublesome scene before them.

"It was an extremely sharp knife, probably eight inches long with a rounded blade edge. Standard kitchen or chef's knife, most likely." Bailey pointed to the clean cuts covering Whitney.

Rebecca leaned forward, noting the white ribs showing through. She stepped back and curled her back, trying to imagine what Whitney had been doing when she was killed. Picking something up? She might have also been bending to get in a car. If there were two killers, she might've been leaning into a car to talk to one of them while the other came up behind her.

"Nothing like that found at the dump site. I searched it myself before forensics showed up. They didn't find anything either. And with the radar team combing every inch of the grounds out there, I'm sure someone would've found it if it was there." Jake watched Rebecca as she moved around the table but didn't say a word about her actions. "Killer might still have it."

"First stab was the cause of death?" Rebecca's gaze was fixed on the puncture marks marring the young woman's pale skin and the carvings on her arms. "I noticed at the cemetery that the other wounds barely bled. There was no blood in the carvings."

Bailey shrugged. "With eight stab wounds, one of which was to her lung, I can't say which wound killed her. Likely, it was a combination of blood loss and suffocation. The symbols were carved long after the heart had stopped beating. By that point, the blood had already started to settle in the chest and stomach. You can't see it with her lying face down, but trust me, it's there. The symbols could have been done at the kill site, or at the cemetery, or somewhere in between."

"Find any other DNA?" Rebecca asked, hoping for a lead.

"None." Bailey shook her head. "Whoever did this left no trace of themselves."

"That might mean that whoever did this had it planned out well enough to wear gloves." Jake's blue eyes were trained on their victim. "Or they were simply wearing gloves and a coat because it's cold out. The cold always adds its own layer of issues to any crime. Or maybe it happened so quickly, there wasn't an opportunity to leave DNA behind."

Bailey raised an eyebrow, clearly impressed by Jake's insight. "Not bad, Deputy."

"Thanks." Jake's mouth quirked up in a half smile.

"While there was no DNA left behind, I did find some fibers on her clothing and in her hair. Several fibers were stuck to the dried blood on her sweatshirt." Bailey pointed to a table that contained evidence bags with Whitney's clothing inside. "Based on the types of fibers, I'm willing to go out on a limb and say Whitney was transported inside a blanket."

Rebecca tried to process this information. It matched what she and Jake had surmised at the cemetery.

"What can you tell us about the time of death?" Jake asked.

Bailey turned to look Kathrine in the eye. "I like this one. Make sure you keep him around."

Jake blushed. Rebecca was sure of it.

"On to your question, Deputy Coffey. The decedent was in full rigor when I first looked at her around two thirty p.m. yesterday. Fixed discoloration in livor mortis indicates she'd been dead at least six hours by then. Liver temp tells me she died between ten on Monday night and one on Tuesday morning, but that could be off slightly since I don't know where she was killed or what means of transportation was used to move her." She jerked her chin toward the door and the world outside. "And the cold overnight temps could be throwing off the calculations as well."

Jake scribbled notes furiously, allowing Rebecca the opportunity to just listen.

"A ballpark for now is fine."

The medical examiner checked her clipboard notes before continuing. "There are layers to the internal pooled blood. That suggests she was moved a few times. Unfortunately, the science isn't precise on this. But it appears she was in different positions after her death. I don't know the order or how often she was moved, only that she was." Bailey pointed to Whitney's right shoulder, which had a darker, fuller line of discoloration.

Rebecca moved closer, examining each of the patterns Bailey indicated.

Bailey waved both hands over the marbled back of the girl. "A tiny bit of pooled blood matched the uneven position she was lying in and didn't match the pattern of dried blood I found on her back, shoulders, and neck. The different patterns indicate the different movements of her body after death."

"The additional stab wounds were inflicted right after the first blow to her lung? Like maybe they weren't aware of the lethal nature of the first strike? Or they just wanted to make sure she was dead." Rebecca was trying to picture the scene, so she'd know what to look for later.

"Correct." Bailey nodded. "No discernible difference in the skin wounds between pre- and postmortem. There's also no hilt or handle marks on the skin, so the strikes were more controlled and not frenzied."

"Eight stabs, but no bruising from the knife or edge of a hand?" Rebecca peered down at the young woman's body. "But where was she killed? And why did she leave her house that night?"

Bailey pulled her gloves off with a loud snap. "That's your job. Mine is done for now. Which is good, since it looks like I have plenty more I'll be dealing with."

Despite there being at least twenty-four additional bodies besides Whitney's at the cemetery, including Randall Krull's Rebecca had to stay focused on Whitney Turner's case. She deserved justice, and her killer needed to be found.

15

The morning sunlight glinted off the shovel in Hoyt's hands as he dug into the cold earth, sweat trickling down his brow. Physical exercise was a great way to chase away the cold, but honestly, he would've preferred to just keep his coat on. It wasn't the hard work that bothered him. It was the reason for it. Twenty-three bodies.

He paused, holding the shovel straight up to gauge how deep they'd dug already. They needed to stop before they got to the depth of the remains. And to make sure he didn't disturb anything, he was forced to dig a couple of feet wider than what they'd seen on the radar as well.

At that point, the techs who were supervising his digging would come in with trowels and spades to ensure the bodies weren't damaged by the larger and heavier tools. Just as they'd done with the site Trent was working. It was more like he was digging a ring for the techs to work in than doing any real work to unearth the victims.

Once the techs took over, their work was fascinating. He didn't understand the intricacies of how they got their measurements, but he understood the end result. Techs drew plans and profiles that indicated the body's horizontal and vertical orientation to other reference points. They plotted those points using GPS.

They were far from done, but the drawings were eye-opening. Anomalies in the ground indicated there were bodies stacked above the coffins that had been properly buried.

Thankfully, Hoyt's phone buzzed in his pocket, allowing him an excuse to climb out of the shallow ditch they'd been working in. He recognized the number on the screen and stepped away from the grave to take the call.

"Special Agent Lettinger? What have you got for me?" Hoyt spoke loud enough for Trent to hear. He was helping the techs by hauling buckets of dirt from another grave so they could sift every particle for evidence. Trent lifted his head and gave a nod, letting Hoyt know he'd heard and understood.

"Hey, Frost. I've been digging into the Krull case like I promised, and I found some interesting information about him." Rhonda's words piqued his curiosity instantly, and he felt a mix of anticipation and dread.

"Go on." Hoyt leaned against a nearby tree as he listened.

"All right, so Krull was a private investigator in the Tidewater area, like I said. He didn't have any kids, but he did have a wife. She's the one who reported him missing to the police in Newport News. And according to his widow, he was digging into something big when he disappeared."

"That sounds promising. Did he—"

"Before you ask, he never gave anyone the details of what he was working on. Even more interesting, when he went missing, so did his computer with all his work files." Rhonda's tone had a steely edge to it. "All his widow could remember about the job was that he'd been going over to the island periodically, but they had no hard evidence linking him to anyone or anything."

"The M.O. matches Dwight Stokely with the missing computer and files like he did with Roger Biggio." That was good and bad news. The good being Stokely was no longer a threat, since he was dead. The bad part was they'd still have to prove it was Stokely who killed Krull. They knew Stokely had buried some victims here, but there was no way to tell if he was the only murderer Abe Barclay had a deal with.

"I'll keep looking into this. I've got the original lead on the case bringing me his case notes now. I'll email you what I've got so far."

"Thanks. I appreciate it." Hoyt frowned as he processed Rhonda's new information. The image of Krull, a private investigator, digging into something big and dangerous before his disappearance, painted a grim picture. What could he have been looking into? Whatever it was, it had to be pretty serious if it got the man killed.

He could check the date of Krull's disappearance and compare it to anything that had happened on the island that might've required a private investigator.

Hoyt took out his radio to contact Rebecca. There was a pause of only a few moments before she answered. "Go ahead, Frost."

"We've got some new intel on the first set of skeletal remains, a man named Randall Krull. Lettinger found his missing persons case file, and he did have a possible connection to the island and the Yacht Club."

"Two bodies!" Trent called out, cutting through Hoyt's conversation. He waved Hoyt over, urgency in his voice.

"Boss, give me a minute. We just found something new." Hoyt jogged over to where Trent waited for him. He stopped at the edge of the grave.

Two bodies were stacked atop one another like discarded

dolls wrapped in a grotesque embrace, as if one had been trying to shield the other. The lower body had just been unearthed, with only a portion of the ribs showing under the original corpse they'd already dug up.

"Boss," Hoyt spoke into his radio, his voice tense, "we've got a problem. We found two more bodies directly under Randall Krull in the first grave."

"Two?" Rebecca's disbelief echoed through the line. "I'm coming over to hel—"

"No." Hoyt cut her off firmly. "You need to keep investigating that dead girl. We'll handle things here."

"Are you sure?" Her hesitancy came through the radio clearly. "I can be there in—"

"With the way you solve cases, you'll have that one wrapped up before we can even finish counting all the victims out here." Impotent anger tightened Hoyt's throat, and he had to pause to clear it. "You're doing something important. No need for you to come here only to watch over our shoulders. We got this."

"All right, but call me if anything else comes up."

"Yeah, Boss." Hoyt clipped his radio back on his shoulder, turning away from the gruesome scene before him.

"Man, this is messed up." Trent shook his head in disgust as they began their examination. "Think we're looking at forty-six victims instead?"

"Let's not jump to conclusions yet." Hoyt inwardly shared the same fear. This was going to be too much for just him and Trent to handle. He hadn't wanted it to come to this. Hoyt sighed, pulled out his phone, and dialed Deputy Viviane Darby.

The sound of her voice was a welcome distraction from the ghastly tableau. "Hey, Frost, do you miss me already?"

"Viviane, we might need your help here. I know you wanted some time off to spend with your mom now that she's out of the hospital, but could you come help us out today?"

"Are you serious?" Viviane's disbelief was evident even over the phone. "Now that Mama's awake and talking, I want to spend as much time with her as I can. I know I helped catch Luka, but I still have guilt about leaving her exposed. She endured a second attack because of me."

"Trust me, it's very important." He glanced at the two bodies being carefully exhumed, their pale bones contrasting against the dark soil.

Viviane sighed. "All right, but it'll have to wait until my dad gets back. I'm not leaving her alone. It's going to be a few hours."

Next, Hoyt called the medical examiner, filling her in on the situation. "We've found two more bodies in the first grave. I'm willing to bet we'll need more help than whoever you can scrounge together."

Bailey whistled. "Agreed. I'll see if I can get Agent Lettinger to send a forensic team to help as well as calling in some favors with a few forensic anthropologists scattered around the state." With that, she hung up.

A flash of movement caught his eye, and he turned to look. "Dammit."

A photographer was lurking just beyond the cemetery fence, snapping away at the grisly scene with a disturbingly gleeful expression on his face.

"Locke!" He tried to keep his frustration in check as he called out. "We need the team that's setting up the tents to kick it into high gear. That vulture's trying to get pictures of the bodies."

Hoyt's mind raced as he contemplated the potential fallout from those photos being splashed across the media. These victims deserved to be treated with dignity and privacy, not to be exploited in tabloids for the morbid curiosity of the public.

"Hey, you!" Trent bellowed at the photographer, striding toward him with purpose. "You need to back off. This is an active crime scene."

"Freedom of the press!" The photographer raised his camera defiantly. "I have every right to be here." Sadly, that was true. They couldn't even take the camera from him.

"Come on, man." Hoyt joined Trent near the fence. "Show some decency. These are real people who've lost their lives, and their families deserve better than having their pain exploited."

The photographer paused for a moment, seeming to weigh his options. Finally, with a sigh, he lowered his camera. "Sorry, gentlemen. I get paid for photos that draw traffic to the website. And these are going to generate a lot of interest."

"Money over decency, huh?" Locke scoffed.

He'd stopped taking photos, but it was clear he only did so because Trent and Hoyt were blocking his view. "You might stop me temporarily, but I'm pretty resourceful."

"Wonderful." Hoyt seethed as the man retreated. A knot of unease twisted in his gut. Everything about this case felt like it was teetering on the edge of chaos.

16

Rebecca set the radio back in the cradle, her fingers trembling slightly as she gripped the device. Hoyt's words echoed in her mind. The graveyard situation was spiraling out of control, the weight of it settling heavy on her heart. But Hoyt was right. She and Jake needed to settle Whitney Turner's case as quickly as they could.

"Marie Allman's place is just around the corner." Jake spoke up, breaking her thoughts.

She turned onto a quiet residential street lined with modest homes and well-manicured lawns. Rebecca took a deep breath as she stepped out of the SUV. The air was crisp and cool, carrying the faint scent of saltwater from the nearby shore.

The sun was still two hours away from the peak of noon, sending long shadows reaching for the house they were approaching. The house itself was quiet, not a single sound coming from it. Considering the time of day, that wasn't unusual. Not everyone was able to get off work the day before Thanksgiving.

"Let's hope someone's here." Rebecca knocked on the door.

Surprisingly, the door swung open right away, revealing a middle-aged couple wearing matching expressions of concern.

"Sheriff Rebecca West." She showed them her badge. "And this is Deputy Jake Coffey."

The man reached out a hand to shake. "I'm Patrick Allman, and this is my wife, Tanna. We heard about what happened to that girl."

Tanna stretched out her hand to shake as well. Her fingers trembled just a bit.

Patrick put his fist on his hip. "I'm assuming you didn't stop by just to wish us an early happy Thanksgiving. What can I do for you, Sheriff?"

"We're sorry to intrude, but we need to speak with your daughter, Marie. It's about Whitney Turner. They were classmates, as you might know."

Patrick's jaw tightened, but he nodded. "Of course. Just… please be gentle with her."

"Nobody wants to cause her any distress." Rebecca spoke reassuringly. "We just need to ask her a few questions."

Tanna fixed them both with a steely gaze. "Marie won't be questioned without us present."

"Understood." Rebecca held her hands up in surrender, earning her a tiny smile from Tanna. "Is it all right if we come inside?"

"Please." Patrick stepped aside to allow them entry. He called out over his shoulder. "Marie, can you come here, please?" Then he took his wife's hand and led her to the couch.

As they waited, Rebecca took in the cozy family room, noting the photographs adorning the walls—smiling faces, joyful memories. The kitchen, where people usually kept knives, was out of sight. If the girls were friends, or even just classmates, it wouldn't be outside the realm of possibility that the parents also had a connection to the girl.

Right now, everyone was a suspect. During her very first case on the island, teenagers dominated the investigation, but it was the parents who proved to be the problem. That was a lesson Rebecca wouldn't ever forget. She needed to know how all these people might be connected.

With eyes that were slightly puffy and as red as her hair, Marie entered the room, her gaze darting between Rebecca and Jake before settling on the floor. It looked like she hadn't been expecting company, considering the wrinkled state of her shorts and the fact that no one would wear a tank top that flimsy on a day so cold.

Tanna called her over, and Marie took a seat next to her parents, her back rigid, hands folded in her lap. Clearly, word of Whitney's death had affected her. That might've been why her parents had asked them to be gentle. A death in a town this small could affect a lot of people, especially those at such a vulnerable age.

"Marie," Rebecca began gently, "we're here because we need to learn more about Whitney Turner. Did you consider yourselves friends?"

"We knew each other, but mostly from being in the same grade at school." Marie played with the hem of her shirt, her voice barely above a whisper. "Just hung out a few times. We were starting to get to know each other, and now she's dead."

"So you heard about what happened to her?" Rebecca watched Marie's reaction closely.

"Of course. It's all over social media." Her eyes welled up with tears. "She died. It's all anyone's talking about."

Rebecca noticed Marie didn't mention how Whitney died. They were trying to keep as much information out of the press and town gossip chain as possible. It was important when interviewing people to see if they slipped up and indicated they knew details of the crime that hadn't been publicized.

When the girl didn't say more, though, she moved on. "Did you ever go to Archive Arcana together?"

"That shop that opened right before summer break? Yeah, once or twice, just to look around. Whitney was really into that stuff." Marie's answer came quickly, almost nervously, and she peered at her mother. "I just wanted to look at the pretty crystals they had there."

Tanna brushed her hand down Marie's hair. "It's okay, baby. We're not upset. Kids your age get curious about things. Just know that none of that is real."

Marie shrugged. "The crystals were real. That's all I really cared about. I'm not like those girls in school who keep waiting for an owl to show up with an invitation in its beak. I teased Whitney about that once, but she just laughed me off. I don't know if she really thought that kind of stuff was real or not." She swiped the back of her hand under her nose. "But now I feel bad for making fun of her at all."

Jake reached into his pocket, pulling out the paper with the drawings they'd found on Whitney's body. "Are you familiar with these symbols? Have you seen them before?"

Marie studied the paper for a moment before nodding. "Yeah, I've seen them at the shop. They have all sorts of weird stuff there. Cards, rocks, crystals, bones, feathers, and vials with all kinds of weird names. It's like a Halloween party that takes itself way too seriously in there."

"Did Whitney seem especially interested in those symbols? Or the things that had those symbols on them?" Rebecca tried to gauge if Marie's gaze lingered on any one symbol. She appeared more confused by them than anything, though it was hard to tell, considering her puffy eyes.

Marie screwed her nose up. "Not that I noticed. But I wasn't looking at everything she looked at either."

"Can you think of anyone who might want something terrible to happen to Whitney?" Rebecca asked, her tone soft but insistent.

A flicker of hesitation passed across Marie's face, her eyes meeting Rebecca's for a brief moment before turning to her parents. Their expressions mirrored her own uncertainty, a mix of fear and sorrow.

Marie's hesitation was palpable as she finally spoke, her voice trembling. "I think…it was the old witch that did it."

Rebecca raised her eyebrows in surprise, and she noticed Patrick and Tanna shared her shock. "What witch are you talking about?" Rebecca needed to verify they were on the same page.

"Th-the old witch in the cottage, by the lighthouse." Marie's eyes darted between her parents and the investigators. "Everyone knows she cursed the island, and that's why bad things happen here."

Rebecca felt a pang of sympathy for the young girl, clearly frightened by the weight of the local legends.

Jake shot her a questioning glance but didn't ask any questions. He'd joined the force on Shadow Island after the mess on Little Quell Island got Deputy Darian Hudson killed. Rebecca had met him at the end of the ordeal with the Lovecraft sacrifices, when he was tasked with taking her statement, and she hadn't officially hired him until right before Abe Barclay turned up hanged at the cemetery. So he wasn't as familiar with the local legends as the folks who'd spent many years here.

"We don't believe in witchcraft in this household," Patrick interjected firmly with a disapproving look.

Tanna nodded in agreement. "None of that stuff is real. Neither are curses."

Rebecca leaned in to make eye contact. "Marie, do you believe in the witch?"

"I didn't before." Her admission was barely audible. "But I do now. Some of the other kids at school said they've seen her. Walking late at night through the trees around the lighthouse. Some of them said you found a dead body in one of those trees. Like it killed her a long time ago. What if that was the witch?"

"That's not what happened, Marie. We didn't find any bodies in a tree. We caught the real flesh and blood bad guy, and he wasn't a witch." Rebecca didn't tell her the rest of that story. Learning what had happened to the descendants of the last caretaker of the lighthouse would not help dispel rumors about curses.

"But someone still died there." Marie didn't seem like she was going to be convinced the supernatural wasn't involved.

Rebecca knew that sometimes rumors or legends held elements of truth. Perhaps Marie knew more than she thought she did. "Why do you think the witch would be angry with Whitney? What could've provoked her?"

"Maybe she didn't like that we were playing around with the occult, or maybe she just wanted revenge for something."

"You said 'we.' How many people are in your group?"

Marie pressed back deeper into her mom's embrace. "I guess it depends on who's available. Just a few of us. Maybe four of us, I guess."

"Have you been to the witch's cottage recently?"

Marie shook her head. "Not recently, no. It's been a long time."

"How long?" Rebecca tried to gauge the girl's sincerity.

"Everyone on the island has been there at some point in their lives." Marie avoided a direct answer.

Tanna shifted uncomfortably in her seat.

Patrick nodded his agreement and then defended his

daughter. "Marie's right. Everyone goes to the cottage at least once. It's a historical site and tourist magnet. Nobody takes that chain across the open doorway seriously, whether they're locals or visitors. And it's practically a rite of passage to go inside and hang out."

Rebecca took in this new information, her mind racing with questions and possibilities about the connection between the old witch and Whitney's death. The investigation was certainly taking a strange turn. Deciding to change her approach, she spoke more firmly. "Marie, where were you this past Monday night, the twenty-third after ten p.m.?"

"Home." Marie answered without hesitation. Her eyes flicked nervously between Rebecca and her parents.

"Can you confirm that?" Rebecca directed the question to Patrick and Tanna.

Both of them nodded vigorously. "Yes, our daughter was with us all evening." Tanna's voice was laced with a protective edge. "It was family game night. Why are you asking about it? Surely, you don't suspect my daughter."

"Sheriff, I think it's time for you to leave." Patrick shifted. "You're upsetting our daughter."

Rebecca observed them closely, sensing their overprotectiveness of Marie. She sighed internally but knew when it was time to back off. "Of course. Thank you for your time."

Patrick escorted them to the front door. Meanwhile, Tanna and Marie disappeared into the depths of the house.

As they stepped out into the cool island air, Rebecca mulled over the information they'd gathered. Marie's account of the old witch, combined with her belief in the curse, added an eerie layer to the investigation. And while she didn't believe in curses or witches herself, she couldn't dismiss the possibility that someone was using the legend to their advantage.

Here we go again.

17

Rebecca and Jake stood on the doorstep of Abigail Miller's home, about to knock.

The door swung open, revealing a teen girl with black hair and dark eyes. She jerked back, almost flinching away from Rebecca's raised fist.

Rebecca cleared her throat. "Hello, Abigail. I'm Sheriff Rebecca West, and this is Deputy Jake Coffey. Are your parents home?"

Abigail shook her head. "No, it's just me and my mom, but she's at work right now."

Rebecca frowned. Even though, according to DMV records, Abigail was technically eighteen and an adult, she was still in high school. Rebecca felt a bit uneasy about speaking to such a "new adult" without a guardian present. However, she pushed the feeling aside, reminding herself that they were running out of time. "Abigail, we're investigating Whitney Turner's case. You heard about it, correct?"

"Um, yes."

"Would you be willing to answer a few questions about her?"

"Oh. Um. Of course." Abigail stepped aside and gestured for them to enter. "Come on in."

The house was spacious, with high rooflines and plenty of windows. As they settled into the living room chairs, Abigail hurried to the kitchen. "Would you two like something to drink?" Rebecca noted that, while Abigail's question was aimed at "you two," the teenager kept her gaze on Jake the whole time.

She studied Abigail. She couldn't help but think Abigail was unsure of how to handle adult visitors without her mother present, despite her attempt to play hostess. Rebecca shared a knowing look with Jake, who seemed to understand. "No, thank you," she replied.

Abigail reappeared and took a seat across from them, folding her hands in her lap. "What do you need to know? I didn't really know Whitney well, but I'll do my best to help."

"First of all," Rebecca leaned forward, "do you know what happened to Whitney Turner?"

Abigail's eyes filled with tears as she nodded. "Yes, it's horrible. I can't believe someone would do that to her." She wiped away her tears with the back of her hand. "I'm sorry, I just…it's a lot to take in."

"Hey, it's okay." Rebecca flashed her a comforting smile.

Abigail sat upright, held her head high with her shoulders back, and smiled back.

Everyone grieved differently, as people liked to say. But grieving people tended to fold in on themselves, even when playing hostess.

"There's no reason to apologize. Now, how well did you know Whitney?"

"Um, I knew her, but just to say hi. There's not a lot of girls my age in town, so I probably know most of them by name. I never saw her at any of the dances or football games, though, so we never really hung out."

In Rebecca's experience, sad people tended to stare at the ground, to get their bearings, but not Abigail. She met Rebecca's gaze straight and steady. That was odd too. It was highly unusual for teens to look authority directly in the eye.

As Rebecca jotted down her observations, Abigail continued. "We'd talk occasionally at school. I feel bad about that now. People are saying Whitney didn't have any friends other than Sara Porter."

"We found some strange symbols near the crime scene. Have you heard anything about that?"

Abigail's eyes widened, and she shook her head. "No, what kind of symbols?"

Jake handed her the page with the hand-drawn symbols.

Abigail nodded. "Oh, yeah, I think one of them is Egyptian. Like a pharaoh's staff or something?"

So far, the girl's behavior was inconsistent. Tears without grief. Surprise that didn't quite reach her keenly observant eyes.

"Do you have any idea why someone would leave these symbols near where Whitney was found?"

"No, but...the witch could've done it." She handed the paper back to Jake and held her gaze on him.

Rebecca latched onto the word. "The witch?"

She turned back to Rebecca. "A lot of kids are saying the witch is why all these horrible things keep happening on the island. She cursed the place before dying. It's like something out of a horror movie."

"Interesting." Again, words without any underlying fear or signs of distress. Was Abigail in shock? No, she had color in her cheeks and her breathing was even. Rebecca put that down in her notes. "What was your opinion of Whitney?"

"She was...nice." Abigail fidgeted in her seat. "Not

particularly smart. It makes sense that the witch went for her. Maybe it was a kind of warning."

"Why does it make sense? And a warning for what?"

"I don't know." Abigail twisted her fingers nervously. "Maybe because the girls went to the witch's cottage a few times? It could've angered the old bag."

This answer bothered Rebecca, because she knew some of the horrible things that had happened at that cottage. "Abigail, do you know of anyone who might've had a grudge against Whitney? Someone who would want to harm her?"

"No, I don't know anyone who would want to hurt her." Abigail's voice trembled. "It must've been the witch."

"Abigail, we're asking everyone this. Where were you late Monday night, say between nine and two in the morning?" Rebecca watched the girl keenly.

"You mean two nights ago?" Abigail held her chin in thought. "Well, I was home…kinda…"

Rebecca waited, knowing silence was often the best way to get someone talking again. She fixed her stare on Abigail… and waited.

But Abigail kept fidgeting, like she was taunting them. Rebecca exchanged a quick glance with Jake and gave him the tiniest of nods.

Jake smiled all the way up to his eyes. "What does 'kinda' mean, Abigail?"

She stopped fidgeting and locked in on the deputy. "What I mean by 'kinda' is that I sneaked out. My mom would freak if she knew, so please don't tell her. But I sneaked over to Carrie's, and we hung out at her place."

"Thanksgiving break, boredom sets in. I get it." Jake offered a disarming, crooked smile.

"It sure does."

"Carrie who?" Jake relaxed in his seat, feeding into the conversation.

"Dugan. She's another girl in our class. But more mature like me."

"And what happened at Carrie's?"

"Well, we were going to have a sleepover, but after I got over there, she chickened out. Said her parents would be really mad that we didn't get my mom's permission."

"Parents." Jake shrugged.

Abigail mimicked him, shrugging too. And then, after a moment, she turned back to Rebecca, meeting her intent stare. "So we hung out for a few hours, and then I came home and sneaked back inside."

At this time of year in the bone-chilling night air, there just wasn't much to do that wasn't going to get a person in trouble. If Abigail had anything to do with what happened to Whitney, she wouldn't be very smart to admit she had no difficulty sneaking in and out of her house without her mom knowing.

"Can you tell me when the last time was that you went to the Old Witch's Cottage?" Rebecca would need to confirm her notes for each girl's answers.

"Uh, I haven't been there in weeks." Abigail's gaze darted around the room. "I'm too scared to go there now. So many other girls have gone missing over the summer."

Rebecca's thoughts raced as she recalled the dark summer months when young women went missing on Shadow Island. She'd caught every person responsible for those heinous acts, but the memories still haunted her.

"Abigail, would you mind giving me your mother's phone number? I'd like to speak with her as well."

"Sure. Her name's Samantha. But she won't be off work until later this evening, and she never answers her phone at work." She went to the kitchen and pulled open a drawer that rattled with stuff, a junk drawer presumably. They watched her grab a sticky note and pen and jot down her mom's number.

"Thank you." Rebecca took the paper from her. She dialed Samantha's number, but as Abigail had predicted, there was no answer. She left a brief message, asking her to return the call when she could.

"All right, we'll be going now. If you think of anything else that might help, please don't hesitate to contact us." Rebecca stood and motioned for Jake to follow.

He nodded, rising from his seat. He kept his eyes trained on Abigail, indicating he was treating the girl as a threat and taking the situation seriously. But Jake always followed protocol.

"Of course." Abigail led them to the front door. "I hope you guys find out what happened to Whitney. Nobody deserves something like that."

As Rebecca and Jake walked away from Abigail's house, the late morning sun tried to warm the quiet suburban street. Both of them processed the information they'd just gathered. It wasn't until they approached the SUV that Jake broke the silence.

"Something's off with that girl." He kept his voice low so they wouldn't be overheard. "It's like she's reading from a script."

Rebecca replayed their conversation with Abigail in her head. "I agree. Like the script said 'sound sad' but she didn't quite know what that looked or sounded like. And then, as soon as you started engaging—"

"Script be gone." He rubbed the back of his neck. "I need a shower after that interaction."

Rebecca laughed. "Plus, throughout the whole interview, she seemed a bit too comfortable talking to the cops. And not genuinely sad like the other girls."

"Exactly." Jake opened his door but didn't climb in,

looking around the small neighborhood they were standing in. "She's hiding something, but it could be about anything. That's the impression I got. Not necessarily criminal or related to this case."

"I'll try calling her mother again later." Rebecca pulled out her notepad and scribbled a reminder to herself. "There might be more to their story than what Abigail told us. Two down, two to go."

Jake shook his head. "Can't hardly wait."

18

Jake and Rebecca pulled up to the Porter household, the familiar white picket fence standing out against the bright noon sky. They exchanged glances before stepping out of the cruiser, steeling themselves for another conversation with Sara and her parents.

Once they approached, Jake gave the door a firm knock.

Sam Porter opened it, his face a mixture of surprise and unease. "Officers, we weren't expecting you again so soon."

"Who is it, dear? Is it a delivery?" Kristen straightened the scarf she was wrapping around her neck as she entered the front room and noticed Rebecca and Jake standing there. "Oh."

"Sorry to interrupt, Mr. and Mrs. Porter." Rebecca began, her tone professional but warm. "We'd like to speak with Sara again, if that's possible."

Kristen frowned, glancing back into the house. "Well, she has a friend over right now, so it's not the best time."

"Please." Rebecca's gaze was unwavering. "It's important." She watched as the Porters exchanged worried glances, but they seemed to recognize the gravity of the situation.

"All right. Come on in." Sam took a deep breath and gestured for them to come inside. "I'll go get her." He disappeared to the back of the house, leaving Rebecca and Jake standing there with Kristen.

Within minutes, Sara appeared in the front room, her friend trailing behind her. Rebecca studied them both, noting the nervous energy radiating from Sara and the uncertainty in her friend's eyes.

"Carrie Dugan?" Rebecca blurted out in surprise as she registered the identity of Sara's friend. Thanks to the pictures that Jake had retrieved from social media on the way to Archive Arcana, she'd known what each of the girls looked like before ever meeting them. Carrie's athletic build and blond hair were a stark contrast to Sara's lanky frame.

She hadn't expected to see Carrie at the Porters' home, but then again, nothing about this case was predictable. Since Carrie Dugan was the next girl on her list of people to interview, maybe things were starting to turn in Rebecca's favor.

"Hi." Carrie's eyes were downcast and her posture tense. Both girls seemed uneasy, but they agreed to answer some questions for Rebecca and Jake.

"I need to talk to both of you. But let's do this one at a time." Rebecca tried to sound reassuring but firm. "Sara, you'll go first. Carrie, while I speak to Sara, you can call your parents if you'd be more comfortable having them here."

Carrie's eyes widened with obvious hesitation, and she glanced nervously at Sara. Sara nodded, giving her a small, tight-lipped smile before Carrie grabbed her coat from a hook by the door and reluctantly stepped outside with Jake.

Once they were alone, Rebecca began her questions. "All right, Sara, I'm curious. Why didn't you mention Carrie, Abigail, or Marie when I first asked you about friends?" She tipped her head in the direction Carrie had gone. "Especially Carrie, who's clearly a close friend."

Sara wrung her hands together, her breathing shallow as she tried to maintain her composure. She was already displaying more signs of grief than Abigail had. "Whitney and I hung out all the time." She avoided making eye contact with Rebecca. That could be from guilt or grief. "But we only saw the rest of our group occasionally. Carrie was never friends with Whitney, so I didn't think it was important to mention her."

Rebecca studied Sara's face, noticing the beads of sweat forming on her forehead despite the chill in the room. "Okay." Her voice was steady even as her thoughts raced. "So how long have you and Carrie been friends?"

"Friends?" Sara continued to avoid eye contact, choosing her words very carefully. "That's a strong word. This is the first time she's come over. But she said she was home alone today and didn't want to be by herself. She didn't have any other place to go." She hunched her shoulders. "I told her she could hang out here. I think it was more about being somewhere where there were adults than it was about hanging out with me. We're all scared now."

"Right." Rebecca's eyes narrowed. "Well, let me ask you this. Have you two ever gone to Archive Arcana together?"

"Look," Sara snapped, her calm starting to crack, "I don't know what you're getting at, but you need to stop asking me questions multiple times and focus on the witch instead."

"By 'witch,' are you referring to Morningstar from Archive Arcana?" Rebecca twisted her question around to the one Sara had dodged, her suspicion growing.

Sara rolled her eyes. "Everyone knows it was the witch from the *cottage* who killed Whitney. You need to find a way to break the curse."

They keep bringing up the damn witch.

She searched the girl's face for a moment, noting how her eyes continued to dart around the room. "All right, Sara. You can go. Please send Carrie in on your way out."

Sara hesitated. For a moment, it seemed as though the girl wanted to say something to Rebecca, but before she could, she turned away, leaving the room to retrieve Carrie and Jake.

Carrie's face was pale, and her body language screamed her discomfort as she entered the room. She looked at the floor as she sat down.

"Did you want your parents here?"

"They aren't home right now. When I called, they said the Porters would make sure everything was okay."

Rebecca nodded to Jake, who was posted by the doorway. He ducked out of sight to retrieve one of Sara's parents. As soon as Sam bobbed through the doorway with Jake, Rebecca began questioning Carrie. "Did you ever go to Archive Arcana?"

"Uh, yeah, once or twice. Just to look around." Carrie shifted her weight back and forth.

Jake held up the paper with the symbols. "Are you familiar with these?"

Carrie hesitated before shaking her head. "No, except...I think I think the pharaoh staffy thing is Egyptian?"

Rebecca didn't correct Carrie. Especially since it was the same thing Abigail had said about the images. Instead, she pressed on with her questions, asking about any potential enemies Whitney might have had.

"Well, it's pretty obvious it's the witch. She hates everyone on the island. I don't know anyone who'd want to hurt Whitney. It must've been the witch."

Déjà vu was giving Rebecca vertigo. The similarities between the teens' reactions could point to some kind of conspiracy between the young women...or it could mean the

Old Witch's Cottage was a story that permeated the very ground of the island.

"Where were you Monday night, the twenty-third?" Rebecca had her notepad out so she could check Carrie's answers against the other girls' responses. "Between nine p.m. and one a.m.?"

"Home." Carrie's gaze was downcast, her voice barely a whisper.

"Were you home all night?"

"Ye-yes…but I wasn't alone. Abigail came over for a while. We were going to have a sleepover, but…well, I didn't like the idea of her sleeping over without my parents' approval. So we hung out for a few hours, but then I…I chickened out. I didn't want to get in trouble, so I made Abigail leave. It wasn't very nice of me, but I was scared." A tear trickled down Carrie's cheek, and Rebecca noted it was the only time any of the girls' sadness had felt genuine.

Carrie's alibi aligned exactly with what Abigail had stated. Still, Rebecca couldn't help but feel like the girls were stonewalling her. She hoped whatever secret they were keeping was about stealing something from Morningstar's shop or had to do with a boy, something harmless in the grand scheme.

"Is there anyone who had a grudge against Whitney?"

"No." Carrie twisted her hands in her lap. "I don't want to say anything bad about anyone. It was the witch. It had to be."

"Enough." Sam Porter's words broke through the conversation. "The girls have answered your questions."

Kristen had moved into the entrance of the room, and her voice was tight with concern too. "They're grieving and miserable. They need space and time to cope."

Rebecca snapped her mouth shut against her natural

protest. It didn't matter. She'd asked her questions, even if she would've liked to dig deeper.

With a sigh of resignation, she gave Jake a nod. As they left the house and got into their vehicle, the weight of unanswered questions hung heavy in the air.

"Rehearsed." Rebecca practically spat the word as she turned the key in the ignition. "The whole thing was scripted, or I'll eat my hat."

"Carrie's statement sounded a lot like Abigail's. She didn't say a word to me the whole time we waited outside. Wouldn't even look at me. What did the Porter girl have to say?" Jake leaned back in his seat and observed the house they'd just left.

"Nothing new or helpful." Rebecca drummed her fingers on the steering wheel, recalling the interviews. "And maybe it's just me being paranoid, but I can only think of one reason all three girls would have the same answers to our questions."

Jake nodded. "These girls know something. And they're much closer friends than they've been admitting."

Rebecca shrugged. "Let's not forget it's school break. They're not at school where conversations would happen organically, either chatting idly at lunch or between classes. But they've definitely made an effort to coordinate their stories."

Jake cocked his head to the side to look at her. "What are we going to do about it?"

Recalling how easy it had been for her to sneak out when she was a teenager, Rebecca wasn't convinced the parents' alibis for their kids were entirely reliable.

"Sara seemed like she was close to telling me something." Her eyes narrowed as she tried to piece together the puzzle. "But we're going to need something solid to justify another interview with her. At least in her parents' eyes."

"Maybe there's something we missed or someone we

haven't talked to yet." Jake scanned their notes from the interviews.

Rebecca nodded, her resolve strengthening. As an investigator, it was her job to sift through all the information and find the relevant clues. And if these girls were hiding something, she'd dig until she unearthed their secret.

"We're not far from the cemetery." She turned the Explorer on and put it in drive. "Let's swing by and check on things."

19

Hoyt leaned against his SUV scanning the bustling cemetery crime scene. They'd had to move their cruisers inside the gate to keep the press out after more medical examiners and crime scene techs had arrived. He watched Bailey and her colleagues work alongside a dozen other experts and was filled with a sense of relief.

Their movements were precise and efficient, like clockwork. Interns in full-body protective gear sifted soil and searched for evidence, while others set up tents to shield the activity from prying eyes and the cold wind. It was like watching archaeologists at a new dig. Except the new digs kept popping up, and so did the tents.

He hoped their dedication would bring an end to this case faster. At the very least, it would shorten the amount of time they had to hide from assholes who were heavy on cameras and light on morals. The photographers had been joined by reporters, and they now dotted the fence line, looking for a good angle so they could record their videos.

He'd been adamant about none of them parking in the street or blocking access, so their vehicles were scattered around as well. With all the cars, vans, and trucks parked outside the small cemetery, it was starting to get crowded.

"Can you believe this?" Trent sidled up next to him, his beefy arms crossed over his chest. "I never thought we'd have this much help."

"Me neither. We're lucky they got here so fast." Hoyt turned his head to look when a car door slammed behind him.

Viviane climbed out of her cruiser, which she'd had to park across the street. She let out a low whistle as she took in the chaotic scene sprawling across the cemetery. The once-quiet graveyard now resembled a war zone, with tents, equipment, and workers in full protective gear swarming over the graves. She spotted Hoyt and jogged over, stopping at the closed gates behind his cruiser.

"Can one of you let me in? And what the hell did I miss while waiting for Dad to get home?" Viviane's hands were planted firmly on her hips as she waited by the gate. "You said you needed help, but you failed to mention just how much help you were calling in."

Trent jogged around the cruisers they'd been using as a barrier and pulled a key from his pocket. He unlocked the gate and motioned for her to come in.

As Viviane approached, Hoyt shifted his feet, trying to find a comfortable position. "Welcome to the shit show. Right now, the rough estimate is around thirty bodies. And they all need to be dug up and the soil around them searched. Bailey had to call in extra help too. Everyone who's available is here. There'd be more if it wasn't the day before Thanksgiving."

"Damn." Viviane leaned against the locked metal gate. "You should've called me sooner."

"We've already managed to recover four bodies without

you. Besides, helping your mom is important too." Hoyt's tone was gentle.

Viviane waved off his concern. "Mama's doing fine. Dad's following her around and doting on her to make sure she doesn't take on too much. But enough about her. What's with all the tents and tarps? They look like they're setting up a base camp, not clearing a crime scene."

"Yesterday, we flagged more than twenty possible body dumps. Today, we started digging them up. Turns out, it takes a small army to get that done. Especially after Hoyt caught a guy taking pictures of two bodies earlier." Trent jerked his chin to where the reporters were lined up, gesturing over the fence while they spoke into the news cameras.

"News travels fast, since more and more of them keep showing up. We've spent the last hour or so just keeping photographers out of the way. I even had to conscript the groundskeeper." Hoyt grinned and stretched out on the hood of his cruiser, using its absorbed heat to warm his back. "He could use a rookie to help him walk the perimeter and keep the riffraff back."

"You called me down here to play guard dog?" Viviane planted her hands on her hips again. "That's messed up. Is that the guy walking along the fence line?"

Hoyt twisted and saw where she was pointing. "Yep, that's him." Behind Graham, he saw the SUV with the large, reflective *SHERIFF* printed down the side. "And that's West. Shit, just what we need."

"What?" Viviane grinned at him. "You think she's going to chew you out for just sitting on your butt doing nothing?"

Hoyt shot up, checking to see if any of the reporters filming their segments had noticed her yet. "No, I think she's going to catch the attention of all those reporters and bring them like a flood to the gate, where they'll start screaming all kinds of questions and trying to get a statement from the 'hero sheriff' about this mess. And then they'll follow her around like ducklings when she won't give them one."

"Which will totally cock up the investigation she's already working on." Trent started to wave at her to keep driving when he froze. "Get her on the radio."

Hoyt grabbed his radio, thumbing the button to connect with Rebecca. "Boss, it's Frost. Don't come any closer. We've got things under control here. I'll call you with an update."

Rebecca's voice crackled through the speaker, betraying a hint of concern. "Why? What's going on?"

"We've got roving bands of reporters and photographers down here, just like you predicted. You're about to get a pack of them chasing you. You certainly will if you turn this way." He kept his gaze on her vehicle, waiting to see what she'd do.

Several of the reporters noticed her stopped at the intersection and started walking her way. The scene reminded him of a zombie movie, with the way they zeroed in on their target.

There was a long stretch of silence, and Hoyt saw the SUV turn the other way.

Seeing their "dinner" scram, the reporters looked around for new prey.

Hoyt surveyed the scene. Reporters and videographers were practically collapsing the cemetery's fence as they pressed against it to overhear a tidbit or catch sight of one of the unearthed bodies. And it was getting crowded inside the perimeter, too, with radar technicians, medical examiners and their teams, and the bodies being unearthed.

Just another day on Shadow Island. Damn, I really do need to retire.

20

Rebecca had a stranglehold on the steering wheel. She was being chased away from her own crime scene. That really ground her gears and made a bad day worse. Checking the rearview mirror, she could see the reporters had turned back to where her deputies were.

"Frost, if you can talk without being overheard, give me an update."

Hoyt's voice crackled over the radio. "We've uncovered two additional bodies, Boss. Reporters are swarming like vultures. Someone was hanging around earlier and got a couple of shots from the first dig site. That must've whetted their appetites, because they've been growing in numbers ever since."

"How's the extraction going?"

"We've got numerous coroners and medical examiners, along with a group of assistants and crime scene technicians from three counties. And I've got Locke and Darby here helping me make sure they're not bothered while they work." Hoyt sounded amused, and she assumed he was teasing at least one of the other deputies.

"Thanks for the update. Don't let all that extra help go to your head, though. We need to make sure the roads stay clear with all those vehicles from the mainland." Out of the corner of her eye, she could see Jake smile at that.

Traffic detail was always annoying—yet so vital. And it never seemed important until an emergency vehicle couldn't get through.

"I'll keep working on Whitney's case while you handle that mess. We need to solve this murder fast. Very soon, you're going to have your hands full with a bunch of victims that need to be identified and next of kin notified."

"No worries. I remember what you told me about delegation." Hoyt changed the subject before she could object. "How's your investigation going?"

"We finished talking to all four girls who knew Whitney. Conveniently, Carrie Dugan was already at Sara Porter's house." Rebecca was still bothered by that supposed coincidence. "They all blamed the old witch. And according to them, there's a rumor spreading amongst their peers that also blames the old witch. Rumors are usually based on something, so it's worth looking into."

Jake spoke up from the passenger seat and leaned forward to speak into the radio. "I wasn't here yet when you guys dealt with that psychopath killer at the Old Witch's Cottage. What's the old legend about the witch these girls keep talking about? Something about a curse?"

Rebecca nodded, recalling fragments of the story, though she wasn't sure how it started. "I remember some things from the Lovecraft crimes, but Hoyt knows more." She cued the radio again. "Frost, can you tell us the legend of the Old Witch's Cottage? And about the witch herself? We need to better understand what these girls are talking about."

There was a long pause on the other end of the radio before Hoyt spoke. "Well, they say an old woman lived in the cottage back in the mid-eighteen hundreds when the island was first being settled by Europeans. She was here before anyone else. And so was the cottage."

Jake raised an eyebrow. "An elderly woman living on her own? That would have been unusual for the time."

Rebecca jumped in. "That's just the story. I don't know if there's any truth to it. Her cottage doesn't seem that much older than the lighthouse."

"She was rumored to have lured children into the attic where she had a fabulous playroom of some kind. Except not all the children who went up into that playroom came down again." Hoyt sounded uncomfortable, clearly not enjoying the retelling of the sinister tale. "However, that rumor started around the same time the locals were trying to get her to sell her house to a wealthy family that wanted to move to the island."

"Let me guess." Jake rolled his eyes, speaking into the radio. "She refused, and so they called her a witch in order to get her kicked her out of town."

"Yep, same story, different town. When someone got in your way back then, you just labeled them a witch and drove them out. Then took whatever they left behind."

Rebecca tried to piece together what could connect Whitney's murder to the witch's legend. "What happened to her?"

"Well, first they built the lighthouse to prevent sunlight reaching her gardens. Which, of course, was a death sentence back then. Your only hope of survival was if you had neighbors with spare food who would trade or sell it to you. And the right environment to grow some of your own." Hoyt's words added an extra layer of horror to the story.

An elderly woman, hated by her neighbors, harassed by the richest families who had intruded on her island, was left to starve to death because she wouldn't give them even more than they had already taken from her.

"But what happened to her?" Jake pushed.

"What do you mean?" Hoyt sounded confused.

"How did the old witch die? Did they kill her? Did she starve to death?"

Rebecca frowned. That part of the story she'd never heard.

"Oh. Um, no one knows for sure. The version I heard was pretty messed up. Like the witches in Europe ages ago, the old witch was tied up and tossed into the ocean. It was called 'swimming a witch' and, ironically, if the accused managed to survive the test, it proved she was a witch. If she drowned, her accusers would know she was innocent."

Jake rubbed his chin. "So she was dead no matter what."

"Yeah. They say our witch survived off the coast for a long time before her head disappeared below the surface. I don't know what they considered a long time, but if you were tied up and treading water, I think five minutes would seem like a lifetime."

"Well, it was a lifetime...to the accused." Jake no longer sounded thrilled with the legend. "But the curse. What was it said to be exactly?"

Hoyt sounded deflated. "There are different versions of what happens if you step in the shadow of the lighthouse. One is that you won't have prosperity, much like her gardens never stood a chance. Another is much worse. Whoever was cursed would die a water-related death."

"Yikes."

"After she cast her curse, that's the end of the story. As far as I know."

Feeling let down, Rebecca turned off the street she was on. "Well, with that refresher course, we're going to swing by the Old Witch's Cottage. Each of the girls has blamed the witch. There might be something there that connects to Whitney Turner's murder."

"Could be." Jake sat back in his seat.

Hoyt still sounded troubled. "You know, even without the witch, the cottage has its own twisted legend. Although no one lives there, there's always been signs of activity inside. There used to be a door. A huge, heavy, solid black door. Like something you'd see left over after a house fire. It shrieked like a banshee if you tried to open it."

A pang of loss hit Rebecca. When last she'd heard this story, Hoyt had been telling her and Darian about the door.

As he got back into the storytelling, Hoyt's voice softened, maybe as he remembered the same thing. "The damn thing was so loud, you could hear it all the way across the island. But the way I heard it was that every time someone closed the door, it would be open the next day. And no one heard a thing. Except when the door didn't open."

Though Rebecca already knew how this part went, Jake was on the edge of his seat.

"When that happened, we all knew it was a bad sign. Because there would always be something behind that closed door when we went to look. And, of course, the door would shriek and squeal when we opened it. So everyone knew something was up."

Beside her, Jake gulped.

"Sometimes, it would be a lost child or someone's pet. Other times, it would be a dead animal. Every now and then, there'd be signs someone had gone in there to do spells or hold seances or whatever. Finally, people had enough, and they removed the door and burned it down on the beach, fearing it carried a curse. Now we just have to worry about stepping over that chain when we need to get in and out."

As they approached the Old Witch's Cottage, Rebecca couldn't shake an uneasy feeling Hoyt's words had engendered. The man sure had a knack for telling ghost stories. She wondered how often he'd told that story to his sons when they were little.

Which raises the question, how much of the original story has he embellished over the years?

The legend was just a story, she tried to reassure herself, but something about it felt dangerous and real. People loved to blame the supernatural to hide their dirty deeds. "The devil made me do it" was a crappy—but often used—defense.

"Thanks for the refresher, Frost." Rebecca set the radio back down.

"Think Hoyt actually believes in the witch?" Jake was staring at her as she straightened up in her seat.

Rebecca managed a small laugh. "I doubt he'd ever admit it if he did believe the witch stories. He's superstitious, but it's usually just about things like fishing or boating or anything else to do with the ocean. Maybe we should call in some ghost hunters to help us with this one."

"Or those radar guys with their fancy tools." As Rebecca pulled into the parking lot, Jake turned in his seat to look at the cottage they'd just been discussing.

"Not a bad idea. We might just find out what happened to that poor old lady who first lived here." Rebecca parked the cruiser and considered the cottage. As unassuming as it looked now, it was a place where darkness had left its mark.

Last time she'd been here, there'd been a head left in the yard, set to stare at its decapitated and flayed body. A maniac had done it for the third time. Before that, he'd painted the walls with a mixture of shit and blood.

Today, those whitewashed exterior walls were clean. They had a slight amber tinge from the layers of protective shellack that was reapplied every few years to preserve it.

"Let's see if there's anything connecting this place to Whitney." Rebecca climbed out of the cruiser. She stood at the edge of the parking lot, gaze fixated on the Old Witch's Cottage.

"Creepy." Jake stepped out to stand next to her. "I can see why all those stories and legends started."

Rebecca walked ahead of him. "Honestly, I've always found it a rather soothing place. It's quiet, calm, a great place to hang out on a hot summer day. In fact, I used to do that as a kid."

"Was that before you knew the history of the place?" Jake fell into step with her.

"I'm not sure. As a kid, I never heard the full story. Only that this place was cursed." Rebecca stopped at the chain that spanned the doorway. She clicked on her flashlight and froze.

There were large circles of dark brown in the pale earth under the chain and more just inside the entryway.

"Shit. That's blood." She bent down to get a better look. There, in the hard-packed dirt, were several overlapping pools of dried blood.

The air was tinged with a musty scent that clung to her senses like a familiar guest. Standing, she swept the flashlight around the interior of the cottage.

Jake leaned over the chain, looking at the inside of the front wall. "These look familiar."

"Crap." Rebecca peered in, too, and recognized them as the same symbols carved into Whitney's body. "Walk the perimeter. Whitney's bike was missing, so if she came here voluntarily, it might still be here."

"Yes, ma'am." Jake stepped away from the wall and began his search.

Rebecca cued her radio. "Dispatch, West here."

Elliot Ping's response was immediate. His voice carried the distinct cadence of someone who rode waves before he operated phones—a surfer boy turned dispatcher. "This is Dispatch, go ahead, Sheriff."

"I need you to contact one of the CSI teams. According to Frost, there's plenty of them over at the cemetery. I'm at the Old Witch's Cottage. Let them know we found a crime scene. This is almost certainly where Whitney Turner was killed."

As Rebecca recalled the fat globules and blood that had stained this cottage only a few months ago, she wondered if this cottage was indeed cursed. And if it was, how did that affect her current case? More questions swirled through her mind.

Why had Whitney come here that night? Did someone lure her here, or did she come here to practice some of the dark arts? Was this location significant or random? Was it merely a twisted inspiration for a sadistic mind?

Standing at the entrance, Rebecca glanced at the chain that spanned the two poles at the doorway to the cottage. A few red-brown streaks dotted the links, and she was pretty sure they weren't from rust. From the size and number of the blood circles on the ground, someone had certainly died here.

So as not to disturb any blood, Rebecca leaned forward to further inspect the walls with her flashlight.

Symbols, just like the ones found gouged into Whitney's skin, were drawn on the walls in black marker.

They used a knife to make them on Whitney but used a nondestructive tool on the walls. Why didn't they use the knife to carve the symbols into the walls for a more lasting mark? Did they value the Old Witch's Cottage more than a human life or flesh?

She turned to look at the parking lot. Jake was just finishing his circuit around the cottage grounds.

"Hey, Boss? I didn't touch it, but there's a bike leaning against a tree a few yards that way." He gestured toward the woods on the opposite side of the cottage. "I don't want to be sexist, but I'd say it's a girl's bike. It's covered in leaves, but you can tell it doesn't have the crossbar that most boy's bikes do."

"Great work. We can photograph it along with the rest of this stuff for the case file, then the techs can check it for prints while they process the scene."

"So what now?"

"I'm thinking that if Whitney was killed here and found in the cemetery, then we need to check every route between here and there." In her mind, she was already mapping various options. "We need to see if we can find any witnesses or surveillance footage. Between that and any forensic clues found here, let's hope we find something to lead us to Whitney's killer."

21

I rolled over in bed to connect to the video chat. My sisters appeared on the screen. Cordelia, Minerva, and Sapphire.

Sapphire looked like she was about to shit a canoe. And she kept looking over her shoulder. At who? I couldn't guess. We were all connecting from our bedrooms, and everyone's door had to be locked.

Minerva seemed fine. She was busy checking her selfie image and fixing her hair. Genetics fucked her sideways. *Good luck with that, Minerva.*

Cordelia rolled her eyes. She seemed to notice too.

It was important to keep our meetings secret, so we never met at the same place twice in a row. We didn't want to create a pattern someone could track.

"All right, let's go." Shit, I sounded weak. I cleared my throat. "I want to know exactly what you told the sheriff. No lies, no sugarcoating."

One by one, they all swore they'd stuck to the agreed-upon story that they believed the witch was responsible for Whitney's death. And they had no idea how or why this was happening. Or any idea who else would've wanted to hurt Whitney.

As they talked, I studied each of their faces for any hint they were lying or hiding anything. I was stoked to see Cordelia seemed fine.

It must've gone well for all of them with the sheriff lady, who seemed pretty clueless. That fine deputy too. But he could come back. I'd smash him if Cordelia didn't get to him first. Especially if he dropped a few pounds.

"That's good. You're all doing great. I'm glad we're all tight. Just stick to the plan."

Cordelia beamed at my compliments. So did Minerva. But Sapphire was quiet, and she seemed kind of out of it.

"But I need to be sure none of you are hiding anything." I paused dramatically, letting my gaze linger on the hot mess before barking, "Sapphire!"

She jumped.

"You look like you're holding something back. Tell me the truth. Did you say anything else to the sheriff? Anything that could put us in danger?"

Sapphire scanned her surroundings before returning her attention to the three faces on her screen. "No. I swear! I didn't tell her anything. I followed the plan. Just like you said. Shit, chill."

I leaned closer to the screen, trying to read Sapphire's expression as she refused to look directly into the camera. Was she telling the truth or just too preoccupied with watching the rest of us on her screen? I couldn't afford to take any chances. The future of our coven was at stake, and betrayal would not be tolerated. This would be easier to figure out in person, but we couldn't risk being seen together.

"Sapphire, I need you to look me in the eye and swear on

your soul and the chance at rebirth that you did exactly as I said. Because if you didn't, you're putting all of us at risk."

Sapphire took a shaky breath and looked directly into my eyes. "I swear it, Blair. I did everything we talked about. We're in this together, right?" Her voice wavered, desperate for reassurance.

Cordelia jumped in. "Swear on your soul and the witch's vengeance that you didn't spill the tea, Sapphire."

"I swear on my soul and the witch's vengeance, I did not tell the sheriff, or anyone else, anything more than what I was supposed to."

I studied the drama queen. "All right. But remember, we can't afford any mistakes."

Everyone seemed to chill for a hot second.

And then Sapphire shook shit up again. "Um, guys? I didn't say anything that would get us in trouble, but I've been thinking…maybe we should just come clean? If we do it now, maybe we can get off easy."

Cordelia and Minerva erupted. "Are you fucking insane?"

"We're as good as dead if we confess!"

"Do you know what would happen to us?"

"The same thing that happened to the old witch!"

"Exactly. The whole town would turn against us!"

"Yeah! They'd tie us up and throw us in the ocean, and I can barely swim on a good day." Minerva's hands were shaking with fury. "Blair, do something! We can't get charged with this."

I didn't have to do anything. It made me look good to not be the one losing my shit. And, honestly, I understood where the hot mess was coming from. Always looking over your shoulder sucked. The pressure from the investigation was getting to us.

"Enough. Listen to me, all of you." They all shut up. "We

made a pact, remember? We stick together, no matter what. We've come too far to turn back now."

They nodded in agreement, but Sapphire's words still hung in the air, threatening to derail our story. "Sapphire, if you say a single word about what happened, I swear you'll be the next one the old witch axes."

Sapphire's eyes widened in terror, and she clamped her mouth shut.

'Bout time.

"Whitney deserved her death for betraying this coven." I had all their attention now. My word was law. Just as it should be. "The symbols were a stroke of genius, honestly. The lady sheriff is chasing her tail trying to find meaning in the worthless BS. I mean, she asked all of you about them, didn't she?"

Each of my sisters in the coven bobbed their heads.

"If you stick to the plan, this'll all blow over. We didn't mean to find that skull at the cemetery, but now the pigs are ass-deep in bodies. It's cash. So just cool your tits." I looked hard at each of them in turn. "But I'm not fucking kidding, if any of you even think about turning on the sisterhood, you'll bite it too. It's coven law. Is that clear?"

Cordelia swallowed hard, her gaze not quite meeting mine. But I had that twat just where I wanted her.

Minerva bit her lip.

But Sapphire…that bitch still looked shook. And cornered animals could be the most dangerous. I'd have to keep an eye on her.

"Remember, we're a coven. We stick together, no matter what. If anyone breaks that trust…they'll pay. I know we're all scared, okay?" There was a knife's edge to my voice, and I could see it reverberate through them. "But we have to trust each other. If one of us screws up, it's over for all of us. Do not press me."

As they all agreed and disconnected, I couldn't shake the feeling that Sapphire was dangerously close to cracking. And it wasn't just her.

Cordelia looked pumped about the idea of coming clean. And I trusted her the most.

Down to basics, I wasn't going to let anyone take away my power.

Those were facts.

22

With a map of Shadow Island pulled up on her phone, Rebecca traced a line with her finger, following the route from the Old Witch's Cottage to the cemetery where Whitney's body had been dumped. Her brow furrowed, weariness seeping into her eyes. A map could show so much and yet reveal so little.

They still didn't even know why the killer picked the Old Witch's Cottage. Whitney could've been a victim of opportunity. Her mother admitted that she'd sneaked out before. Maybe Whitney had left to meet a boy. Or maybe she hadn't even gone out to meet someone and instead just wanted to escape the house after having a fight with her mom.

A teen needing to blow off steam could wind up anywhere. And on a cold night, riding her bike, when stores were closed, this cottage might've been the only shelter Whitney could find.

She could've walked into something she wasn't expecting or been tailed by someone with ill intent. Or maybe this was a mugging gone bad. Not everything had to be a conspiracy, after all.

We just don't know enough about her yet. I need to get those girls to talk to me more.

Jake had been busy digging through the girls' social media accounts. So far, he hadn't learned anything useful. There were no indications of any bullying or stalking by an online predator. Sara's social media was the most limited, and that was likely due to her protective parents.

Finding a girl's bike at the cottage strongly indicated that the blood belonged to Whitney. But the bike could've been planted there to try to throw off the investigation. Rebecca wouldn't let herself get tunnel vision. Every clue mattered until they learned it didn't.

Jake, who'd been coordinating with the forensic team working on the possible murder scene, walked over to where she was leaning on the cruiser. "What are you thinking, Boss?"

As much as she might've disliked being called *Boss*, Hoyt's continued use of the title had spread to everyone else, and she'd learned to accept it.

"There are several stores and commercial buildings between here and the cemetery, but almost none between here and Whitney's house." She pointed to both places on the map. "Let's check along the commercial route and see if there're any cameras we can get access to. There are no street cameras, so we'll have to rely on the businesses."

"What are we looking for?" Jake looked up from the map, already searching the area.

"Maybe we'll catch a glimpse of Whitney on her bike or someone following her. Or see something like a vehicle driving erratically. I dunno, trying not to be seen while hauling a body."

"Sure, I hear ya."

The hunt for evidence often meant searching through everything one piece at a time. Or, in this case, one block at a time. The SUV's engine hummed to life as she pulled away from the curb, embarking on their canvass of the town. Rebecca drove, her gaze flickering to every storefront, every alleyway, while Jake kept his eyes peeled for the telltale signs of modern vigilance—security cameras.

Many of the businesses were advertising Thanksgiving specials, while others simply announced they were closed for the holiday. As they approached the dry cleaners, Rebecca noted a dapper turkey not only wearing a Pilgrim's hat but the whole outfit, clean and pressed.

"Nothing at the dry cleaners." Disappointment laced Jake's words as he tapped the passenger window. "And the camera outside the pawn shop is facing the wrong way."

"Keep a lookout. Someone has to have one. Those things have been sprouting up all over the island in the last year." Rebecca peered through her side window while still keeping an eye on the road.

The storefront of the consignment shop featured mannequins wearing close approximations of male and female Pilgrim outfits. No camera there, though.

"Here's another one. Amanda's Wash and Fold." Jake sighed as they approached another corner. "Never mind. The camera's busted."

As the road curved, they saw fresh paint, indicating where some construction had been recently completed. A charred paper turkey had blown free of its perch and rested along the side of the building.

That was the site where one of Kurt Archer's pipe bombs had gone off.

"Of course." Rebecca's tone was dark. Archer's random act of violence had destroyed surveillance cameras that might have prevented a murderer evading detection. That was how the world worked.

It was almost as if the universe itself were conspiring to keep the truth buried. She couldn't shake the image of Leonard Blyberg and his team, sweeping the cemetery grounds with their radar, uncovering secrets meant to stay hidden. Until Whitney Turner's case was solved, she couldn't help the rest of her team.

"Wait, stop the car." Jake pointed to a convenience store they were about to pass.

Rebecca slowed the SUV and pulled over, her eyes narrowing. The store's front door listed its Black Friday hours. And above that door was a camera, its lens pointing out toward the street like an unblinking eye.

"Looks inactive, but let's check." Rebecca didn't let hope bloom. She'd learned the hard way that optimism in their line of work was often a prelude to further disappointment.

Jake jumped out of the SUV, approaching the entrance with quick steps. Rebecca waited while he opened the door and popped his head inside. It only took a moment before he turned back to the vehicle, shaking his head.

"It's a fake. They put it up to stop kids from hanging out front and vaping." Jake got back in and put on his seatbelt.

"All That Crepe is just ahead. We'll check there." Rebecca pulled back onto the street.

The café was a quaint structure nestled on the corner of a less-traveled street, its patio embraced by wrought iron railings and dotted with mismatched tables. Every third spindle of the patio fencing had a melamine sign with a rolled crepe, open at one end to look like a bountiful cornucopia. A sign above the door with the name in fanciful font swung gently in the afternoon breeze.

Rebecca's attention was immediately drawn to the security

camera perched like a hawk above the establishment, angled out over the road that led toward the cemetery's solemn gates. Looking closer, she saw a red light glowing next to the lens.

Hope, that rare and often deceitful visitor, fluttered in her chest as she pulled over again.

"Could be something." Jake climbed out and approached the entrance.

There was a neon sign of a steaming coffee cup in the front window. "Might as well get a refill while we're here." Rebecca followed, pushing open the door and joining him as he went in.

The smell of fresh coffee greeted her like an old friend. She scanned the room, noting how empty it was. The full garbage cans let her know there'd been plenty of people coming through earlier in the day.

The manager hovered behind the counter, his apron stained with the day's work, and there was a fine dusting of flour on the hairnet covering his short brown hair.

He smiled as they walked up. "Y'all looking for some crepes for dinner tonight? We're sold out at the moment, but we've got more batter mixing now. I know no one wants to cook the day before Thanksgiving."

"Sadly, I'm on the clock, so just a coffee for me. No time to make dinner plans." Beside Rebecca, Jake looked wistful. "I'm Sheriff Rebecca West, and this is Deputy Jake Coffey. We're investigating a case, and we'd like to check your surveillance footage from this past Monday night."

The middle-aged man, with the look of someone who'd seen more than his fair share of island storms, grabbed the pot of coffee and motioned to her travel mug.

Rebecca popped the top off, and he filled it up, waving her off when she reached for her wallet. "I'm Cecil. Nice to meet you, but your money's no good here. Law enforcement gets free coffee in my shop. Follow me and I'll pull up the camera feed for you."

One good thing that had come about in the wake of the Yacht Club's demise was that everyone in town was a lot more willing to help the police now. Rebecca and Jake stepped behind the counter to follow Cecil as he turned away.

They wove through a maze of worktables in the kitchen. The gentle hum of an old soda machine accompanied their steps as they passed the rows of round crepe griddles.

Cecil keyed in a password on a dusty computer tucked away in an open office area. There wasn't even a chair, showing how little time this man spent at his desk. He opened a folder on the desktop.

"Here we go." He gave a pleased head bob. "I'm sure you know how to work this. I need to get back to my prep work. Dinner rush is going to start soon enough."

As the video feed played, Rebecca watched the slow progress of cars driving past the café under the well-lit street. No one had braved the evening on a bicycle—at least not via this route—so Jake took to pausing the video on every automobile while she wrote down a description of each one and its license plate number as it passed the creperie.

The minutes ticked away with mechanical indifference, broken only when the manager came over and set a cup of steaming coffee in front of Jake with a silent nod.

Considering they had no way of knowing what vehicle they were looking for, what time it would've passed, or if it had even come this way, they continued searching and documenting until the time stamp on the video matched the time the body was found by the caretaker of the cemetery.

Rebecca glanced around, finding Cecil standing over a cutting board and a case of leafy greens. "Thank you for your cooperation. Hopefully, the information we gathered will prove useful."

"I'm happy to help." Cecil looked over his shoulder, hardly slowing in his chopping.

"Would you be able to email us this footage?" She pointed at the screen.

The rhythmic tacking of the blade on the cutting board stuttered and halted. "Uh, I...well, I'm not too good with computer things." He grinned suddenly. "But my nephew, he's a wizard with this tech stuff. He starts his shift at six. I'll get him to send it over when he comes in, if you can wait that long."

"I can make a copy to take with us if you'll give us permission." Jake pulled a thumb drive from his pocket.

"Permission granted." Cecil waved at the computer. "The less I have to do on the computer, the better it is for me."

A few clicks later, Jake pulled his thumb drive out of the port. "Got it."

"Thank you again."

"Of course." Worry lines creased Cecil's forehead. "You sure you don't want a few crepes? I could have them cooked up in just a few minutes."

Ignoring Jake's eyes wandering to the rows of sweet fillings for the crepes, Rebecca shook her head. "The sooner we get this sorted, the sooner we can close this case and help a grieving family."

At her words, Jake's gaze snapped back to the manager, and he nodded in agreement while patting his stomach, earning him a chuckle.

"Well, if either of you change your mind later, we'll be open late tonight." He gave Jake a knowing smile.

As they stepped out from the mustard-colored walls of the café, the grit of the island's streets grated beneath

Rebecca's boots, the sandy texture grounding her amid the swirling uncertainties of the case.

Back in the Explorer, Jake pulled the laptop over and began entering plate numbers from the list they'd made. Rebecca started rolling forward again, looking for more cameras they could use.

She paused a few times but was getting close to the end of the street when Jake lifted his head.

"Uh, Boss, the black 2012 Ford Focus we saw on the video is registered to Samantha Miller."

"Abigail's mother? Was that one of the vehicles heading south, in the general direction of the witch's cottage? What was the time on that?" Rebecca frowned. She hadn't spoken with the woman yet, but it looked like it was time to change that.

"Yes, it's Abigail's mother, and the time stamp was ten seventeen that night. I went ahead and checked insurance, just to double-check, and Abigail's shown as a driver for that vehicle."

Rebecca slowed down, glancing over at Jake. "And we couldn't see who the driver was because of the reflection on the windows."

"Abigail said she sneaked out and went over to Carrie Dugan's house for a sleepover that never happened. And Carrie told us the same thing."

"But we don't have any idea where Samantha Miller was Monday night, since we haven't been able to speak to her." She flicked on her blinker. "Let's go visit the Millers." She took the next turn, which would lead them back to the Millers and possibly their killer.

23

"Remember, we don't want to spook her. We already know she was out for part of the evening. So we have to find out if her alibi is a lie or not." Rebecca's gaze never left the front door, where a festive wreath hung incongruously amid the gloom of the oncoming night. "We need to get access to the car first."

Jake nodded. "Understood."

They turned their attention to the black Ford Focus nestled in the driveway, now wreathed in suspicion with its suggestion of a friend's possible involvement in Whitney's murder.

Rebecca pressed the cold plastic of the doorbell, listening to the chime sing through the interior of the house. It felt like a prelude to a revelation, and she wondered whether it would be Abigail or Samantha Miller who would greet them.

The door creaked open, and there stood Samantha Miller, her features etched with worry lines deep enough to tell their own stories. "Sheriff? Is everything all right?"

"Mrs. Miller, we're sorry to bother you. As I'm sure you know, we talked with Abigail earlier in connection with the murder of her friend, Whitney Turner. We have a few more questions for Abigail, and we'd like to speak with you as well." Rebecca kept her voice as soft as the evening shadows all around.

She noted the tightness in Samantha's jaw, the way her knuckles whitened against the door frame. Clearly, she didn't know about their previous visit. Was Samantha too busy, or had Abigail withheld the information from her mom? Or was the woman reacting to having to answer questions for herself?

"Abigail isn't home right now. She's with some friends." Samantha's forced smile flickered across her face. "I'm glad she's been making friends since we moved here. It's good for her."

"Ah, that's right. You're new here. What brought you to the island, Mrs. Miller?" Rebecca asked the question to keep the conversation going. Their preliminary research had filled in a few of the details, but both of the Miller women were still enigmas. If Abigail wasn't home but the Ford Focus was, then maybe Abigail didn't drive the car as much as her mother did.

"It's Miss, actually. And that's none of your business." Her response was curt, and Rebecca reeled inwardly from the unexpected shutdown. Noting the abruptness, she filed it away. Another piece in the puzzle. To Rebecca, the question seemed innocuous, but to Samantha Miller, it was clearly a loaded one.

Samantha followed up her rudeness with an explanation. "Abigail's father, he's…out of the picture. We came here to start over. Why do you need to speak to Abigail, if you've already talked with her?"

"We've discovered Abigail may have been out driving at a time she claimed to be at Carrie Dugan's house for a sleepover." Rebecca paused for a beat. "Unless you were the one driving the Ford Focus between ten Monday night and two Tuesday morning?"

"No, my friends picked me up for an early dinner before a night out on the mainland. Why are you tracking my car?" The accusation was sharp, tinged with anger and disbelief.

"We weren't. In fact, we were surprised when we checked the area where the crime happened and noticed that car." Jake pointed to her Focus in the driveway. "It drove through at a time when Abigail told us she was at the Dugans'. You can see why we'd have more questions for her. We're trying to establish timelines."

"Abigail was at the Dugans'." Samantha's stance was unwavering. "She told me so, and I believe her."

Suspicion prickled at Rebecca. That detail didn't line up with Abigail's statement, since she'd said her mom would freak out if she knew she was staying overnight with Carrie. Rebecca produced her phone, tapping on the screen to bring up a video she'd had Jake transfer from the laptop to her phone on the short drive over.

"This is surveillance footage from a local shop." She held the device up so the woman could see the grainy image of a car passing by. The license plate was unmistakable. "As you can see, this is clearly your vehicle. It's registered under your name with Abigail as a driver. If you weren't the one driving it that night, then it must've been Abigail. Can you give us the names of the friends who picked you up? That way, we can check your alibi as well."

Samantha's face lost color, her breath catching as if she'd been plunged into icy waters. "You think Abigail..." Her voice trailed off, laden with unspoken fears. She didn't even seem worried about her own alibi, leading Rebecca to believe she was telling the truth about being out with friends.

Her worried reaction was more like a mother trying to protect her child, because she knew she hadn't been using her own car that night—and had already given that information up.

"We're not making any assumptions." Rebecca held up her hands. "But we need to account for every detail. Can you give us the contact information for the friends who picked you up?"

Samantha nodded and rattled off three names with phone numbers, which Rebecca wrote down. "I…Abigail said she went to a sleepover. I believed her…" She faltered, and Rebecca noticed the use of the past tense. Samantha's fingers twisted around each other as she wrung her hands. There was something there—an uncertainty, a crack in the facade.

Before they could probe further, Abigail's voice called out from the back of the house. "Mom, I'm home!"

Samantha Miller turned, and Rebecca could see over her shoulder as Abigail closed the back door and looked around.

Abigail's guarded expression betrayed the turmoil beneath the surface. Rebecca observed the set of her shoulders, the cautious way she closed the distance to the front door. "What's going on?"

"Hello, Abigail." Though triumph leaped through Rebecca's heart, she kept her demeanor cool as a cucumber. "We have some additional questions for you."

"You said you were at Carrie's house, but they have pictures of you driving in town, Abigail." Her mother glared at Rebecca.

"I was over there, like I told you. Chill, Mom. Then I was out driving." Abigail faced off with her mother.

"That's not what you told us earlier." Rebecca frowned at the girl's flippant answer.

"You asked me where I was that *evening*. I think this is a matter of how we interpret the word. That *night*, I was home, because in the *evening*, I went over to Carrie's expecting to stay." Abigail looked at her mother for confirmation. "You know I sometimes go for drives." Then she turned to Rebecca. "I didn't realize that was a crime."

Samantha's face scrunched up in confusion.

Rebecca raised an eyebrow, prompting her to elaborate.

"I was at Carrie's until after ten that night. Which is what I told you. I'm not sure of the exact time. Then she flaked on me and sent me home. I did some driving to clear my head after that." Her words tumbled out, laced with a defensive edge.

"Why didn't you mention this earlier?" Rebecca kept her tone measured but insistent. She saw the flicker of panic in Abigail's eyes before the girl masked it with indignation.

"Because I didn't think it was relevant. That and...if I told you everything, I was afraid I'd look guilty." The reply was timid, and Rebecca sensed the undercurrent of fear in her voice.

"Where exactly did you go on your drive, Abigail?" Jake's pen was poised over his notepad. The catch on the top was pressed down. It wasn't an ordinary pen.

Months ago, Richmond Vale—the former chair of the Select Board and a corrupt man who worked for the Yacht Club—had implied he'd block Rebecca's request for body cameras through his equally corrupt buddy, the county treasurer. She'd resorted to buying spy pens with video and audio recording devices hidden in the barrel instead.

Abigail wouldn't get away with pretending to answer a different question this time.

"Just to Atticus Beach. I sat in the car, watching the waves. And then I came back." Abigail crossed her arms, as if warding off their questions.

Rebecca's thumb swiped across the screen of her phone, bringing up the satellite image of the island with its jagged coastline. The map rendered every street and landmark in stark clarity. She traced the route from the Miller residence to Atticus Beach. It passed the All That Crepe café. It could be a coincidence that Abigail had been in the area, but Rebecca wasn't buying it.

Her voice betrayed none of the frustration simmering within. "What time did you leave for your drive?"

"Right around ten or so. It wasn't like I looked at the clock when Carrie sent me packing." Now Abigail was hugging herself, as if bracing against a cold only she felt.

"And returned?"

"An hour, hour and a half later, maybe."

The feasibility of the timeline nettled Rebecca. The camera didn't cover the other side of the road, so they'd have no idea when she returned. It was possible, all too possible, yet it provided no firm ground on which to build their case.

And the small island meant homes tended to be clustered in certain areas. All the girls lived within a few blocks of each other. Anyone heading north to that neighborhood could also appear to be heading toward the cemetery.

She pocketed her phone with a faint sigh. The proximity of Atticus Beach to the Old Witch's Cottage and the cemetery was an inconvenient truth—one that tangled the narrative further into knots of maybes and what-ifs.

"Did you see anyone while you were out? Talk to anyone?" Rebecca watched a flicker of annoyance cross Abigail's face.

"No one's ever out at night. It's a stupid little town." Abigail's words were laced with a bitterness that seemed older than her years.

Rebecca noted the response, another piece of the puzzle that refused to fit neatly. Without a witness, without a receipt, without a stray fiber or a drop of blood, Abigail remained shrouded in layers of adolescent defiance and half-truths.

"Mind if we take a look inside your car?" Rebecca anticipated the objection, even as she asked the question.

"You can't do that without a warrant." Abigail's retort was a rehearsed line delivered with a mix of smugness and fear.

"But if your mother agrees...?" Rebecca turned to the mother, whose hands wrung the fabric of her sleeves where she was clutching her own arms. Hopefully, she would be more cooperative.

"I'm afraid I'll have to insist on a warrant." Samantha's voice was firm in the defense of her child.

"Getting one won't be difficult. It would look better for you if—"

"Still no." Samantha's jaw was set in stubborn defiance.

Rebecca exchanged a glance with Jake, who gave a subtle nod. They both knew where this was heading.

"All right." Rebecca conceded the setback with a tilt of her head. "We'll see about getting that warrant."

The crunch of late-autumn leaves beneath their soles was the only sound as Rebecca and Jake left their doorstep.

Rebecca's voice was tinged with urgency. "Get started on that warrant for the car."

As they approached their vehicle, her hand hovered above her radio. She braced herself against the SUV, feeling the cold metal through her jacket—a stark reminder of the chill that had nothing to do with the weather—before cueing her mic.

"Frost, it's West. What have you got for me?"

The weariness in Hoyt's voice was palpable even through the radio. "Boss, we've unearthed ten now. Ten bodies."

Rebecca felt a leaden weight settle in her chest. Her breath hitched as the number echoed in her mind. Ten lives snuffed out, buried secrets clawing their way to the surface. Including Randall Krull, there were potentially thirty possible corpses, but she'd hoped some of those would be anomalies in the radar system or roots, anything but actual bodies.

Once again, "hope" had done her dirty. Ten confirmed corpses proved that true.

"Any…any ID on them yet?" She struggled to keep her composure.

"We only have the first one, Randall Krull, from Bailey's analysis. We're still processing the rest of them." Hoyt's voice was flat, the usual vibrancy of his spirit extinguished by the grim task at hand. "But this is…it's a lot, Boss."

"Keep me posted." She ended the call, clipping the radio back onto her shoulder.

She sagged against the SUV and closed her eyes, allowing herself a rare moment of vulnerability. The whispers of the waves reached her, a chorus of voices from the past, urging her to decipher them.

24

Sapphire's fingers trembled over the luminescent screen of her phone, the soft glow casting shadows across her huddled form on the bed. The door was a steadfast sentry, bolted shut, offering an illusion of sanctuary in her dimly lit room. As she traded texts with Cordelia, the weight of the last two days settled heavily in her chest.

I can't pull my shit together and I just wanna wake up to graduation. Sapphire hovered her thumb before adding—*I wish magic was real*—and hit send.

But it wasn't. And now, she was stuck in a coven that pretended it was. Everything was just so screwed up. Reality didn't even make sense anymore.

Cordelia's reply was instant. *It's not that simple, Whitney got what was coming.*

The words sliced through Sapphire's already frayed nerves, and she blinked against the sting of unexpected tears. Whitney—bright-eyed and brimming with mischief, now just a memory shrouded in tragedy. She scrubbed at her cheek, her heart clenching for the friend she missed so fiercely.

Blair did this, not us, why shouldn't we turn her in?

Because Blair is dangerous and that bitch will cut us if we do.

Her mind flashed back to Blair's pale face and cold eyes, the veiled warnings that made her skin crawl. Sapphire choked down the fear, imagining the sharp edge of danger lurking just beyond her locked door.

Are we supposed to live in fear forever? FML, I can't do that!

She hoped for some sliver of an ally in Cordelia.

Better scared than dead, Whitney just challenged her and she was axed the same night.

If we confess we'll be safe, the police will protect us.

The glare of Sapphire's phone screen burned her eyes in the dark room as she awaited Cordelia's response. Scrubbing her eyes, she wiped away more tears. She'd asked the question that had been gnawing at her insides. Now it seemed to hover in the charged silence between each notification chime.

Sapphire couldn't stand the silence and asked the question that had been haunting her. *Would Blair actually hurt us? I don't think she's got the balls, there's no way with the cops watching like this.*

The three dots danced on her screen, taunting Sapphire with their promise before vanishing without a word. She stared at her friend's profile picture at the top of the screen inside the small circle. Her tan face, blond hair, and big smile implied her friend was carefree. She used to be pretty and fun, and all the boys liked her. But no one of their group was fun or carefree anymore.

If Cordelia had an answer, she wasn't prepared to share it. Or maybe, just maybe, she was hesitating because she was thinking through what Sapphire had suggested. She stretched her long legs while she waited for her friend's response.

"Come on. You know I'm right. Why are you being so slow?" Her whispered question reverberated in the darkness.

She'd used the excuse that she was tired to go to bed early, but if anyone overheard her talking, they'd know she was faking. And then they'd wonder why. And then…they'd ask even more questions that Sapphire really wanted to answer but didn't have the courage to.

Minutes stretched like hours until, finally, the screen lit up once more.

Texts can be traced, we can't talk here. Cordelia followed it immediately with a second message. *Meet up?*

Are you serious? Cops are fucking everywhere! Sapphire's stomach bubbled into a froth of fear and frustration at the very idea.

You started it! I'm not gonna talk on text!!!

Sapphire scowled at the reasonable response. Cordelia was right, but she hated it anyway.

F that, I'm calling you.

What if someone overhears you talking? About Whitney…

Sapphire wrapped her arms around herself, trying to stifle the shiver that wasn't just from the night air seeping through the window cracks. The cold was nothing compared to the chill of fear that settled over her.

Fine, where? I have to walk so…

Cordelia wrote back instantly. *I'll pick you up.*

Fine, end of block by blue house.

Slipping out of bed, Sapphire moved with deliberate silence. She dressed quickly, layering for warmth, her movements fueled by a cocktail of trepidation and determination.

This is good. Cordelia was finally growing a dick. *Maybe she won't be Blair's bitch anymore. Maybe we can both be free of her shit.*

Her heartbeat was a pounding drum in her ears as she

opened her bedroom door and slipped out, tiptoeing toward the door. She was ready to freeze if she heard any sounds growing closer. But as she waited at the end of the hallway, the house was silent as a cemetery.

Sapphire walked through the kitchen and crouched next to the back door, waiting for the signal.

The glow of her phone screen cast a spooky light on Sapphire's tense features as it vibrated with an incoming message.

Btw, delete all texts about this and sisterhood and coven.

Her friend's warning knifed through any remaining illusion that this was a normal conversation. With deft fingers, Sapphire navigated her messages, erasing each one— a digital exorcism of fears and secrets shared.

Pocketing her now-sanitized phone, she moved like a shadow out the back door.

The night air hit her with an icy slap as she eased the door shut behind her. The world outside her home was shrouded in darkness, save for the pale luminescence of the streetlamps casting long shadows across the yard. Every rustle of dead grass underfoot sounded amplified in the silence, and the cold bit through her layers, nipping at the resolve that armored her heart.

Gripping her winter coat tightly, she crouched down to slip under the windows. As she circled around the house, the front lawn loomed wide before her, a nocturnal ocean she had to cross to reach the sanctuary of Cordelia's car. It sat down the block with the engine off, no brake lights or headlights if anyone happened to look out.

"Hey." She ducked into the passenger seat, keeping her head low, as if to ward off the darkness. "Let's get out of here. Hurry!"

Following her demands without a word, Cordelia rolled

the car forward. She was even smart enough not to press the gas too hard, so the engine stayed quiet.

Sapphire kept her eyes locked on her home, watching it recede into the distance. Once it was out of sight, she felt like she could finally breathe without worrying. She blew out the breath she'd been holding.

Sitting up, she inhaled deeply and reached for her seat belt. "Thanks for picking me up. It's colder than a witch's tit outside." She started to giggle at the silly phrase her grandpa had always used.

The laugh died in her throat as she turned to Cordelia.

"Cordelia? What's with the hoodie?" Cordelia was too vain to ever put her hood up. She reached for it and yanked it down to reveal the pale complexion and hard eyes of their coven's leader.

Blair.

Before she could grip the door handle to jump out, pain exploded across Sapphire's chest.

She sucked in a breath and looked down in confusion. Crimson bloomed like a grotesque flower all over her cream-colored sweater, with the handle of a knife sticking out.

Is that the knife that killed... Sapphire's mouth opened, but no sound emerged—only a gurgle of betrayal.

Then Blair yanked the knife out, causing her to choke on a scream.

The knife went back in. And again.

And again...until the edges of Sapphire's vision blurred, and the suburban streets spiraled away into a blue oblivion.

25

I rolled down the window to let in some fresh air. That bitch stank, in life and in death.

"You should've known better than to cross me! Cordelia messaged me as soon as you started whining."

I smiled as I remembered, with a flicker of satisfaction, how Cordelia spilled the beans about Sapphire's BS. I ran to her house to see the messages for myself. I couldn't believe it. The snake.

She'd let me in through the window. I was there when Sapphire tried to turn her against me, watching her effed-up texts come in. Then, together, we planned how to deal with the problem, sealing Sapphire's fate.

The look in Sapphire's eyes when she yanked down the hoodie...and right before I stabbed her...solid gold.

"I can't believe you actually fell for that. I thought you were smarter." I checked the rearview mirror where the night swallowed the road behind me. "Cordelia's brainless... stands to reason. You can only be so smart when you're that hot. But you? You're even dumber than she is."

Killing Sapphire was harder than I thought it'd be.

Physically, it was exhausting stabbing someone in the chest. And from my position behind the steering wheel, well, getting that thing through the lining of her rib cage over and over...

At least I was right-handed, and she didn't have any titties I had to work around, so that was a relief.

Ha. I cracked myself up.

I tried not to freak out as I thought about next steps. Once Sapphire's body was found, Cordelia and Minerva would lose their shit, but there was no way anyone else would challenge my authority. I had them on lock now.

There'd be no more doubts about my dedication to keeping our secrets.

The coven would remain intact.

"Scared little mice." I snickered, a thin smile curving my lips. "They'll think twice before stepping out of line."

I glanced again at Sapphire, whose sightless eyes stared out into nothing. I didn't feel a thing—no guilt or sadness, just a rush of relief for dealing with Sapphire's bullshit. I had to remember to make her cuts look like Whitney's body. Consistency was key.

"Girl power." I rolled my eyes, thinking of the big shot sheriff. Sure, she'd taken down a bunch of one percenter perverts.

Yet she still hadn't caught me.

She hadn't stopped me from killing Sapphire.

And she wouldn't figure it out either. I'd covered my tracks.

Tonight's mission was nothing more than a tiny wave in the ocean. Sapphire's disappearance would be forgotten in no time, just like all the other useless girls who'd gone missing on this island.

The marshes greeted me with a cold hiss of grasses as I pulled to an abrupt stop. The tires sank slightly into the wet earth, and the moon cast a ghostly light over the waterlogged landscape. I heard the distant, haunting calls of night birds and the soft lapping of water against the shore.

I turned off the ignition, the silence amplifying the pounding in my chest.

"All right, Sapphire." I smiled at the girl who had, until recently, called me friend. "Let's get you taken care of."

Climbing out, I walked around the car and opened the passenger door. The cold wind was brutal, since I'd left the house wearing only the shorts and tank top I usually slept in and the pair of boots I'd slipped on for the messy task ahead.

Grabbing her sweater, I began to drag Sapphire's limp body out of the car.

"Damn, you're heavier than you look, heifer." Beads of sweat formed on my forehead, despite the chill in the air. Sapphire's dead weight resisted every pull.

My boots squelched in the mud as I half walked, half stumbled toward the water. My breath was visible in puffs of white. When I reached an area shrouded by shadows and dune grasses, I let go, watching the body slump awkwardly into the ankle-deep water.

"Time for your last makeover."

I pulled the small, sharp blade from her chest. It took a while to yank off her sweater and toss it into the deeper waters. The tide could haul that out for me.

I needed to get to her arms.

Carefully, I dug the knife in and carved symbols into her skin, just like I'd done to Whitney. It was important they matched, considering how differently this kill was going down. I totally understood how even the tiniest details could fuck up a seemingly perfect plan. Which was why I kept at Sapphire, even after I knew she was dead.

Leaving the bitch partially exposed seemed risky, but it was calculated. After the failure at the cemetery, I'd looked up new ways to get rid of a body. And lucky me, dumping a corpse into the ocean was easier than digging a grave.

Exposed flesh would entice scavengers, hasten decomposition, and obscure evidence, according to the internet. Stepping back to get a better view of my former friend, I imagined bugs and birds picking away at her, stripping her of any leftover beauty. All that would be left was a gross mass of decay. They'd need dental records to figure out who she was.

With that happy thought, I said my goodbyes. "Have fun in hell, Sara. Say hi to Whitney for me."

26

The rising sun was brightening the town when Deputy
Frost's cruiser sliced through the crisp November morning.
He'd barely noticed the usual hustle of early risers darting
into the grocery store or scurrying to complete their holiday
errands. His mind was elsewhere, replaying yesterday's grim
discoveries.

Of the bodies they'd discovered, they were now up to
sixteen unearthed so far. Each one a life stolen and hidden
away in deceitful graves. He thought of the radar team, led by
Leonard Blyberg, who hadn't even processed all the data
from the flagged locations yet. They were still working on
imaging the rest of the cemetery, including landscaped beds
and areas where there were no graves.

But his thoughts were selfish. Tonight, once his workday
was over, he could go home. He'd be greeted by his loving
wife, eat Thanksgiving dinner, relax, and enjoy her company.
A moment of melancholy threatened to squeeze his heart
when he recalled that his boys wouldn't be there this year.
They were both busy but had promised they'd make the trip
home at Christmas.

He understood they had lives, but that didn't make their absence any easier. In true form, Angie had been gracious, though he knew it hurt her too.

But the poor souls who'd ended up buried unceremoniously wouldn't be enjoying any more holidays with their loved ones. And their families would have their lives upturned—again—by police officers explaining they'd found the body of a missing family member.

As he approached the cemetery, the thrum of activity struck him immediately. It was a hive of forensic endeavor. More tents were being erected. Each new body needed a new tent to fend off the prying eyes of the media.

Thankfully, Graham Ricky was working with them. His alibi had checked out, and the caretaker was just as concerned about his cemetery being overrun by overzealous reporters as Hoyt was. The man was the exact opposite of Abe Barclay. Considering how many of Hoyt's friends and family were interred here, that was a welcome change.

When Hoyt pulled up to the closed gates, Graham was standing guard, his presence a barrier to the indiscriminate flood they were sure would descend once again.

"Morning, Graham." Hoyt rolled down his window to greet the man, despite the cold.

"Hey, Deputy Frost." Graham's eyes were bloodshot but alert. "Deputy Locke's already here. I think he's over at the second row of tents, talking to that Coastal Ridge M.E. woman. I don't remember her name."

He was talking about Bailey Flynn. It was a bit of a surprise to hear she was already on-scene. "Thanks. We'll try to get this wrapped up as fast as possible and get out of your hair." Parking amid a sea of other vehicles, Hoyt took a moment to steel himself before climbing out.

He surveyed the scene of assembled medical examiners,

hard at work while police tape fluttered like morbid ribbons in the breeze.

The brisk morning air was tinged with the metallic odor of freshly turned earth. As Hoyt approached the area where Bailey Flynn and her team were already hard at work, he noted the precision with which each member moved.

A coroner's assistant knelt beside a half-exposed skeleton, meticulously measuring the length of femur bones protruding from the dirt. Bailey had explained to Frost that the measurements helped them calculate the size of the skeleton. That allowed the techs to estimate the size of the bodies, meaning they could excavate the bones without damaging them.

"Make sure we double-check those against the database." Bailey's voice carried an authoritative yet respectful tone. She caught Hoyt's eye and gave him a nod, not slowing in her task.

"Got it." One of her team members documented the jawline of the remains in front of him, his focus unwavering.

"Let's keep it moving, people! We've got a lot of ground to cover." Bailey rallied her team as they continued their solemn work.

Hoyt stayed out of the way as some of the skeletal remains, each a silent witness to an untold story, were gently placed into large black body bags. The sound of a zipper closing echoed somberly through the field, a finality that resonated deep within him.

"Morning, Frost." Trent's voice broke through Hoyt's reverie. The deputy's beefy frame seemed to sag under the strain, but his intention to support his colleagues shined clear in his gaze.

"Morning."

"Ready for round three of exhuming bodies?" A shadow of a smile crossed Trent's face.

"Let's just hope we find some answers today." Hoyt clapped Trent on the shoulder. "For the victims' sakes."

As he turned away from the forensic tableau, the incessant clicks of camera shutters grated against his nerves. The reporters had gathered like vultures, eager to feast on any scrap of information they could pry loose.

"Deputy Frost!" one of them called out, their voice piercing through the hum of activity. "What can you tell us about the investigation? Any leads on who's responsible?"

Hoyt felt their lenses trained on him, tracking his every move with predatory precision. He remained stoic, refusing to give them the reaction they hungered for.

"Is it true that a former FBI agent is behind this?" The shouted question was so absurd it bordered on the offensive.

Internally, Hoyt seethed. Rebecca didn't deserve to have her name dragged through the mud, not now, not ever. But outwardly, he maintained his composure, his face a mask of professional detachment. He even managed to flex his fingers to prevent them from balling into fists.

"Please direct all questions to our press liaison." Hoyt's voice betrayed none of the turmoil churning inside him. "We're focusing on the investigation." That was by far his favorite answer to give.

He'd probably heard it while watching a cop show or something like that. It had popped up in his head yesterday when they yelled other stupid questions. Shadow Island Sheriff's Office didn't have a press liaison. Hell, the *town* didn't have a press liaison. But it was fun to think about them wasting time looking for one.

Boots crunched on the frost-encrusted grass path, and he looked up to see a bleary-eyed Viviane approaching. Her head hung down.

"Morning, Vi."

Viviane looked up, her russet-brown eyes betraying her inner turmoil. "Morning, Hoyt." She lifted her chin, a smile tugging at the corners of her lip before a yawn took over. "Sorry about that. I didn't get much sleep last night, and the coffee hasn't kicked in yet."

Hoyt smiled, pleased that a lack of sleep was the reason for her weariness. "Ready for another day in paradise?"

Trent offered a nod, the corners of his mouth twitching in what could've been the beginning of a smile or a grimace —perhaps both. "Hopefully, it'll be our last one in this little slice of heaven."

"Let's focus on what we can control. Bailey and her team have the forensics handled. We're here on guard duty, traffic control, and whatever else they need us for." In attempting to rally his team, Hoyt was drawing on a fortitude he wasn't sure he possessed. "We do our part and make sure nothing interferes with theirs."

"Speaking of control…" Trent trailed off, nodding toward the gaggle of reporters crowding the perimeter, their lenses glinting.

"Leave them to me." Hoyt winked. "You two keep your heads down and work. I'll handle the vultures."

With that, he strode forward, intercepting a particularly aggressive journalist who was trying to argue his way past Graham.

As he stepped out of the protective line of tents, camera flashes burst forth.

"Deputy, any word on the number of victims?" one reporter called out, trying to provoke a response.

"Ma'am, I'm going to need you to step back." Hoyt moved up next to Graham, holding his hand up. "This is an active crime scene, not a press conference."

Seeing the uniform, the woman who was trying to get

through the gate shifted back, lifting a recording device. "Is it true that—"

Hoyt shook his head, not saying a word. Regardless of how he responded, they would keep pressing with their questions. What they didn't know was that, at least for now, he didn't have many answers to give.

27

When Rebecca woke, the gray light of dawn was seeping through her bedroom curtains. With a practiced motion, she reached for her phone, her thoughts already threading through the intricacies of the case consuming her.

Humphrey, her adopted chocolate lab, grumbled from his spot at the foot of the bed, stretching his legs. Flopping his head down, he stared at her, tongue lolling out.

Her phone screen blinked to life, but not with the email she'd been anticipating. Her search warrant for Abigail's car was still in limbo, the Thanksgiving holiday not helping the speedy pursuit of justice. A sigh escaped her lips as disappointment settled over her like a wet blanket.

Swinging her legs off the bed, Rebecca's feet hit the cool hardwood floor. The chill nudged her fully awake as she padded into the kitchen. Humphrey followed along, eager for his breakfast.

She'd settled into an automatic routine of feeding Humphrey his morning kibble, giving him his first scratches and pets of the day, then brewing a carafe of coffee. The coffee pot's soft gurgling was a welcome sound, the rich aroma of Brazilian dark roast filling the room like an olfactory embrace.

She poured herself a cup, cradling it between her hands for warmth, and took a tentative sip. The bitterness on her tongue served as the slap to the senses she needed to fully wake up.

As she stood at the kitchen counter assembling a modest breakfast of scrambled eggs and toast, Rebecca's mind spun a web of next steps. If the warrant continued its bureaucratic crawl, she'd have to find another angle. Time wasn't a luxury they could afford.

Her planning was shattered by a clamor rising from outside. Humphrey jumped up on the back of the couch, not quite growling as he shoved his head between the curtains to get a look for himself.

Pulling back the curtain, Rebecca's eyes widened at the sight of reporters swarming the sidewalk, their cameras and microphones like weapons at the ready.

"Are you kidding me? It's bad enough they have to pester me at work. Now they're at my house too?" *And on Thanksgiving.*

Humphrey hopped down and spun a quick circle before facing the door. He was ready to bolt outside and chase off the intruders. Or get pets. While Humphrey was a great guard dog, and he'd defended her against an attack from an assassin in her own home, he was more of a lover than a fighter.

Shaking her head, Rebecca set her coffee mug down with a clink against the coffee table. She strode to her bedroom, purposefully donning a pair of jeans and a blazer—armor against the onslaught of prying questions and flashing cameras.

Putting on her uniform was out of the question. If anyone snapped pictures of her, she wanted it to be clear she was not on duty and that they'd come to harass her. It wouldn't stop them, but it would put a damper on their plans, at least. She stepped into her sneakers, the cushioned interior warming her feet.

Upon opening her front door, the air carried the salt of the sea mingled with the persistence of the press. They turned as one organism, sensing movement from their prey, and Rebecca steeled herself. Humphrey whined, sniffing at the door, asking to be let out. Rebecca thought that was a good idea and clipped his long running leash on.

Maybe he'd be a really good boy and leave a steaming mess on their shoes.

The morning sun cast long shadows across the lawn as Rebecca stepped out onto her porch, the tranquility of dawn splintered by the cacophony of questions hurled at her from the sea of reporters.

Humphrey barked softly, hopping down the stairs when he didn't sense any danger from the throng. Clearly, he didn't understand their threat, though his movements did at least send the intruders scattering as he snuffled at each of them.

"Sheriff West, can you comment on your departure from the FBI?" one reporter shouted, thrusting a microphone in her direction.

Another chimed in. "Is there a connection between your move here and the Yacht Club?" Their voice carried a mix of curiosity and accusation that made Rebecca's skin bristle.

In the yard, Humphrey broke off from his sniff session to anoint the posts of the porch, staring at the assembled reporters as he relieved himself.

Rebecca crossed her arms, her posture testifying to years of training honed to keep calm under pressure. Looking down at them from her spot on the porch, she frowned at the seemingly random questions.

What did any of that have to do with what was happening

now? Had they really come to her house to ask about her past instead of what was going on over at the cemetery?

"I left the FBI for personal reasons. And none of those reasons had any connection to Shadow Island." She hadn't even known about the Yacht Club until after arriving here.

"Did your last investigation in D.C. lead you here? Were you undercover?" The questions came rapid-fire, each more probing than the last.

They were trying to piece together fragments of her past, constructing a narrative that had no basis in reality. "My move here has nothing to do with past cases or my time in the FBI."

"Are those bodies in the cemetery more victims of the Yacht Club?" The inquiry sliced through the hubbub, striking at the core of Rebecca's fears. The ongoing excavation at the cemetery had unearthed more than just bones. It was resurrecting a nightmare the island thought recently buried.

"That's an ongoing investigation, and I'm not going to talk about it. Besides, you've all run extensive pieces on my history, so I'm not sure why you're asking questions about my previous employment. It's all out there, open records. You're not getting anything new from me this morning." She didn't bother to hide her annoyance as cameras were pointed at her. In fact, she turned to glower at a few of them.

Humphrey spun around, digging at the ground and kicking bits of sod and grass toward the people interrupting his morning routine.

As some reporters opened their mouths to interject, she raised her hand. "And I'm going to ask you to stay off my lawn. This is private property you're trespassing on, and I don't want my grass trampled. The cold and salty breeze is hard enough on it."

The throng of journalists recoiled slightly, perhaps sensing the ire behind Rebecca's words. She held their collective gaze a moment longer, ensuring her message was clear, before turning and making her way back inside.

"Why aren't you at the cemetery, Sheriff? What about the exhumation of all those bodies?" Their words chased her like hounds on a foxhunt.

Inside her chest, frustration roared like a caged beast, its claws scraping for release. She yearned to throw herself into the thick of that investigation, to stand shoulder to shoulder with the team unearthing grim secrets. But she was relieved the press seemed unaware of her current case. That somewhere on this quaint island a killer was hiding.

Humphrey huffed a few times, not quite barking, before running up the stairs to join her. Opening the door, she followed him inside and away from the chorus of shouted questions she was ignoring.

With the door closed behind her, Rebecca sagged for a brief moment. Her kitchen felt like a bunker. Unclipping Humphrey, she hung his leash on the hooks near the door and headed for the kitchen again. She topped off her coffee, the dark liquid promising a temporary reprieve.

Its bitter scent was grounding, a reminder there were still simple, predictable elements in her world. Humphrey came over and stretched to press his chin on her leg as he stared up. Running her fingers through his wavy coat, she relaxed.

The phone's shrill ring sliced through the silence, and Rebecca's heart hitched. Seeing *Dispatch* on her screen, she answered, already bracing for what could only be bad news this early in the morning, on a holiday. "This is West."

"Boss, sorry to bother you at home again." It was the *again* that upset Rebecca…the fact that this happened so often and with so little time between emergencies. Elliot Ping got right to the point. "We've got another body. This one's been identified. It's one of the girls you interviewed. Sara Porter."

"Dammit." The word came out as a low growl. Rebecca

had to take several deep, slow breaths before she could respond. She could hear Elliot fidgeting on the other end of the call, his chair squeaking as he waited. "Send me the address. I'm on my way. And call forensics to meet us there too."

Humphrey sighed and wandered toward the bedroom.

"Yeah, Boss. I…" He sucked in a harsh breath. "I'm sorry your day had to start this way."

Rebecca checked the clock on the wall. "Your day started the same way. We're in this boat together. Don't worry about it."

Elliot mumbled something before hanging up.

She snatched her travel mug from the drying rack and filled it. There was no time for the chaos outside, no space for the media's insatiable hunger for tragedy. Coffee in hand, she went to her room and pulled on her uniform.

"Kelly will be here soon to take you for a walk." A fun-loving woman who lived less than a mile away, Kelly Hunt pitched in to watch Humphrey whenever Rebecca was overwhelmed at work, bringing her golden retriever Brody with her so the dogs could have playdates.

Rebecca leaned over and kissed Humphrey on the nose. He smiled, his tail swishing back and forth, just above the comforter. His eyes were filled with so much love, she couldn't help but give him a second kiss and a snuggle.

Braced by her dog's unconditional love, Rebecca turned away, walking out the front door before locking it behind her. She moved with purpose, not slowing for anything or anyone, plowing through the sea of reporters.

They're here because they have a job to do, she reminded herself, even as she gritted her teeth. *An important job. They care that lives have been snuffed out, even if it's hard to remember that when they're a noisy mob. A noisy, extremely inconvenient mob.*

The crowd of reporters parted, albeit reluctantly, some still calling out, trying to snag her attention with their pointed questions.

"Is this related to the cemetery, Sheriff? Why aren't you there?"

"Any comment on the teenage victim?"

Their words bounced off her like rain on a metal roof.

Rebecca drove away from the tumult, the rearview mirror reflecting the thwarted journalists she'd left in her wake. A silent prayer slipped through her clenched teeth—a hope that none of them were tracking her, that she could reach Sara without bringing the circus along.

28

The morning air was heavy with salt and the distant cries of seagulls. Rebecca's tires splashed along the half-mud, half-dirt road leading to the crime scene, each turn bringing them closer to a reality she wished she could have prevented.

As she pulled up to the scene, Rebecca killed the engine and sat for a moment in silence. Her gaze lingered on the untamed swaths of marsh grasses dancing in the breeze— nature's indifferent backdrop to human cruelty.

If she'd gotten that warrant yesterday, would she even be here today? Could a piece of evidence have stopped the killer from striking a second time? She'd never know. But the question was added to the growing list of what-ifs that plagued her.

Following her from case to case, those questions reminded her to cross all her t's and dot all her i's. A mistake could cost someone their life. And that was a guilt she'd never be able to shake.

She reached over to the glove compartment, where she found the familiar shape of her camera, its weight a solid reassurance in her hand. When she stepped out of the SUV, the cool bite of the wind brushed against her cheeks as she pocketed the camera and made her way toward the fluttering yellow tape ahead.

"Sheriff, we really should stop meeting like this." Jake's voice was low as he concluded his conversation with a middle-aged woman clutching a dog's leash. The woman's face was drawn, eyes wide with the shock of her morning walk leading to a macabre discovery. She wore a pair of mud-spattered, stalk-covered sneakers, which showed just how far into the marsh she'd gone to retrieve her dog.

Beside her, a white-and-gray dog with brown spots stared up. His ears were tucked down, as was his tail, wrapped around his back legs and pressed tight against his stomach. He leaned against the woman's legs, either begging for forgiveness or comfort.

"Coffey." Rebecca acknowledged him with a nod, her attention shifting between the two. "What've we got?"

"Early morning walker." Jake gestured with a thumb toward the woman behind him, who was petting her dog mechanically. "She found our victim while trying to keep her dog from chasing rabbits. Her dog found the remains and drew her in barking his head off. They're both pretty shaken up."

With a deep breath, Rebecca turned to Jake. "Let's see what we're dealing with. Elliot's called in forensics and the medical examiner, and they should be here shortly. But we can still get the initial photographs taken before they arrive."

Jake nodded gravely to the woman. "Thank you again for your statement, ma'am. Take it easy for a while. You've had quite a shock."

As they started walking, the marsh grasses parted reluctantly, a whispering sea of yellow that seemed to hold its breath as Rebecca stepped through them, doing her best to stay on the high spots to avoid destroying any evidence that might've been left behind.

With each step, she took another picture, documenting her path in. The earth beneath her boots was soft, giving way too easily, reminding her of the first time she'd walked these marshes, searching for a different teen girl's body.

Jake's footfalls squelched behind hers, their silence a mutual understanding that words were unnecessary burdens in the face of what awaited them.

They broke through a waist-high tuft of grasses that had already been trampled once, showing canine footprints in the surrounding mud. Beyond the plants, a fully clothed form lay crumpled at the water's edge.

As had been reported, it was Sara Porter. Grass was entwined in her hair, laid over her body, and piled on her chest. And both arms were flung wide, as if to embrace the sky above her dead, staring eyes.

Through the ripped-up and creased blades of grass, Rebecca spotted white marks on her outstretched arm. The same random occult symbols that had been left on Whitney's body had been carved into Sara's, hopefully also after her death.

This time, the killer appeared to have been in a hurry. The occult symbols carved into the flesh were jagged and uneven. Rushed. The "witch" was getting careless…or perhaps desperate. Rebecca pointed her camera with practiced movements. The lens clicked and whirred as she focused on the cruel etchings on the girl's arms.

Rebecca gestured to the marks while capturing shot after shot. "Looks like our killer was in a hurry. Maybe they're feeling the heat?"

"Or they're spooked." Jake crouched, inspecting the wounds. "Might've thought someone was coming. It's hard to tell with the dog tracks messing everything up."

"Don't blame the dog. He was being a good boy. It looks like he was trying to get to her. Probably sensing something was wrong."

Jake snorted, and she narrowed her eyes at him. He held his hands up, palms out, and stood. "Not saying he wasn't a good boy. He did find her. I just keep forgetting how much of a dog lover you are. It's kinda sweet."

Not sure how to take that remark, Rebecca continued to document the scene. Her thoughts wandered back to yesterday when Sara had sat across from her, eyes wide and fearful, talking about the witch's revenge. "She was close. Close to telling us something big. Now we'll never know."

"Too bad she didn't. We would've been able to keep her safe."

That was a thought Rebecca had too often. "It's always the same, isn't it? We saw this a lot with any case involving the Yacht Club too. People would get involved, then get worried about getting charged or getting a reputation as a snitch. They'd rather take the risk of dying instead of just coming clean."

Rebecca lowered the camera with a sigh. She was dealing with teen girls now, and they were just as scared and reckless as some of the Yacht Club lackeys had been.

Squelching muck beneath vehicle tires announced the arrival of the Bailey Flynn's team. A hum of more vehicles from farther down the road announced the forensic techs not far behind. Response time was fast when everyone was already on the island at the cemetery.

Before she could start that way to greet Bailey, her phone chimed, letting her know she'd gotten an email. Straightening, she pulled her phone from her pocket. "The warrant for Samantha Miller's vehicle's been approved. As soon as the forensic team gets here, we can go serve that."

"Considering how protective Abigail was of her mom's

car, I'd be willing to bet there's going to be plenty of evidence there."

"Let's hope so." Rebecca stared at the dead girl at her feet and wondered if the warrant's delay had cost a girl her life. "So long as they didn't manage to scrub the interior clean last night."

29

The doorbell echoed through the empty house, followed immediately by heavy, rapid-fire pounding on the door. My heart caught in my chest as I pictured SWAT breaking down my door, storming in to arrest me.

I almost ran out the back before I pulled it together. There was no way the cops were here to arrest me. I'd played my hand right.

Back in Cordelia's car, a grim satisfaction had settled over me. The drive back to town to drop off the car was easy and carefree. It was like I'd left all my problems buried in the marsh.

Before pulling into the driveway, I killed the headlights. Then I left Cordelia's keys on the seat—another part of the plan—and walked toward my own vehicle discreetly parked a safe distance away.

At home, I'd cleaned my muddy boots with the hose behind the house before dumping them in the closet. Then I peeled off my gross shorts and tank and threw them in the wash, adding a ton of detergent and an extra rinse, just like I did with my mom's car blanket that we'd rolled Whitney in.

Finally, I'd jumped into a steaming shower, trying to burn away the cold and wet of the outdoors.

"Good old Sheriff West. Doesn't even know who she's dealing with." I'd scrubbed under my nails. *Let her try to find evidence to convict me.*

Even the blanket we'd wrapped Whitney in was now resting at the bottom of the ocean, tied up with rocks. I'd tossed it off the pier after backtracking to the cottage for my epic game changer early Tuesday morning.

They had nothing on me.

And running wouldn't do me any good anyway.

Taking a moment to catch my breath and make sure I didn't look scared, I walked to the front door and swung it open.

It wasn't the cops. Instead, Cordelia stood there, a mess of anxiety with her chest heaving and eyes wild.

"Blair, why…why isn't Sapphire answering my texts?" Her voice squeaked, on the edge of hysteria.

"I think you know why." The words slipped out like the flick of a blade, smooth and sharp.

Her face drained of color, leaving her looking like she'd seen a ghost. Maybe she had, in a way. "What did you do to her?" Cordelia's entire body shook, quivering like a stupid jellyfish.

"Come on." I leaned against the doorframe and batted my lashes. "What did you think I'd do after the texts you showed me last night? Isn't that why you showed me what she was saying? I told you what I'd do to anyone who betrayed the coven. And Sapphire was trying to betray the coven. You should've seen this coming."

This was the part of the game where I relished every moment—the fear, the shock, the certainty. I wasn't just talking trash or making shit up when I told them what I'd do to traitors. And now, she finally got it. I said what I said.

"You can't just…you're saying you…" She couldn't even string a complete thought together. Poor thing. Her brain was scrambled eggs.

"Let me spell it out for you, then." Sneering, my voice dropped to a dangerous purr. "This is why you don't fuck with me. I'm not playing make-believe. This is very real."

The pretty little thing looked as if I'd slapped her, her wide eyes reflecting the monster she saw in me.

I knew I should be careful, keep it together, but the power high was fucking thrilling.

"No one can cross me and walk away." My laugh was bitter, cold. "You've always been naive, Cordelia. Too soft. But this is the real world, and in the real world, there are consequences."

She stumbled back, her whole body radiating fear and panic, but there was no way out. Not for her, not for the others. Her desperate breaths escalated into pants. Then she focused on me, and something dark overcame her.

"You're a murderer!" Cordelia screamed and then lunged, fingers clawing, aiming for my face in blind fury.

She tried to slap me, but I ducked out of the way, and she was too slow to correct her swing.

I started to laugh, but she brought her hand back around, catching me in the cheek with her knuckles.

That shit stung. I jumped forward, gripping her shirt and pulling her off-balance. We both stumbled back into the house.

We were a tangle of limbs and rage, crashing into furniture, knocking over a lamp. The back of my legs hit the couch, and I lost my balance, but I pulled her with me. I twisted to the side and rolled over, slamming her onto the floor.

I released a full-on scream, letting my anger spill out like a wild thunderstorm. I'd take her down with my bare hands, and she'd regret—

"Enough!"

The command boomed from the doorway, authoritative and sharp as broken glass. Cordelia and I froze, our bodies still locked in conflict, as Sheriff West barged in, her gun pointed at both of us.

Her hot deputy, I couldn't remember the guy's name, was at her heels. He had his gun out too. I got off Cordelia, fixing my gaze on the sheriff and slowly raising my hands. How much had she heard? Any of it? I didn't think so. But she must have arrived not long after Cordelia did.

"Care to explain what this is about?" The sheriff glared at both of us, her expression filled with angry confusion. She kept her gun trained on the center of my chest. The hot guy had his on Cordelia. I bet she loved that.

We stood up slowly.

"What are you two fighting about?"

"She borrowed my hoodie and won't return it." As angry as Cordelia might've been, she didn't even hesitate to lie to protect me. I immediately forgave her for everything she'd done during our fight. She was my real best friend. "So I tackled her to force her to give it back. Then we fell."

"I told you. I don't know where it is. It's probably in the wash. I'll return it as soon as I can find it." I snapped back at Cordelia even though I wanted to hug her. Now was the time to put on a show for the cops, and Cordelia was doing exactly that.

"We can deal with whatever's going on here later." The sheriff held up a piece of paper. I wasn't going to spoil my image by acting concerned enough to read it. "I have a warrant to search your mother's car."

"Go ahead." My words were ice, my demeanor

unflappable as I crossed to the buffet and tossed the sheriff my set of keys with a flick of my wrist.

Sheriff West caught the keys and walked outside. I shot a warning glance at Cordelia, so she'd know to keep up the ruse before I followed the sheriff out of the house.

As they combed through my mom's car just a short distance away, I leaned against the doorframe, arms folded, the very picture of nonchalance. They'd find nothing. There was nothing to find.

"Confident, are we?" The sheriff's voice cut through my reverie, her eyes searching mine for a crack in the armor.

"I have nothing to hide, so why wouldn't I be?" I matched her steely gaze.

"Most people would be sweating right now."

"Most people aren't me." My smile was a razor's edge, slicing through the tension.

I watched as my heart continued to beat a steady drum of assurance while the sheriff emerged from the car empty-handed. But the hot deputy kept searching, following her orders like a dog. He wouldn't find anything either.

"Nothing to say?" Sheriff West probed, her tone suggesting she expected more.

"Nothing you want to hear."

It was a game of chess, and I was always two moves ahead. Let them look, let them doubt. I was going to get away with murder, and there was nothing they could do about it.

"Looks like you missed a spot." Her tone was as cold as the water I'd dumped Sara in.

"Excuse me?" I feigned ignorance, even as a serpent of dread coiled tightly in my gut.

"Deputy Coffey found something interesting." Her head turned toward Deputy Hottie, who was taking pictures of the inside of my car.

My mind raced. I had been thorough. I was sure of it.

The hot deputy was talking to his lady boss, but I couldn't make out what he was saying.

"There's a line of blood in your back seat where the seat meets the back. And my deputy pulled a short black hair out of it." Rebecca's words slithered like a snake ready to strike. "Care to explain?"

"Explain what? Your desperate attempts to pin something on me?" My voice was a snarl, a lashing out against the tide turning against me. "I give my friends rides all the time. Who knows how many hairs fall off while the windows are down and we're cruising through town. And that blood could've come from anyone, at any time. It's my mom's car. I just use it from time to time."

"But that's…" Cordelia's voice quivered as she joined me on the porch, her pale face a mask of horror.

I shot her a look that could kill. "Stay out of this!"

"Actually, she's part of this. We're contacting your mother now about the items found in the car. We're also letting her know that we're arresting you." The sheriff stepped closer. "You're in deep trouble. You admitted to us that you drove your mom's car on the night of Whitney's murder, and now we've found blood in the car. That's enough to detain you until I get more answers about what Deputy Coffey found in your mom's vehicle."

Sheriff Rebecca smirked at me, and I wanted to slap the expression off her face. Who did she think she was to look at me like that?

"Coffey, cuff her." She started reciting the Miranda rights at me, like I was some kind of common criminal.

Deputy Hottie moved forward and turned me around, pulling my hands behind my back. The metal was cold on my wrists, making me shiver, but at least he wasn't forceful or rough. Did that mean he liked me, or that he didn't see me as a real threat? I hoped it was both.

After checking my pockets, he took my phone and handed it to his boss before leading me away. My brain scrambled for more things to clear my name. My excuse for the hair was solid but the blood…that was a rookie mistake.

A lesser bitch would panic. Not me. Already, I saw how this turn of events worked to my advantage. Now that I was arrested, the cops would pay close attention to every word I said. The sheriff didn't realize she had just handed me the perfect opportunity to control the narrative.

30

Abigail Miller sat hunched and handcuffed in the back seat of Rebecca's vehicle, her eyes hollow pits of defiance and anger as she stared at the back of the front passenger seat. Rebecca knew the quiet would gnaw at her prisoner, urging her to spill her secrets.

Jake leaned against the SUV. He'd just finished his call to get forensics and a tow truck out to their latest scene.

Rebecca spared a momentary thought for the forensic teams. They were working so much overtime the last few days, and today was Thanksgiving. "Stay with Carrie," she instructed Jake. She didn't believe for a moment the girls' fight had been about a hoodie.

There hadn't been a knife during the altercation, which made it a different kind of attack than the ones that had killed Whitney Turner and Sara Porter.

That didn't mean Abigail wouldn't have grabbed a knife to end the fight if they'd gotten there a little bit later.

"It's time we got to the bottom of this and find out what these girls have been hiding."

Resting his hands on his belt, Jake approached Carrie

Dugan so he could escort her into the house. "I called Carrie's parents, given that she's a potential victim and a minor. They should be here shortly."

Even from this distance, Rebecca could see the shock in the girl's eyes. She didn't seem too beaten up from her fight with Abigail, but her tan face was pale, and every now and then, her body shook with shivers.

"Good thinking. Maybe she'll be more willing to answer questions now that Abigail's attacked her."

As if summoned by their collective concern, a car careened into the driveway, disgorging two frantic figures. Carrie's parents were the embodiment of parental fear, their faces etched with lines of dread as they raced to envelop their daughter in protective arms.

It was Rebecca's first glimpse of the couple—a stark introduction under the cloud of suspicion and violence. "Mr. and Mrs. Dugan." Rebecca nodded with a mix of professional courtesy and empathy. "I'm Sheriff Rebecca West."

"Of course." Shock painted Louis Dugan's features. He was the only one who looked up as his wife continued to run her hands over her daughter, still standing in the front yard. Carrie had started to silently weep, her arms still wrapped around her own waist. "What's happened? Is Carrie…"

"We came here to serve a search warrant for Samantha Miller's car. When we arrived, we noticed the front door open. As we approached, we witnessed Abigail and your daughter in a physical altercation inside the front room. We separated them." Rebecca watched confusion and concern ripple across both their faces.

"Honey, why were you fighting with Abigail? Did something happen?" Louis turned to his daughter.

Rebecca stayed quiet about the hoodie excuse, waiting to see what Carrie would say now. But she remained silent.

Andrea Dugan wrapped her arms around Carrie, holding

her tight to her body. "I don't understand. Why did you need a search warrant for Abigail? What has she done?"

Rebecca quoted the party line when it came to ongoing investigations, just like she'd done with the reporters on her lawn. "I'm afraid I can't disclose the details. We're simply trying to gather as much information as we can, and a search warrant is one way we can do that. Someone is harming people these girls know, and we won't stop investigating until they're caught."

What little color remaining in Carrie's cheeks drained away.

Shouldn't Carrie be happy they were closing in on a suspect? Rebecca knew the girl was hiding something, but she didn't know what.

Before she could ponder that further, the Dugans both spoke at once. "We appreciate you trying to find the person responsible," and "Thank you so much. We'll all sleep better once the monster is thrown in jail."

Her parents' statements hit Carrie like a physical blow. She swayed where she stood and likely would've fallen if she wasn't being held in place by her mother.

"I'm sure Carrie doesn't want to see anyone else hurt." Rebecca pressed on, gently but firmly. "A testimony could make all the difference."

"Could you do that, sweetheart?" Louis urged, his voice trembling.

Carrie's gaze was locked on the sheriff's cruiser, and Rebecca turned to see Abigail staring back. Carrie opened her mouth, closed it, then finally crumbled into sobs.

"I-I can't," she stammered through tears. "It's too much."

"Carrie, we need the truth." Rebecca nodded to Jake, and he gently guided the mother-daughter human bundle inside the home and out of Abigail's view. Once they were all inside the front door, she resumed her questions. "Anything you say could be pivotal. Why did you come over here? Did Abigail call you? Ask you to meet her? Did she say anything? What started the fight?"

Carrie shivered and shook her head, her fingers digging into her sides. "The witch," she choked out, her voice ragged with fear. "The witch did it."

"Sweetheart, what do you mean?" Andrea gave her daughter a tighter squeeze and shot Rebecca a protective glare.

"I told you, it's the witch!" Her scream echoed out the front door as tears poured down her face. She collapsed, dragging her mother to the floor with her.

"Carrie!" Andrea tried to support her daughter, but the girl had gone completely limp.

Her father jumped in, wrapping his arms around them. "Sheriff, I'm sorry." He shook his head. "My daughter's been through enough. She needs to see her doctor, not be interrogated."

As the family huddled together, Rebecca stepped back, giving them space. Her mind worked furiously, piecing together the scant shards of truth amid a mosaic of deception and fear. The girls had all blamed a witch. And they had from the beginning.

Even now, Carrie continued to mumble "the witch" through her tears as she clung to her mother with her eyes screwed closed.

What did it mean? It could be the confused accusation of a frightened girl or a clue staring Rebecca right in the face. Even the legend never made any mention of the witch still being alive or coming back from the grave or anything like that.

But if they weren't blaming the island's historical witch, who were they talking about? None of this made any sense, especially considering that the runes carved into the two girls had nothing to do with the type of spell craft associated with the island's witch.

"Okay." Rebecca relented, her gaze never leaving the Dugan family. "Take the time you need, Carrie. You can take her to get evaluated. Abigail is going to come with me so I can ask her some questions. Hopefully, she'll know something that will help us figure out what happened here."

"Thank you. Thank you." Louis spoke politely, but he didn't look up at her. He just knelt beside his wife and child as she continued to sob and shake, urging her to get up so they could go outside.

Rebecca moved over to where Jake stood by the front door, leaving the parents to care for and comfort their daughter while they waited. After all, she had Abigail. Considering Abigail's self-assured and combative attitude, Rebecca was certain they'd apprehended their killer.

31

"Coffey, stay with the Dugans and wait for the techs. Call for an ambulance if they think she needs one. I'm going to take Abigail for a little drive to see if I can get her to talk. Carrie doesn't need to see her sitting here anyway. Let me know if she calms down after we leave." Rebecca strode over to her SUV, pulling the keys from her pocket.

"Will do, Boss." Jake moved to stand next to Abigail's car.

Climbing in the driver's seat, Rebecca's gaze lingered on Carrie. Louis had managed to coax her outside onto the porch, where the girl's frame was dwarfed by her parents' protective embrace. She then turned back to the task at hand. The sound of the SUV coming to life broke the silence that had settled over the scene like a thick fog.

"Where are you taking me?" Abigail's voice, small and unsteady, filtered from the back seat through the partition.

"Where people like you deserve to go." Rebecca smoothly accelerated away from the curb.

With the recent destruction to the sheriff's station, their new holding cells were no longer fit for keeping prisoners, but there were rooms at town hall where she could lock someone up while the investigation continued. The doors had been retrofitted to allow for the rooms to be secured from the outside.

Yes, she could outright charge Abigail for assault. But she wanted to chat with her about other, bigger topics.

For example, there was the matter of the blood in Samantha Miller's car.

Rebecca drove past the turnoff to town hall, continuing toward the open sea. It was a calculated move, taking the longer route, betting on the mounting pressure to pry loose the truth from Abigail's lips.

And why was Carrie at Abigail's? While borrowing clothes and not returning them might lead to a fight between friends, or even a physical altercation, Rebecca was certain that was not what had happened today.

She wished she'd gotten a warrant to go through Abigail's phone, but she didn't have enough evidence for that. Maybe she'd called Carrie over to attack her. But then why leave the door open? And why would Carrie lie about it?

They hadn't gotten through to Samantha Miller's friends, so her alibi was still unproven. It could turn out the mother was the killer—that would explain blood in the back seat of her car. In fact, Rebecca had no hard evidence Abigail had ever driven the car, except that she had access to the keys and admitted to it. But, clearly, so did Samantha Miller.

"Please, Sheriff…I don't know what you want me to say." Abigail broke the silence, her voice cracking with desperation or deceit—Rebecca couldn't be sure which.

Rebecca kept her eyes on the road as they passed the sign pointing toward the beach. The vast expanse of the ocean stretched out to one side, its waves crashing in a rhythmic persistence that mirrored the pulse of the investigation.

"Look, I told you everything already." Abigail appeared uncomfortable as she tried to sink into the back seat with her hands cuffed behind her. "I didn't hurt anyone. And Carrie attacked me. I don't know why you think I did something wrong."

The SUV glided into a public parking spot at the beach, the seagulls' cries echoing the turmoil that swirled inside the vehicle. The cruiser's tires rumbled over the shell-laden parking lot, coming to rest at the shore. Rebecca turned off the ignition and faced the girl in the back seat.

Abigail sank father into the seat as best she could, her body language betraying her defeat.

Rebecca watched as Abigail's slender frame shuddered with sobs. Her tears might've been genuine, but sorrow could easily be a mask for fear or guilt.

"We found blood and hair in your car, and your car was spotted on the route to the cemetery around the time Whitney was killed. You admitted to being out, to driving that car at that time of night." Rebecca presented her statements matter-of-factly, allowing the evidence to hang in the air between them.

"That could be from anyone!" Now there was a quiver of uncertainty in Abigail's protest, a crack in the facade. "For all I know, someone's fucking tampon leaked while I was giving them a ride. And how am I supposed to know whose hair is in my back seat? It's a hair. It could be mine or anyone I've given a ride to."

"Anyone who happens to match the DNA we find, you mean." Rebecca scrutinized Abigail's face, glad she'd activated her pen camera before beginning this conversation. "We're going to test them both. You can be certain we will find out who they belong to. It's a holiday, so it might take longer than normal, but we'll have results within a few days. The lab won't take long to process the evidence. Whose blood is in your back seat? It'd be better for you to tell me now."

"Please...I don't know anything about that blood." Abigail's words were rushed.

"That's fine." Rebecca shrugged, as if dismissing the girl's statement. "We've got Whitney's DNA on file. When that blood matches hers, we'll have more than enough to tie you to the scene. You have no alibi. Once we have the DNA showing she was bleeding in your back seat, any jury in the country will convict you. You'll be going to prison for the rest of your life. And you have a lot of life left."

Perhaps it was cruel to threaten a high schooler, but Rebecca needed Abigail to open up. Especially if she wasn't the killer.

The salty air wafted through the cracked window as Rebecca stared down Abigail. The girl's eyes, once so defiant, now danced with panic and indecision.

"What happened to Sara last night?"

"What are you talking about? I texted her just this morning to see how she's been holding up with everything." Abigail lunged forward to stare at Rebecca through the divider with wide, nearly hysterical eyes. "Why are you talking about Sara? What happened to Sara?"

"Show me." Rebecca climbed out of the cruiser and opened the back door, the girl's phone in hand. After getting the code to unlock it, she held the device up so Abigail could see the screen.

After receiving permission and then instructions from the teen, Rebecca navigated to a screen that displayed a message sent at nine thirty that morning. *Hey Sara you ok? HMU, we'll grab lunch.*

No response followed.

Rebecca scrolled back through the older messages.

All the texts before that talked about school, classes, and boys they thought might be cute. The conversation went as far back as the first days of school. There weren't very many messages, showing the girls didn't text much. That didn't mean they didn't talk much, but if they did, it wasn't likely over text.

Rebecca didn't see any of the dedicated chatting apps on the phone, but many social media platforms could be used to send direct messages. All of which could be deleted later. For that matter, contemporary cell phones allowed people to selectively delete parts of text conversations. The lack of damning messages meant little.

"This proves nothing." Rebecca scrutinized the digital exchange. "You could've trashed what you didn't want me to see. Or you and Sara talk with a different app most of the time, and you sent this one as a cover for today. I know you're a smart young woman, and I think you might find yourself in a lot of trouble. Let me help you, so it doesn't get to that point."

Abigail's desperation was plain. "Please, tell me what happened to Sara. I thought this was all about Whitney. Why are you asking about Sara now?"

"Maybe we can get you cleared of suspicion if we pull the records from your provider?" She was curious to see how the girl reacted. "I can get a subpoena easy enough."

"Go ahead. What you see there is what I said to Sara. The phone carrier's only going to prove I'm telling the truth."

"Let's not make this harder than it has to be." Rebecca softened her voice to offer a sliver of solace. "Truth has a way of surfacing, no matter how deep it's buried."

Abigail's sniffles punctuated the silence, a feeble chorus set against the relentless whisper of the sea. Rebecca leaned against the open door of the back seat, waiting to see what would happen next.

"Fine, I'll talk." Abigail's voice broke through the calm, her words tumbling out between sobs, each syllable heavy with defeat. "It was Carrie."

Rebecca offered a smile, knowing she needed to win her suspect's trust. "Carrie?" she echoed. The same girl who only an hour ago had been in shock, balled up on the floor in the fetal position. None of that had seemed like an act.

"Everyone thinks she's so...so timid." Tears streamed down Abigail's cheeks. "But she's not. She's brutal, forceful. She's been pulling the strings all this time." She choked on a sob, her whole body shaking. "She wanted to lead us, to be the one in charge of our little group. But Whitney resisted, because she didn't want to do what Carrie told her to do. So Carrie killed her."

Interesting. Curious as to what the young woman would say next, Rebecca waited for her to continue.

"If something happened to Sara, maybe she knew something. That's why I've been saying it was the witch. I'm scared, Sheriff. Scared of Carrie, scared of ending up like them..." Abigail wiped away her tears with her shoulder. "She said she'd curse me next if I didn't follow her rules. When I tried arguing about it this morning when she came over, she attacked me."

Rebecca processed the information, finding it both ludicrous and plausible. Somehow, Abigail's unlikely story made the grim puzzle pieces fit with the evidence they'd found. "Is that why there were occult symbols carved into Whitney's and Sara's bodies?" She watched closely for any telltale signs of deceit.

Abigail's eyes widened, her skin paling to an ashen hue at the mention of the carvings. "Sara's dead too?" She leaned forward, gagging, her body convulsing as if she might retch onto the floor of the SUV. "No, no, I didn't know. You never said anything about..." She gasped as a particularly rough retch shook her, and Rebecca stepped back to avoid being puked on. "They were...carved up?"

"Before they died." Rebecca trained her eyes on Abigail's

face, gauging her reaction to the lie about the carvings happening while the victims were still alive.

Abigail retched again, this time leaning out the open door. Spit trickled out of her mouth, but nothing more. Then the girl lifted her head, and Rebecca could see her eyes were bloodshot, tears streaming down her cheeks. It wasn't showy, like Carrie's reaction back at Abigail's house. And that made it even more believable.

The visceral response appeared to be from genuine shock. It seemed these details were news to her. Rebecca felt a shift within herself—a begrudging acknowledgment that perhaps Abigail might not be the culprit. Or was she trying to protect her mother? A family where the dad was no longer involved might leave Abigail fearing the loss of her only remaining parent.

"Then there's the blood...and the hair found in your back seat." Rebecca watched as Abigail crumpled further under the weight of implication.

"It...it wasn't me. But it could be Whitney's. Carrie demanded to use my car that night." Abigail paused, her breath hitched in fear. "She told me she needed to borrow my car, and I had to drive it over right away. I was too afraid to say no. Carrie can be real nasty if you tell her no. And she said it was an emergency. But whatever happened after, I swear, I don't know. I drove it to her house and waited there for her to come back." Fresh tears spilled out of her eyes. "God, I should've said something earlier..."

The story was plausible, filled with cracks and crevices of doubt, but plausible nonetheless. Abigail's terror seemed genuine, her ignorance of the true horrors inflicted upon her friends believable.

The girl's voice held a new edge, one of desperation. "Sheriff, I didn't do this. I'm just caught in the middle of whatever sick game Carrie's playing."

"How am I supposed to believe you when you've been lying to me this whole time?" Rebecca shook her head, feigning sorrow she didn't fully feel. She knew she should, if Abigail was telling her the truth. But she wasn't quite there yet.

"Sheriff, I've got it." Abigail sat up straight, staring at her. "I can prove I'm telling the truth."

"Prove it?" Rebecca barely kept the skepticism from her voice. She'd been led on wild goose chases by this kid before. "How?"

"The murder weapon from when she killed Whitney. I don't know what it is, but I do know *where* it is." Abigail leaned forward. "She told me. Boasted about it. Maybe it's even the same one that she used to kill Sara? I don't know."

She contemplated the weight of Abigail's words—the desperation, the detail. Could this be another diversion? "Let's say I believe you. We find this supposed weapon, and what? You're suddenly innocent?"

"No. I did lie to you. I did cover for Carrie. And I loaned her my mom's car. I even tried to clean it to hide anything that might've been left. I'm pretty sure that's illegal." Abigail whimpered, shaking her head, strands of hair sticking to her damp cheeks. "But I didn't kill anyone, and I'm not making this up. Please, you have to believe me."

Rebecca wasn't sure who to believe anymore. Once upon a time, she'd thought she was good at knowing when people lied to her. But then she'd learned the truth about Ryker, that he'd been lying to her for months. Sure, there'd been moments where things felt off, but she'd disregarded those instincts.

Now she wasn't sure about anything. Except hard evidence backed by science. "If you're playing me, Abigail, it will only get worse for you. I'm trying to help you before this spirals out of control. Understand?"

Abigail bobbed her head. "I understand. I can also explain to you why Carrie keeps saying the witch did it."

That was something Rebecca would very much like to know.

Abigail must've read it on her face, because she elaborated. "She gave the murder weapon to the witch."

32

The shadows that wreathed the Old Witch's Cottage seemed uncanny in the early afternoon sunlight, lending the desolate place an even more sinister air. Rebecca had alerted Elliot to her plan and asked him to notify Jake. She had no problem being there alone with a cuffed suspect, but she wasn't an idiot. Procedures existed for a reason.

Why do so many of my cases bring me here?

Rebecca had never believed in the old legend of the witch or the curse said to infuse every shadow on this property. And yet, all the weird and creepy cases with their twisted turns seemed to lead to this doorstep.

The SUV rolled to a stop, the small stones of the Old Witch's Cottage parking lot popping beneath its weight. Rebecca let the engine idle and sat for a moment, staring at the rearview mirror where Abigail's reflection was nothing but a quivering mass of fear—or was that deception? Now that her passenger had put Carrie in her sights, Rebecca needed to consider if the pieces fit together.

Carrie, with her unassuming demeanor and grief-stricken eyes, had never pinged Rebecca's radar for suspicion. Of course, neither had Ryker, and look how that turned out. Clearly, she needed to recalibrate her settings. She replayed every interaction with Carrie in her mind, searching for a crack in the facade.

With a deep breath, she stepped out into the bracing afternoon air. If Carrie was the killer, she'd find out soon enough whether what Abigail was saying was true. Stepping outside the driver's door, Rebecca fixed her passenger with a steely gaze. "Where is it?"

"I'll take you to it."

"Not a chance. You're going to stay in the back seat until I can investigate the scene. Now, you have one shot at this, Abigail. One. Tell me where it is."

Abigail swiped at her tear-stained cheeks by lifting one shoulder. Her eyes, red-rimmed and swollen, met Rebecca's with a desperate kind of clarity.

"It's behind the cottage. She said there's three trees in a row. It's hidden in the stuff growing around the trunks of the trees."

Rebecca closed the driver's side door and went around to the other side of the Explorer to grab the camera. She collected the evidence kit from the cargo area before heading for the cottage.

The path to the backside of the witch's cottage was a narrow strip of sandy soil, meandering between gnarled trees and tangled undergrowth. Rebecca's boots crushed brittle leaves beneath them, her ears tuned to the sounds around in case this was a setup by Abigail. No one would be able to sneak up on her, at least.

With no other trees matching the description Abigail provided, Rebecca donned latex gloves and meticulously searched through the underbrush and drifts of leaves too sodden to blow away. There, amid the darkened leaves and the loam, glinted something sinister—a knife, its blade smeared with dried blood, a macabre testament hidden away.

Given the importance of this find, Rebecca called in a forensic team. She was not going to let any lawyer claim the evidence was improperly handled. Then she started taking pictures.

The forensic team had been to this crime scene once already, when they'd processed the scene for the dark rings of blood on the cottage's dirt floor. And they'd hauled away the bike Jake had found. The blood had been a match to Whitney Turner, and the bike had her fingerprints and some skin cells in the handlebar grips. But no other DNA was found on it.

Considering how far the three trees were from the actual cottage, Rebecca assumed the techs had stopped their search of the area sooner. She couldn't blame them. They had their hands full at the cemetery and couldn't be expected to comb the entire woods.

When a new team of techs arrived, they made short work of logging and bagging the bloody knife. Then they turned their attention to searching through the rest of the area between where the knife was hidden and the cottage. Nothing would escape their attention this time.

Rebecca scrutinized the crimson-stained blade within the clear evidence bag. Its straight edge and width matched the wounds she'd seen on Whitney's body in the morgue. And it could've created the wounds she'd seen that morning on Sara's body.

There were layers of dried blood rimming the metal. And the plants she'd found it in would have protected it from any salt spray and appeared to have preserved the evidence.

The weight of the knife in her hand was a grim reminder that evidence was the only thing Rebecca could trust. Still, she'd like to hear what else Abigail had to say.

She returned to where she'd left the girl sitting in the cruiser.

"You claimed Carrie told you about the knife's hiding place. Why didn't you tell anyone?" Rebecca let her disbelief show in her face and tone. This girl was hiding information. She didn't have any proof of it, though, and that bothered her.

"I didn't have the guts to challenge her. I didn't even call for help when she attacked me earlier. Probably the only reason I'm still alive is because you showed up to check out my mom's car." Abigail's laugh was hollow, devoid of humor. "I'm alone most times. My parents…Dad left us so long ago, I don't even remember his face. Mom's always out with her friends or with the next love of her life. All so she can pretend nothing is wrong."

"That must be rough," Rebecca said, trying to relate to the girl, to show sympathy. She needed to build rapport with her.

Abigail shuddered. "That's why I joined Carrie's group. I thought I finally wouldn't be alone anymore. It's just me, and Carrie knows that. Even if I'd told my mom, if she was around long enough to talk to, she wouldn't have believed me." She shook her head vehemently, her hair falling into her eyes. "But I don't want to play Carrie's game anymore. Not if it's already killed two girls who could've been my friends. I joined to make friends, not to watch people die."

Rebecca watched the young woman as she spun a story of vulnerability entangled in a web of deceit and violence. This tear-stained girl could truly be a pawn in some sinister game…or she could be lying through her teeth. Rebecca knew all too well the masks people wore, the facades they presented.

As she stood in the shadow of the lighthouse in front of the old cottage steeped in lore, a chill ran down Rebecca's spine. She pushed aside the memories of Kevin Garland's Lovecraftian book of human skin and Mason Alton's obsession with the lighthouse.

A passing cloud momentarily dimmed the limited daylight, and Rebecca's thoughts turned back to the present, sifting through every encounter, every piece of evidence.

Closing the cruiser door, Rebecca stepped away to radio Jake with updates.

"If forensics missed the knife the first time they were out there, how were you able to find it?" Jake's mic cued again immediately as he answered his own question. "You got Abigail to confess."

She nodded, even though he couldn't see her affirmation through the radio. "I've got Abigail in custody. She swears she wasn't the one who killed Whitney or Sara. In fact, she seemed surprised to hear that Sara had been killed."

"Do you believe her?" Jake's voice changed, and she realized he'd switched to his onboard radio.

"Let's just say I don't disbelieve her. Everything she's saying could be true." With deliberate movements, Rebecca twisted the knife around, trying to catch the light just right. She thought she could make out a curve of blood on the handle as well as the blade. A curve about the size and shape of someone's fingertip. "I'll let forensics tell me if it was Abigail who used the knife, or Carrie, as Abigail claims."

"And we'll let forensics tell us if the spring-fresh blanket in the trunk of Samantha Miller's car matches the fibers on Whitney." There was a grim sort of anticipation in Jake's tone.

"Affirmative."

"On my way."

Just as she signed off, her phone buzzed. Rebecca answered without looking at the screen. "This is Sheriff West."

"It's Bailey. I've got a time of death window for you."

"Your timing's perfect, per usual."

Bailey gave a light laugh. "*Timing.* I see what you did there. Anyway, the window looks like ten p.m. to midnight, maybe a little after since it's colder this time of year. But she was wrapped, so could be a little earlier too."

Rebecca couldn't resist giving her a little hard time. "A little before, but maybe a little after. Very precise."

"I'm here to serve."

They said goodbye and disconnected.

As she waited in the stillness for Jake's arrival, Rebecca's mind churned with the pieces of the case. Earlier, the puzzle seemed to be taking shape. But now, all the pieces had scattered, forcing her to start fresh.

The image of Carrie during their previous interview flickered in her memory—a mask of complete hysteria, perhaps too well-fitted. Why hadn't she pointed the finger at Abigail, if the girl was the real culprit?

The skepticism that chewed at her was a familiar companion, one that had served her well in the past. But this time, it gnawed deeper, burrowing into the marrow of her intuition.

Trust but verify was the old adage, though trust was a currency in short supply these days. Rebecca thought maybe it was time to bypass trust and verify twice instead.

33

When the sun cleared the patchy clouds, light spilled down onto the cottage parking lot, casting a pleasant cocoon of warmth where Rebecca's SUV blocked the constant sea breeze. At just past two, the only people in the area were the techs processing the nearby trees, searching for evidence. She considered what to do with the young woman in the back seat.

As Rebecca leaned against the hot metal of her idling vehicle, she pulled out her phone with a sigh and dialed Hoyt. He hadn't answered on the radio, and she assumed he'd turned it down so the surrounding reporters wouldn't be able to overhear. The line clicked, and his voice, edged with the weariness of long hours, filled her ear.

"Boss? What's the update?"

"We found the murder weapon." Her gaze never left Abigail through the back seat window. "It was hidden in some undergrowth in the woods near the Old Witch's Cottage. It's got dried blood on the blade and what looks like a fingerprint on the handle. The techs picked it up to be tested. And it was Abigail Miller who told us where to find it."

"Damn." Hoyt's surprise was evident through the phone. "That's...unexpected. That means she's involved in this whole thing?"

"Yep, though she says she was only told about it after the fact by Carrie Dugan, who she claims is the person who killed Whitney. I'm expecting results from the techs in a couple of hours."

"Kids killing kids." Hoyt sighed heavily. "Well, listen, I've got news too. We've unearthed twenty-four bodies at the cemetery and still no IDs on any of them but Krull."

"Twenty-three unidentified bodies..." The news settled in Rebecca's stomach like lead. She glanced back at the ocean, its surface deceptively serene. "We're looking at one hell of a monster."

"Monster or monsters. We'll keep digging, but for now, it looks like we're both in the same boat. Waiting for DNA to give us the answers we need."

"Waiting is the worst part of this job." It seemed all they could do in their two twisting cases was wait—wait for evidence, wait for answers, wait for justice.

She turned back to Abigail, who glanced away, as if seeking an escape from reality. The girl's vulnerability scratched at Rebecca's resolve.

Abigail might just be a kid caught up in a nightmare, and any decision Rebecca made regarding the girl would leave its mark. In which case, she'd like to cause the least amount of damage possible until she knew the whole story.

The sound of tires squealing caught Rebecca's attention. A media van was braking hard to make the sharp turn into the lot, aiming her way.

"Dammit." The vultures had found her again. She'd

thought the historical site would've been far enough away from the cemetery that no one would spot her sitting there.

"What is it?" Hoyt sounded concerned.

"A media crew found me again. I'm going to have to get out of here before the rest of them catch on and start swarming."

Hoyt laughed. "Oh, no. That would be so terrible." His words were intentionally stilted and brimming with sarcasm. "How awful it must be to have a single media team tracking you down."

She snorted, knowing he was dealing with the rest of the rabid fleet while only one vehicle had pulled up behind her SUV. Like a hound catching the scent of fear, a reporter brandishing a microphone, followed by his camera operator, hustled toward her.

His questions flew fast, battering against her resolve. "Sheriff West, can you comment on the major excavation going on at the cemetery? Is the girl in the back seat somehow connected to that?"

Rebecca's jaw clenched as she held up her hand and measured her breath. "I need you to step back and move your vehicle now. You're interfering with an ongoing investigation."

"Come on, Sheriff. The public has a right to know!" The reporter, a man with golden-blond hair, tried shuffling closer to Rebecca as she reached for her door handle. "Is this place being investigated for something else, or is it connected to the bodies you've been pulling out of the cemetery? Why aren't you at the cemetery, Sheriff West?"

Rebecca rounded on him quickly, not liking the way he was trying to crowd her to get what he wanted. She raised her volume but lowered her pitch. "Move your van now, or I'll arrest you and your crew for interfering with a police investigation and have your vehicle towed. Do you understand me?"

The man reluctantly waved to the driver of the van, and it slid just far enough out of the way to make room for Rebecca's SUV. As soon as it did, she opened her door, ignoring the blond man, and dropped into the seat. She threw the idling cruiser in reverse and pulled out of the lot.

After updating Jake that she was on the move to avoid the media, Rebecca allowed herself a moment of introspection. The deaths of Whitney and Sara—two lives extinguished too soon—weighed heavily on her conscience. Rebecca and her team had worked hard to protect young people just like them from the depravity of the Yacht Club. Now the girls were turning against each other.

And for what? A petty power struggle among kids that wouldn't even matter in another year or two.

As she drove toward town hall, Rebecca's mind drifted to the weight of duty. Each name added to the list of the deceased was a stark reminder of the threat that still loomed over them all. And now, with the Yacht Club's collapse, it seemed the island's own hidden darkness was finally coming to light.

It was just as she had warned Wallace when she'd first learned of the Yacht Club's existence. Letting criminals get away with their crimes only emboldened others. Now that the Yacht Club, the worst of the worst, was gone, the pinch hitters were filling the vacuum left behind.

All while they were still trying to deal with the cleanup from years of criminal activity left unchecked.

Thirty. And still counting.

The tally Hoyt had given her earlier echoed through her mind. Had all those people been murdered and buried by just one hired killer? That might mean each death was ordered by the Yacht Club. Or Stokely could've been working for more than just them. There was also the possibility he wasn't the only one burying people in the cemetery.

Those were answers they'd have to unearth as well.

"What was all that about?" Abigail's voice shook. "Did they take my picture? Are they going to tell lies about me in the news?"

"I highly doubt it. They can take pictures if you're in a public space, but right now, they aren't aware of any case you're connected to." Rebecca hoped so, for Abigail's sake. "They were just looking for answers to a different case." She raised her gaze to look in her rearview mirror.

Abigail was staring out the window while chewing on her bottom lip. The girl looked drained.

"Abigail, I can imagine how overwhelming all of this must be for you."

The girl nodded. Her foot tapped a staccato rhythm against the floorboard.

"Okay, since our station is under repair, I'm taking you to town hall to formally take your statement."

But as they rounded the bend in the road, Rebecca spied two media vans camped out in front of the building.

"Uh, change of plans. Look, some of those reporters are staking out town hall hoping for a quote from me about our other case." Rebecca pondered her options and checked Abigail in the rearview mirror. "We can't go to town hall right now, but we need to wait for the results from the knife. That means we'll need to grab an early dinner and eat it in the car. Is that agreeable to you?"

A beat passed, punctuated only by the distant cries of gulls and the soft hum of the engine as Rebecca maneuvered away from town hall before the media spied her SUV.

Abigail's gaze met Rebecca's in the rearview mirror, a glimmer of fear giving way to a hint of hope. "Dinner sounds good to me. Could I just get a burger with no pickles? Please."

Rebecca's fingers scrunched the greasy paper bag, extracting the last few crumbs of her onion rings as she watched the waves at Atticus Beach over the steering wheel. After getting food, hiding out at the beach had seemed like a good way to keep away from their media stalkers.

Plus, the beach was always a good spot for contemplation. Rebecca did not yet have the full story, and she wasn't beneath using a burger and the relaxing sound of ocean waves to pull it from her prisoner.

The sharp tang of fried food lingered in the air, and in the back seat, Abigail nibbled on her burger, the 'no pickles' request honored to a T. Rebecca had taken the time to switch Abigail's handcuffs to the front so she could eat. Only the sound of wrappers crinkling and the soft tinkle of the chain accompanied the sound of chewing.

"Boss, you there?" Jake's voice crackled through her radio, breaking the stillness within the cruiser.

"Go ahead." Rebecca brushed salt from her fingers onto her khaki trousers. She turned in her seat so she could see Abigail, wanting to gauge the girl's reaction to whatever news Jake had for them.

"Got news on the murder weapon. The kitchen knife Abigail led you to is a match for Whitney's wounds. And we've got blood, her type, on the blade."

The words hit Rebecca with the weight of an anvil.

"DNA results?"

"Tomorrow. But here's the kicker…we pulled prints off the handle. They're Carrie Dugan's."

In the back seat, Abigail gasped. This was the proof that

her friend was, in fact, a murderer, and the things she'd been told were, in fact, true. It had to be both reassuring and terrifying for the girl.

"They're sure they belong to Carrie?" Even though Jake's news matched Abigail's story, Rebecca still found herself surprised by the facts. "How did you make the match so fast?"

"Shoplifting incident from two years back. Carrie was caught red-handed and booked but was only given parole, which she's already served." Jake's voice was steady but carried an undercurrent of disappointment. "Uh, Boss, there's one more thing. Can you go radio silent?"

Intrigued by his request to prevent Abigail from eavesdropping, Rebecca didn't hesitate to do so. She put in her earpiece. Meanwhile, she noted Abigail leaning forward, trying to hear the conversation not intended for her ears.

"Okay. Go ahead, Coffey."

"Samantha Miller's hired an attorney. He's notified us that we need to either press charges against Abigail or release her immediately."

"Then he's a bad lawyer. The Commonwealth has seventy-two hours to bring charges. Well...seventy-one hours, at this point. Anything else?"

"No, ma'am."

Rebecca focused on the hum of her cruiser's engine for a brief moment. "I'm on my way to the Dugans. Meet me there." She glanced up once again to watch Abigail. "Did you know anything about her criminal past?"

Abigail shook her head. "I didn't. If I'd known..." She chewed her lip again. "I'm not sure I would've been her friend. Or if I had, I would've been more cautious. Did I put my friends in danger by convincing them to join a group run by a criminal?"

Rebecca didn't answer. She wasn't sure she had a good

response to that question. Because even though she'd told herself she would believe whatever the evidence said, she still felt conflicted when it came to Abigail. The girl had been nothing but cooperative since she'd been taken into custody, but there was still something that left Rebecca uneasy.

She wasn't sure if it was about Abigail herself or the case in general.

Pulling up to the Dugan's house, Rebecca found Jake standing in the driveway. She parked on the shoulder of the street. "I'll be back in a few minutes." Abigail wasn't going anywhere, since she couldn't open the door from the inside.

Jake's gaze was fixed on a metallic-green Subaru Outback at his side. Rebecca stepped out onto the driveway.

"This car insurance shows Carrie as the primary driver. Take a look at the front passenger seat." Clearly, Jake had peeked through the window before Rebecca had arrived. "Does that look like blood to you?"

She leaned in, her breath fogging the glass briefly before revealing what had caught Jake's eye. The passenger seat was streaked with pale marks, like someone had scrubbed it with a chemical that had bleached the fabric.

Which didn't do much to hide the splotches of brownish red that covered the edge of the seat. The old blood on the floorboard seemed to have been completely left out of the attempt to hide evidence.

She'd wanted evidence. Now it was staring her right in the face. "A botched cleanup job?"

"That's what it looks like to me as well." Jake straightened. His attention shifted to her SUV and the girl in the back, currently doing her best to look out through the barred windows at what they were doing. "Seems we were wrong about Abigail."

"Or whoever did the cleanup screwed it up on purpose because they wanted us to find it." Rebecca's mind raced through different scenarios, each more unsettling than the last. "Let's get this over with."

She turned for the front door, the inside lights just starting to show through the windows as the sun approached the horizon. Once there, she rapped hard.

The door swung open, revealing a pale and frazzled Andrea Dugan. Her eyes, rimmed with red, indicated her distress as she sized up the officers on her porch. "Yes? Did you need to follow up with Carrie to get her side of the story about what happened earlier?"

"Mrs. Dugan, whose car is that?" Rebecca pointed to the Subaru they'd just been inspecting.

Andrea peered out the door. "Technically speaking, I suppose it's my husband's. But only Carrie drives it. We only have one set of keys. Why? Is something wrong with it?"

One set of keys? That made it easy to narrow down. "I need to speak with Carrie."

"Of course. But Carrie said she didn't want to press charges against Abigail. If that changes things at all." Andrea turned and called for her daughter. "I told her she's not allowed to hang out with that girl anymore. I know emotions are high right now, and so are tempers. But that doesn't excuse anyone who attacks their friends like that."

Andrea continued to dither on until Carrie shuffled into view. The blond girl's shoulders were slumped. Given her athletic build, she was probably strong enough to drag a dead body out of her friend's back seat and into the cemetery. Or out of her own front seat and into the marsh.

Carrie slowly raised her head, first looking at her mother, who was frowning at her, before shifting to look at Rebecca standing in the doorway.

Rebecca noted the young woman's expression, which appeared to be a mixture of remorse and fear. "Carrie, would you care to explain why there's blood all over the front seat and floorboard of your car? You didn't fight Abigail today because of borrowed clothing, did you?"

"Blood? What?" Andrea's head whipped back and forth. "Honey, what's she talking about?"

Carrie bit her lip and didn't answer.

Rebecca heard Jake shift his feet behind her. Carrie hadn't moved, but something about the way she was holding herself made Rebecca think she was about to run for it. Jake must've noticed it, too, and was getting ready. "Does the dried blood in your car belong to Sara Porter?"

Andrea gasped at the question, but her daughter didn't even flinch. A single tear rolled down Carrie's cheek, carving a path through her despair as she nodded, a silent admission that spoke volumes.

"Did you kill Whitney?" Rebecca's question sliced through the tension.

Another nod from Carrie as more tears trickled down her cheeks. "Yes. I'm sorry, Mom. I didn't mean—"

"Carrie Dugan, you're under arrest for the murders of Whitney Turner and Sara Porter." Rebecca grabbed Carrie's arm and pulled her out the door. As she read Carrie her rights, she secured the cuffs around her wrists behind her back.

Rebecca glanced at Andrea as she finished Mirandizing Carrie. The woman was still staring at them, open-mouthed and unmoving.

"God, no!" Andrea's emotions finally let loose, and her cry shattered the moment. "Carrie wouldn't, not my baby, not—"

"Ma'am," Rebecca interjected, her tone firm yet not unkind, "we have her confession, and there's blood all over the inside of her car. Once we get DNA results from the lab, we can verify your daughter's confession. We also have her fingerprint on a murder weapon. You can come to where we'll be holding her if you wish, since she's a minor, but she is being arrested."

Rebecca felt the weight of every word. *Kids killing kids*, like Hoyt had said. Something about their youth made it so much worse than when adults were involved. Four young lives had been destroyed, and for what?

It was all just so senseless.

"Deputy Coffey," Rebecca turned her head slightly, not taking her eyes off Carrie, who was now a portrait of resignation, "take Abigail home, please."

"Sure thing, Sheriff." Jake spun on his heels toward Rebecca's SUV to release the young woman who'd made Carrie's arrest possible.

As Rebecca led Carrie away, she kept her head down, not even looking at Abigail as Jake walked past them, escorting her to the front of his cruiser. Abigail's head, conversely, was held high, her face a perfectly blank canvas, as if she hadn't a care in the world.

Rebecca tried to reconcile her unfeeling expression with the girl's earlier statements. She was supposedly terrified of Carrie and had only recently gained enough courage to speak out. If she was so unbothered now, why hadn't she spoken up when Rebecca and Jake had appeared at her house after Carrie attacked her?

She helped Carrie duck her head as she placed the girl in the back of her SUV. Slamming the door, she watched Jake's cruiser drive away.

Something's not right here. But I still don't know what it is.

34

Rebecca headed straight for town hall. In the rearview mirror, Andrea Dugan's sedan was a persistent shadow, keeping pace with the SUV. The back seat was silent except for the occasional shuffle of fabric against the hard plastic barriers. The sound seemed overly loud in the tense quiet as Rebecca tried to figure out what still had the girl on edge.

"You don't know what she's like. You don't know what she's capable of." Carrie's voice broke the silence, her words spilling out like marbles on glass, discordant and oddly paced.

"Who?" Rebecca heard the telltale sound of Carrie shifting in the back seat.

Chancing a quick glance over her shoulder, Rebecca noted Carrie tucking her face farther away, her body folding inward, as if to shield herself from the weight of the truth. Rebecca's intuition prickled again. Something wasn't right.

"Who?" Rebecca was firmer this time. The SUV took a corner smoothly, the centrifugal force pressing them gently against their seats. "Abigail?" Rebecca ventured the name, threading it into the air between them. She checked Carrie's reaction, once more stealing a quick look over her shoulder.

A nod, almost imperceptible, but there. Rebecca exhaled slowly, her mind racing through the implications. "You need to talk to me, Carrie. What are you trying to say? I'm never going to get to the bottom of this if no one's willing to speak up for themselves."

But Carrie clammed up, her silence a fortress that refused to yield any further secrets.

Town hall loomed ahead, an aging structure of red brick and white stone trim that stood as testament to the island's history. Rebecca eased the cruiser into the asphalt parking lot. She parked, and before she could kill the engine, Andrea's car skidded to a halt beside them. The woman was out of her vehicle in a flash, her agitation evident as she shifted her weight from foot to foot.

With a deep breath, Rebecca stepped out and walked around to open the back door. She was worried she'd have to fight her way past Andrea, and that would be a bad scene for everyone.

Carrie didn't resist at all as Rebecca took her arm and guided her out of the back. Handcuffed and subdued, Carrie glanced at her mother before focusing on the ground once again. If there had been any fight left in Carrie, it had fled, perhaps at the sight of her mother's agitation.

"Come on." Rebecca escorted Carrie by the elbow. They entered through a side entrance, Andrea trailing close behind, her sneakers slapping a staccato rhythm on the linoleum.

The back hallways were a labyrinth of identical doors and echoes. This area of the building was seldom used except for storage or by those who sought privacy. Rebecca led them to one of the rooms she'd had reserved while the sheriff's station underwent repairs. It smelled of dust and faint mold, which was the main reason they'd been meeting at Trent's house instead.

Rebecca unlocked one of the doors, revealing a sparsely furnished space that held a table, two chairs, and a security camera perched in the corner. Andrea swept past her into the room, her gaze sweeping over the interrogation setup with thinly veiled distress.

"Right in here." Rebecca gestured for Carrie to take a seat. Once Jake arrived, she'd remove the girl's handcuffs, but not before. Moving to the camera to start it, she watched the young woman closely. Rebecca noticed how her gaze lingered on the camera before settling on the table's smooth surface.

With that handled, Rebecca turned to Andrea, the woman's face contorted in a mask of maternal indignation.

"My daughter could not possibly be involved in any murder." Andrea had been so quiet to this point that Rebecca had started to think she wouldn't have to fight or argue with the woman.

Rebecca straightened her shoulders and sucked in a long breath. "Mrs. Dugan, Carrie's fingerprints were found on a murder weapon, a knife, with the victim's blood still on the blade. You heard her confess."

"Which victim? I heard from my friend on the way over that there was another body found in the marsh this morning. Are you trying to say my daughter killed her?" Andrea's voice was sharp, demanding clarity. With her shock now over, she was an angry mama bear, willing to do whatever it took to protect her cub. And she was trying to use gossip to bolster her defense.

Technically, Rebecca was accusing Carrie of killing both victims, as she'd stated when she arrested Carrie. But she decided to go along with Andrea to see how she would respond. So far, they didn't have any proof Carrie had killed Sara.

Which was likely why Andrea, in her shock, was focused on that murder, not realizing clearing her daughter of Sara Porter's murder wouldn't absolve her of Whitney Turner's.

"The one from last night."

Rebecca's gaze never left the mother's face as she searched for any flicker of truth or lie. There was an awful lot of finger-pointing happening, and she didn't want to have to go through this again later.

"That's impossible!" The words burst from Andrea like steam from a pressure valve. "I was with her all night. She's been so stressed lately, and after what happened to her friend…she was consumed with grief."

At the table in the center of the room, Carrie observed the contours of their clinical surroundings. The black dome of the security camera seemed to hold her attention, or maybe she was watching her reflection in it. It was as if she didn't hear or didn't care about her mother defending her.

"Explain." Rebecca offered her a reassuring smile, hoping that would be enough to urge the woman on.

Andrea's gaze wavered before reconnecting with Rebecca's. "Last night, Carrie came out of her room around eleven, saying she couldn't sleep. I'd just finished prepping today's meal, which is how I knew what time it was. We snuggled up on the sofa together to watch some holiday movies. I stayed right beside her until she fell asleep around one this morning."

"And…" Rebecca prompted. So far, the estimated time of death for Sara was mostly a guess but the window would be tight for Carrie to have committed the crime, even it was a "little before" ten, transported Sara's body to the secondary location, carved the symbols into her, and gotten home and cleaned up before joining her mother.

With every word, Andrea seemed more confident. "I didn't leave her side all night. And I didn't fall asleep until early this morning because she kept whimpering in her sleep, and I had to soothe her. Does that sound like the reaction of a heartless serial killer? No, it does not. My daughter couldn't have done this."

Murderers didn't come wrapped in a one-size-fits-all bow. Rebecca knew that all too well.

A memory flashed through her of cuddling on her couch with Ryker as they settled in for a night of binging television shows. Her head resting on his chest, listening to his even breathing and the beat of his heart. The warmth of his arm draped protectively over her.

Dammit. Now is not the time.

Andrea breathed in deep through her nose. "After the sun came up and I needed to start on the pies, I helped her to bed. She didn't leave the house. I'm positive of it."

Rebecca processed this information, connecting the different pieces of data she'd gathered. She knew better than to take alibis at face value, but she also recognized genuine distress when she saw it. Andrea's account could be the truth…or just another set of lies meant to protect her daughter.

In the silence that followed, Rebecca's mind raced. Abigail had been insistent that Carrie used her car that fateful night. But what if Abigail was the one behind the wheel? What if—

The door opened with a whisper, and Jake entered. His brows knit together in silent inquiry as he carefully observed the room's occupants.

"Deputy Coffey, perfect timing. Come here." Rebecca gestured to the silent prisoner. "Please stay with Ms. Dugan.

If you want, you can uncuff her." She pointed to the door. "Mrs. Dugan, I need to speak with you outside."

With a last lingering look at Carrie, who now appeared small and lost within the stark confines of the interrogation room, Andrea turned to follow Rebecca. Her maternal concern was palpable, a living thing that filled the space and trailed after them as they exited.

Rebecca secured the door behind them with a soft click as she twisted the key in the lock. "Can anyone else corroborate your story?" She held her breath, anticipating the answer.

"Who would watch us in our own home?" Andrea's reply came mixed with frustration and a hint of scorn.

"Maybe your husband?"

The woman shook her head. "He was asleep before any of this happened."

Rebecca's gaze sharpened as she leaned forward. "Do you have any proof of this? Perhaps video or phone calls? And I need to remind you that lying to the police is a crime, even if you're doing so to protect your child."

"Proof?" Andrea's voice rose with incredulity. "How on earth would I be able to prove when and where my child and I fell asleep?"

The evidence Rebecca had so far was pointing to Carrie. But her gut was telling her there was more to this than she'd uncovered so far. There was still the blood in Abigail's car, and the blanket fibers, though the test results on that weren't back yet.

She needed more physical evidence.

A memory that had been niggling in the recesses of her mind finally broke free. "A doorbell camera." She straightened. "You have one, don't you?"

A flicker of understanding sparked in Andrea's eyes, brightening into a momentary relief. "Yes, we do! And it would record us if we'd left the house!"

From that particular door, at least.

"Your front porch," Rebecca ventured, her mind painting the scene in crisp detail, "has no bushes there, nothing to obscure the view to where Carrie's car was parked, correct?"

"That's right."

"Can you show me the footage from last night?" Rebecca watched as hope seemed to inflate Andrea's posture. She didn't bother explaining that it would be insufficient to prove Carrie hadn't left the house. After all, the girl could've gone out the back door or through her bedroom window like Whitney had done.

But the camera would show the driveway. And something about the terrible attempt to clean the car was still bothering Rebecca. If Carrie was their suspect, why didn't she do a better job of cleaning her car? She could've put it in the garage, where it wouldn't be seen by anyone walking past it.

"Of course, but…" Andrea's sudden eagerness faltered, her shoulders slumping. "I don't have the app on my phone. It's all on the home computer."

"Coffey." The door quickly opened in response. "Can you keep an eye on Carrie while I go back to the Dugans' house to retrieve their doorbell camera footage?"

"Yeah, Boss." Jake tilted his head to where their prisoner was seated. "You want her to just sit in there for now?"

"For now, yes. The video camera in the interrogation room is already going, so anything she says will be recorded." Rebecca nodded to Mrs. Dugan and waved a hand in the direction of the parking lot. "Let's go see if your camera caught anything useful."

Andrea didn't need any more pushing and spun around to race out the way they'd entered.

Silently, Rebecca trailed behind. Regardless of what the footage showed, Rebecca knew that even if Andrea provided Carrie with an alibi for last night, she hadn't yet offered one for the night Whitney was killed. And that was the murder that Rebecca had physical evidence for. No matter what Andrea showed her, Carrie was still a killer and would be imprisoned.

However, if Carrie did have an alibi during Sara Porter's murder, that meant there was still another suspect out there. Rebecca shivered, afraid she'd let her go free earlier that day.

35

Rebecca stopped her SUV in front of the Dugan house, once again parking on the shoulder.

Andrea had rushed from town hall once she'd been given the tiniest hope of proving her daughter's innocence. She'd damn near sprinted out of the building, jumped into her car, and raced home.

On the way over, Rebecca had received the forensic report.

The blood Jake found in Carrie's car matched Sara's blood type.

Rebecca noted the front door of the Dugans' house standing wide open, a telltale sign of distress she couldn't ignore. As she got out of the cruiser and stepped onto the porch, her heart raced with anticipation. "Mrs. Dugan?" Her voice echoed through the empty foyer. "Can I come in?"

"Yes!" Louis Dugan shouted, his face flushed as he emerged from the back hallway. Carrie's father was visibly agitated. "Andrea says you can come in. She's bringing the laptop. It's Thanksgiving. What the heck is going on?"

As if on cue, Andrea raced into the front room, her eyes

wide with hope and determination. She held a silver laptop tightly in her arms, as if it were a lifeline.

Rebecca's gaze shifted between the two parents, weighing the consequences of her next words. "Your daughter, Carrie, has been arrested for murder."

The color drained from Louis's face, but Andrea seemed to steel herself, tapping anxiously at the laptop.

"I can prove she didn't do it." Andrea's fingers flew over the keyboard. With an excited cry, she pulled up security footage from the previous night. "Look, this is our front yard and driveway. Here's when Louis came home. None of us left the house after that."

She gestured for Rebecca to come closer as she started the video again. The first couple of times the clip started, there was nothing but darkness and the occasional leaf fluttering past the camera, activating the motion sensor.

"Sometimes, it catches a leaf falling and records that." Louis explained the sensitivity of the camera as Rebecca observed with a critical eye.

"Wait, here!" Andrea exclaimed as another video clip started. This time, it clearly showed Abigail Miller walking around the side of the house to the driveway. The girl nonchalantly approached Carrie's car, got in, and drove away, leaving the headlights off.

Rebecca paused the image with the brake lights frozen on the screen. Anger swirled inside her as she stared at the still.

Both girls had thrown each other under the bus, indicating they shared their guilt. But her assessment about Abigail had been right. She'd forced herself to let her go due to lack of evidence. Everything had pointed to Carrie, except Rebecca's intuition.

Which she'd doubted because of her experience with Ryker. Before, she would have dug deeper until she found what needled her suspicions. Not given up so soon. Now it turned out she should've trusted her instincts. She still could. That was something anyway.

To be fair, though her instincts had pointed to Abigail from early on, Rebecca had spent the afternoon dining with a killer and then had Jake drive her home like a damn chauffeur. Just because she lacked evidence hadn't meant she needed to swing so far in the other direction in the treatment of who she suspected.

She should've been thrilled they had this evidence against Abigail. But the girl was no longer in custody and could be anywhere.

Andrea was still trying to process what she'd witnessed. "Abigail stole Carrie's car?" she choked out. "That's why you found blood in it. It was her and not my daughter."

Rebecca shook her head. "I don't think she stole the car." She rewound the video, pausing it at the moment Abigail approached Carrie's car and opened the door with ease. "See? It was unlocked. Unless Abigail is a hot-wiring expert, Carrie must've left the keys for her before telling you she couldn't sleep."

"We-we've told her to stop leaving the keys in the car, Louis stammered, his face pale. "Of course, we thought it would get stolen, not be used in a murder."

That story wasn't enough to acquit Carrie of aiding in Sara's murder, but a jury could quibble over that detail.

"One way or the other, I need to ask her some more questions about what we just saw." Rebecca's brow furrowed in thought. It was possible Abigail pressured Carrie into loaning her the car. And she needed to talk to Abigail to get her side of the story.

"It still proves it wasn't Carrie who killed that girl last night. Knowing that, you'll let Carrie go, right? Because the murders are linked, and she didn't leave the house when it was happening." Louis's inquiry came out pitiful, each word more desperate than the last.

"Sorry, but no. Carrie might not have killed Sara last night, but her prints are still on the weapon that killed Whitney." She shook her head. "We can't rule anything out yet."

Rebecca watched in real time as Andrea's delusions crumbled. The woman collapsed over her computer keyboard with a sob. She must have finally realized her daughter was a murderer and going to jail. Possibly for quite a long time.

Louis held onto his wife. "We'll get her the best attorney. There has to be some mistake." He looked up at Rebecca, his face contorted with confusion and fear. "Sheriff, please, just leave."

After watching them send the email with the camera footage to her, Rebecca left the distraught couple to their grief and headed for Abigail's house. On the way, she radioed in the latest update on the case and where she was going.

Tires screeched as Rebecca parked her cruiser in front of Abigail's residence. She hurried to the front door and knocked, her knuckles rapping against the wood with urgency.

When Abigail's mother opened the door, her features darkened with anger. A football game was playing on a TV in a distant room.

Before Samantha Miller could ask whatever question she was trying to piece together, Rebecca snapped, "Where's Abigail?"

"Where is she? That's a stupid question, isn't it?" Samantha sneered, her voice rising. "You arrested her, didn't you? Shouldn't you know where she is?"

Rebecca's mind raced, analyzing the situation. She needed to find Abigail before it was too late. "No, we detained her for questioning, but then we released her. She was brought here by a deputy. When was the last time you saw her? What time did you get home?"

"I don't know. I got home an hour ago. I had to get cleaned up before our Thanksgiving dinner tonight."

Rebecca sniffed the air, noting there was nothing to indicate anything was cooking. Then she noticed Samantha's rumpled clothes. "If you came home to clean up, why are you still wearing yesterday's outfit?" It was a shot in the dark, but it found its mark.

Samantha straightened. "I've just gotten home. I wanted a moment to relax before I took a shower."

"You need to stay home. Call me if Abigail comes back or contacts you." Rebecca turned to leave as she gripped her radio. "Coffey, what was the status of Abigail Miller after you dropped her at home?"

After a brief silence, Jake's tone came through laced with concern. "Uh, status? I dropped her off and didn't stick around after I saw she'd made it inside safely. What's going on?"

Rebecca ignored the question for the moment. "Dispatch, I need you to put out a BOLO for Abigail Miller. She's missing, and we need to find her ASAP. I need all hands looking for her."

"Copy that, Sheriff." Elliot's voice crackled through the speaker. "Any leads on where she might be?"

"None yet, but every available deputy needs to search the island thoroughly. Keep me updated." With shaking fingers, Rebecca released the radio.

36

The last vestiges of twilight bled from the sky, casting Oceanview Cemetery into shadow. The finality of dusk settled heavily upon Hoyt's shoulders as he watched his team, their faces drawn with fatigue, pack up their tools. The clink and clatter of metal against metal marked the end of another long day's work. Medical examiners shuffled past him, burdened with the weight of their equipment and the somber task still at hand.

A few of them offered "happy Thanksgiving" as they passed, but their tone was bitter. No one had been happy about having to spend the holiday working. And it certainly didn't feel like anyone had anything to be thankful for.

"Bailey." Hoyt's voice was tinged with a weariness that seeped into his bones. "What's our count?"

Bailey, her face etched with the day's grim labor, peeled off her mask and approached him. "Twenty-nine," she replied, her eyes reflecting the toll of each soul accounted for. "We're nearly done exhuming the remains already discovered, but…"

"Yeah." He understood all too well. It wasn't just about

numbers. Every digit represented an untold story, a family shattered, a life cut short before its time. There was no solace in the near completion of their appalling collection. The real work was yet to come—the painstaking identification and the delicate task of giving names back to the nameless, of returning them home and then finding who killed them. This was only the beginning.

Hoyt's radio broke the silence, piercing the quietude of the cemetery with a rapid clicking as someone toggled their mic repeatedly. He stared around, noticed that Trent and Viviane were also looking confused, and realized what was happening. "Hey, Boss, you trying to get our attention?"

"Yes."

"Sorry, I had to turn it down with all these assholes following me around with their giant microphones on poles, and I forgot to turn it up again. But if you're calling to say we can knock off because it's a holiday, don't worry. We're already mostly done here."

"Sorry, Frost. No rest yet. I've got a BOLO out on Abigail Miller. Her picture should be attached to it." Rebecca's voice crackled with tension. "Wanted for killing a young woman last night. She was dropped off at her house after questioning this afternoon and hasn't been seen since. Now I've got evidence linking her to at least one murder, and I suspect she was involved in the first one as well."

"Understood." Hoyt pinched the bridge of his nose, feeling an oncoming headache. "I'll grab the others and start a grid search of the island."

Dammit. He thought about how much radio chatter he'd missed while he'd been so focused on playing security guard, even as Rebecca and Jake worked a double homicide.

He wouldn't ever absolve himself of the guilt he carried over the Yacht Club's unchecked reign of terror if he kept ignoring what was right in front of him. His blind eye had nearly brought down the island and all the good people who inhabited it. The blame for that rested on him and Alden Wallace. But he wasn't going to blame a dead man.

Waving his arm, he signaled to Trent and Viviane, telling them to come in. None of them had their radios on loud enough to be heard, having followed his lead in turning theirs down.

Putting his back to the gathering darkness of the graveyard, he dialed Angie, bracing for the disappointment he'd hear in her voice. He spoke before she could, just so he wouldn't have to hear it for a moment more than necessary.

"Angie, love, I'm sorry. It's going to be a late night. I'm not getting home in time for Thanksgiving dinner." Knowing their sons hadn't made the trip home for Thanksgiving made breaking the news even harder. He was leaving her alone...again.

Her response came through calm and soothing, a balm to his frayed nerves. "I understand, dear. This will give me a chance to call my mom. You know she loves to talk. Do what you need to do. I'll keep dinner warm."

"Thanks, babe." His heart clenched with gratitude. The unwavering support she offered was the lifeline that kept him afloat amid the chaos. "I'll wrap this up and be home as soon as I can. Say hello to your mom for me. I love you."

Angie chuckled. "Of course you do. I have your dinner. And you won't get it 'til you come home and give me a kiss."

Hoyt smiled, his night suddenly not seeming so terrible. Then he remembered the young lives lost and felt guilty for smiling in the face of such tragedy.

37

The hushed corridors of town hall swallowed Rebecca's footsteps as she made her way back to the makeshift interrogation room. Naturally, the place was a ghost town on Thanksgiving. Most of the residents of the island were likely dozing in front of their televisions after overeating by now. But not Rebecca and not her dedicated deputies. At least the medical examiners and everyone out at the cemetery could salvage part of their holiday.

Carrie hadn't said much earlier, but Rebecca was determined to make her talk now. She rapped twice to give Jake a bit of warning before opening the door.

Jake was rising from his seat when she walked in, and she waved for him to stay there. The camera light showed red, and Jake held up the notepad he'd been reading over.

It was Carrie's confession, detailing everything that happened the night Whitney had been killed. It included the symbols, when and where they were carved, how she'd tried to hide the body in the cemetery, and how she'd returned to the cottage to leave the knife hidden there.

The only part not spelled out was why she had done such a vile thing.

Balling her fists up, Rebecca leaned on the table, her knuckles inches away from Carrie's arms. She figured the best way to start would be to surprise the girl. "Carrie, I know you didn't kill Sara."

Carrie's lips parted in shock. "What?" The word tumbled out, fragile as glass.

"Abigail did it. We have proof." Rebecca locked her gaze onto Carrie's. "You don't have to cover for her anymore."

"It doesn't matter." Carrie's voice was a whisper lost in a storm. "I killed Whitney."

Rebecca leaned forward, her instincts honing in. She was already certain of that but wanted to hear what Carrie could reveal. "Tell me everything."

The fluorescent glow of the overhead lights in the temporary interrogation room seemed to cast more shadows than illumination. Those shadows carved deep lines of remorse on Carrie's face as she struggled with the weight of her confession. And then, like a dam bursting its confines, Carrie crumbled as tears poured out of her already red eyes.

Rebecca straightened, unmoved, but didn't back away. She'd seen this happen before and wasn't going to do anything to stop the girl from pouring her heart out now.

"Abigail is evil. Like really, seriously evil." Carrie's voice was barely above a whisper, tainted with dread. "She's always been a bit bossy and controlling, but ever since we started the coven, she's been pulling our strings. And we're supposed to just go along with whatever she says like we don't have brains of our own."

Rebecca tilted her head, probing for clarity. "The coven? What exactly is that?" Based on the name, she could already guess how the Old Witch's Cottage played into the whole thing.

Carrie's fingers twisted together, knuckles whitening. "It's…it was supposed to be fun. Just a bunch of us getting together, talking about old legends, the witch trials. And looking into spells we could use…to make better grades, get good luck for a day. A way to feel powerful, you know?"

Rebecca nodded. "I understand."

She glanced up. "But Whitney…she took it seriously. Believed in it. The rest of us, not so much. We wanted to make a statement. Like…like 'fuck the patriarchy.'"

"And Abigail?" Rebecca prompted.

"She didn't really believe in it, either, but she still took it way too seriously. She'd insist on wearing certain colors on certain days. Or meeting based on the moon's cycle or something. It was little things at first, so we just went along with them. But Abigail just turned into a real control freak." Carrie breathed out the word as if it were toxic. "That's all she ever craved. And she got it. She controlled every one of us."

Rebecca could see where this was leading. She waited Carrie out, letting the teenager fill the silence.

"Whitney wanted to do a new spell, but when she showed it to us, the instructions said it had to be performed by the head witch of the coven. That's when Abigail declared that she was the head witch."

Rebecca recoiled internally at the pettiness of the motive that had led to such irreversible consequences.

A shudder passed through Carrie's frame. "Whitney said we should vote. Said that Abigail didn't even do spells or anything. That if we were a coven, we needed someone who knew witchcraft better than her." Her voice broke, filled with pain. "That made Abigail furious."

Everything Abigail had done was now starting to make sense. Even the way the girl had tried to play host when they'd first gone to question her was just another way for Abigail to control her surroundings and interactions.

Carrie's haunted gaze met Rebecca's. "I don't even understand why I did it. When she told me to meet her that night to talk to Whitney, I didn't even question it. And when she handed me the knife and told me I had to remove Whitney from the group...I just did it. I killed her."

And there it was. An official confession.

Carrie dropped her face into her fists, clutching her hair. "And then she acted like it was no big deal! She told us to cry! To act like we were torn up about it. Am I crying now because I'm sad? Or am I crying because she told me to?" Strands of hair came out as she pulled her hands away from her face. "I just don't know anymore! But I can't stop remembering how it felt to carry Whitney into the cemetery and try to dig up that grave to hide her. And then we saw that skull sticking up."

"What did you do then?"

"Abigail said we couldn't bury her, there wasn't enough time. So..." Carrie paused and hiccupped. "She told me to carve symbols into Whitney's skin to make it look like the old witch did it. No one outside of the coven even knows about us, so she swore no one would suspect us."

Two lives lost over a power struggle in what's essentially an after-school club.

Rebecca paused, her lip curling. She glanced at Jake, who was watching the confession with an equal measure of disgust. "Do you have any idea where Abigail might be now?"

Carrie shook her head, her hair wild, sticking to her forehead despite the chilly room. "I don't know. I really don't. She doesn't tell me what she's doing, only what I'm supposed to be doing."

As silence settled between them, Rebecca's thoughts churned. If Abigail was banking on no one outside the coven connecting them, there was still one person who knew about Abigail and Whitney's relationship.

Marie Allman.

An icy realization crept down Rebecca's spine. There wasn't a moment to lose. She had to find Marie before Abigail's twisted need for control claimed another victim.

"Is Marie part of the coven?" Jake's question followed Rebecca's line of thinking.

"Yes. But she doesn't know anything about this except that Whitney is dead because she betrayed us. And that she's supposed to cry and say she didn't know Whitney very well." Carrie's fists clenched on the table in front of her.

"Where did the coven meet? And how often?" Rebecca could guess but wanted to be sure.

"Sometimes we met online, but we preferred to meet at the Old Witch's Cottage. It was really important for all of us that no one knew what we were doing. My mom would've gone apeshit if she thought I was practicing magic. Abigail would call us up and tell us what time to meet. That's how we got Whitney to meet us that night too."

Rebecca only had to glance at Jake before he nodded at the door, letting her know without a word what she had to do next. She stepped outside and dialed the number for Marie's parents. Thankfully, the call was answered on the second ring.

"Hello?" Valerie Allman had picked up.

"Mrs. Allman? This is Sheriff West. Is Marie home? I need to speak with her right away."

"Hold on, Sheriff. We've just finished dinner, and she went to her room for a nap, I think. It *is* Thanksgiving, you know." That last bit came out sounding more than a bit miffed.

"And I wouldn't be interrupting your holiday if it wasn't very important, ma'am."

A brief pause was followed by the distant muffled sounds of a mother calling out to her child, the everyday symphony of family life playing its tune. But the melody was broken abruptly, transforming into a discordant note of panic. "Oh, god...I thought she was in her room, but she's not there. Her window is open too. She's gone! My husband just went outside to look for her."

"I need you to stay there. Call me if she shows up again or if she contacts you. We're going to search for her." Rebecca tried to calm the woman even as she started running for the exit. "Have you seen her friend Abigail recently?"

"No. I don't know anyone named Abigail. What makes you think she's her friend?" Valerie's voice was a high-pitched combination of confusion and terror. In the background, Rebecca could hear her opening and slamming doors as she searched for her child.

"I'm sorry, but I'll explain later. I'm going to look for your daughter now. Please let me know if you hear from her." Hanging up, she felt the cold bite of the island wind against her face as she stepped out of town hall and dialed her next call.

"Hey, Boss, what's up?"

"Frost, I need all units to converge on the Old Witch's Cottage, now. Bring everything you've got. I think Abigail's going to meet Marie Allman there. And I think she's going to kill her."

38

The Old Witch's Cottage stood in front of me, its outline blending in with the deep, eerie shadows of night as if it were also trying to hide. I had ditched the hot, blue-eyed deputy with a convincing enough smile and slipped inside my house only long enough to grab my bike from the garage.

My car, now a piece of evidence in their pathetic investigation, was off-limits. That was fine. It had served its purpose of linking Carrie to Whitney's death.

As I pedaled through the familiar streets, no one gave me a second glance. The cool air bit my cheeks, but the burn in my thighs was a welcome distraction from the chaos of the night. Carrie, the dumb bitch, was under arrest because of me. If she had the brains to save herself, she would've spoken up by now. But she didn't, and that silence was sealing her fate.

I trusted her to keep her mouth shut, not out of loyalty but out of self-preservation. She was neck-deep in Whitney's blood just as much as I was. Sure, I might've pushed her toward it, but Carrie was the one who actually stabbed

Whitney and helped me drag her body across the cemetery grounds.

Carrie was just as guilty as I was. More, maybe. There was no reason for her to turn on me. Doing so would only make her look worse.

I rested my bike against the gnarled wood of the cottage's tree line, not far from where I'd ditched the knife with Carrie's fingerprints on it. A damp chill lingered in the air, carrying the scent of wet moss and decay.

There was just one person left who knew what had happened.

Marie had been quiet, too quiet since the interviews. It made my skin crawl, that silence. She never fought back as hard as Sara or Whitney.

I wouldn't be able to pin this murder on Carrie. Not with her in custody, with a bunch of cops watching her every move. But that didn't mean I wouldn't get away with it.

The sheriff and her deputies believed every lie I fed them, and I had them eating out of my hand. Hell, the sheriff even bought me dinner because she felt so bad.

Yeah, I had this on lock.

The moon loomed over me like a giant eye as I sneaked into the shadow of the witch's cottage. I'd sent the text an hour ago, practically daring Marie to show up.

Come alone. Urgent. We're all that's left.

Marie—or should I say Minerva—would be arriving soon, if she knew what was good for her.

A single light pierced the shroud of night, and I turned to see someone walking up to stop at the edge of the clearing.

What a good girl.

"Minerva?" I faked a relieved smile as the shape started moving again. "I'm glad you came."

"Hey, Blair." She pointed the light up so it would

illuminate her face. "What's going on? Why are we meeting here? Did something happen?"

She was such a chatterbox, I was surprised she hadn't already spilled the beans. Minerva was a loose end and the final nail in Carrie's coffin. "Can't stay out here, can we?" I gestured to the open doorway. "It's not safe. Let's go inside, and I'll tell you then."

Minerva scanned the clearing. "Okay." She walked past me, only pausing a moment to step over the chain that still carried a vibrant yellow knot of crime scene tape the nerds had missed when they took the barrier down earlier.

Like a lamb to the slaughter.

A smirk tugged at the corner of my mouth. My hand slipped into the depths of my jacket, fingers grabbing the handle of my knife.

Just as I planned.

Checkmate.

39

Rebecca cursed under her breath when she saw a string of headlights approaching.

It had only taken moments after calling Hoyt before he radioed back to warn her that he, Trent, and Viviane were being followed by most of the reporters who'd been camped out for the last couple of days.

Apparently, seeing the cemetery mostly empty and the deputies all leaving at high speed meant they weren't willing to just go back to their offices without getting some answers. And on an island this small, it was nearly impossible to shake a tail.

A burst of dust billowed out from the tires, mingling with the shadows cast by the trees surrounding the Old Witch's Cottage. Those trees had only recently been used to form a yellow ring of crime scene tape, as had the posts in front of the door. Every inch of the area surrounding Whitney Turner's blood had been a crime scene. Rebecca hoped it wouldn't turn into one again tonight.

"Damn vultures can't even wait 'til the case is settled." Anger bubbled in her veins as she exited her cruiser. Then she noticed a light in the witch's cottage—not a reflection from a headlight, but a shifting patch of illumination.

A second later, it vanished.

As Rebecca unsnapped her holster, Hoyt slid into the parking space next to her and popped out of his cruiser like a jack-in-the-box. Trent and Viviane pulled up and joined them. Hoyt's eyes narrowed at the swarm of reporters that descended like locusts.

They started asking questions before they even got out. "Deputy Frost, what's going on?" one journalist shouted, thrusting a microphone in Hoyt's face. "Is this related to the serial killings buried in the cemetery?"

"Back off!" Hoyt roared, shoving the reporter aside. "You're obstructing an investigation!"

The other deputies, including Viviane and Trent, followed suit, pushing away the invasive journalists as they pulled in and got out. Trusting her deputies to keep the hordes at bay, Rebecca signaled to Viviane, the only one looking at her, that she was going in.

"Stay behind the cruisers!" Hoyt warned the reporters, his voice growing more authoritative. They hesitated before begrudgingly retreating as they continued to yell their questions.

Rebecca had her hand on her gun and her focus firmly on the opening to the cottage, the only way in or out. She continued out of the parking lot, walking in an arc to get a better view inside.

Trent and Viviane were suddenly at her back, forming a wall between her and some reporters.

"Back up! Do not cross over to this side of the cruisers. You all need to stay back." Viviane's normally happy tone was replaced with harsh authority.

"There's no way we're sneaking up on anyone now," Rebecca grumbled to Trent, who was beside her now, before raising her voice and turning. "If anyone dies tonight, I'm going to be making a statement to the press naming every photographer, newspaper journalist, and television anchor out here, as well as recommending charges on anyone I legally can."

"I'm taking names, Boss." Viviane brandished her notepad.

The threat of being name-dropped managed to finally get through to them, and the crowd that had been pushing against her deputies gradually eased off.

Rebecca approached the doorway of the cottage. The bright lights from the cameras and media van headlights glinted on the chain across the entrance, partially illuminating the interior. Thanks to the added light, she could see Abigail's face behind Marie's shoulder. They were against the back wall, their expressions a mixture of fear and confusion.

Marie's hands were clutched around a small flashlight while Abigail's were hidden behind Marie's body.

Rebecca stopped just short of the chain that cordoned off the open doorway. "Marie, Abigail, step away from the wall. We need to get you girls out of here and away from the reporters." Rebecca wondered for a moment if she should be glad the press had followed them out. Perhaps their ruckus had confused Abigail enough to delay her plans to turn on the remaining member of her coven.

"What's happening?" Marie's voice was trembling.

"Right now, you two are trespassing. We need you to leave, immediately." Rebecca carefully stepped over the chain as Abigail moved farther away from Marie, pressing herself against the wall. She couldn't reveal her suspicions about Abigail just yet. Both Whitney and Sara had been killed by knife wounds—and at this distance, Abigail could kill Marie before Rebecca would have a chance to fully draw her gun.

Viviane was just behind Rebecca on her right, doing her best not to block the light from the reporters and their vans. But then the headlights in the doorway went dark, and Rebecca stole a quick glance behind her. Hoyt and Trent had hopped the chain to prevent the media from filming what was happening inside the cottage, she guessed. But their presence had the unfortunate side effect of plunging the one-room building into darkness.

"Who are all those people outside?" Abigail had put on her scared and meek voice.

"Reporters." Rebecca squinted. Hoyt and Trent had moved away from the doorway, forcing her to adjust her eyesight, again, to the stark lighting and contrasting shadows caused by the overeager media. "Remember how they were bothering us earlier? Apparently, they don't take Thanksgiving off, and they keep following me and my deputies wherever we go."

Behind her, Viviane flicked on her flashlight and pointed it at the ground, helping to offset some of the contrast created by the bright lights from outside the cottage.

Rebecca continued to assess the risks. "Ladies, we got a call about trespassers out here, and they followed along like the pests they are. Right now, we need to get you two out of here and back home. I'm sure you'd like to spend the rest of the holiday with your families. You've probably got delicious pies waiting for you."

As she spoke, she studied both girls carefully in their spots near the opposite wall of the cottage. Marie's eyes were wide with fear, while Abigail seemed to be calculating, searching for an escape. Tension hung thick in the air, as if the very atmosphere was waiting for the next move. Rebecca had to tread carefully. One wrong step could fatally endanger Marie.

She held her breath, hoping her deception would hold up

under the girls' scrutiny. To her relief, it seemed as though they believed her—at least for now. Half a step back, Viviane was mirroring her movements, staying out of Rebecca's way.

Abigail's face was initially unreadable. Suddenly, her expression shifted to one of desperation, and she screamed. Backing away, she pointed an accusing finger at Marie.

"It's her! It's been Marie all along. I was wrong! She's the one who killed Whitney! Carrie was just her scapegoat. I came out here to talk to her about it, and she admitted everything!" She screamed so loud, the reporters outside were likely feasting on her statements.

Yep, Rebecca heard the excited drone of collective voices as they sensed headline news happening.

Marie's eyes widened in terror. "What? No! I didn't do anything!"

"Enough! Carrie's already confessed to both murders. Abigail, you don't have to be afraid anymore. That case is closed and neither of you need to worry about it right now." Rebecca did her best to look exasperated, an easy task, given the circumstances.

Right now, she needed to convince Abigail she wasn't a suspect so she wouldn't do anything stupid because she was afraid of being caught.

"I know you're scared, Marie, but right now, you're still trespassing. I need you to step toward me so we can escort both of you out of here safely. One at a time now. Let's go."

Marie didn't move. Rebecca's mind raced as she assessed the scene. Unable to shake the nagging feeling that something was about to go horribly wrong, she had no choice but to proceed carefully. One wrong move could send the entire situation spiraling out of control, and she couldn't afford to let that happen. There wouldn't be any more deaths in this little friend group if she had anything to say about it.

"Abigail, hun, don't worry." Viviane coated her words in

sugar. "We'll get you out of here too. None of this is your fault. I'm sorry the media jerks are making things way more complicated. Let's get you home so the sheriff and I can finally have our Thanksgiving dinners. Okay?"

"I'm sorry." Marie's tears streamed down her cheeks as she stepped away from Abigail. "I didn't know this was trespassing."

"It's all right, hun." Rebecca tried to copy the way Viviane sounded, but she couldn't pull off saying "hun" without it sounding weird and forced. Her heart was pounding in her chest. But outwardly, she remained calm, a pillar of strength in the face of danger as Marie put some distance between her exposed back and Abigail's hidden hands. "Now let's get you both out of here."

The air in the Old Witch's Cottage charged with electricity as Abigail's mouth fell open. Marie was now a few feet in front of her but still yards away from Rebecca, Viviane, and safety.

Rebecca saw it in her eyes, the split-second shift.

In one swift movement, Abigail brandished a knife from behind her back and lunged forward. She grabbed Marie by her coppery red hair and yanked her back. Even though she was bigger than Abigail, Marie was pulled off-balance.

"It wasn't me!" Abigail's voice cracked with desperation as she brought the knife down and pressed the tip of it against Marie's throat. "It was the witch. The witch killed Whitney and Sara. She's possessing me now! Please, she just wants to be set free!"

Marie screamed at the top of her lungs.

"Shut the fuck up, Minerva!" Abigail screamed back.

Rebecca's instincts kicked in, telling her this wasn't the right time to pull her gun. Viviane was by her side and must've sensed it, as she, too, stood steady.

Despite the adrenaline coursing through her veins,

Rebecca's voice was steady as she addressed Abigail. "Drop the knife, Abigail. It doesn't have to end like this."

But Abigail only tightened her grip on Marie, who didn't make a sound, though she looked increasingly terrified as she tried to wriggle away from the sharp knife.

That worked to her disadvantage as Abigail yanked her hair harder, prompting a squeal. She pressed herself more firmly into Marie's back, causing the knife to create a bigger indent in the poor girl's neck.

"No one's making you do anything you don't want to do, Abigail." Rebecca tried to remember everything she'd learned about the girl. The main thing that popped into her head was Abigail's pathological need to exert control over her surroundings. "We can help you. But you need to let Marie go and drop the weapon."

Abigail's eyes flickered with uncertainty, but she refused to relinquish her hold.

Rebecca held her hands up, showing they were empty. In her periphery, Viviane shifted her weight. She knew the young deputy was not just a crack shot but also fast on the draw.

"What do you want, Abigail? We don't want anyone else to end up like Sara and Whitney."

At Rebecca's words, Marie's expression shifted. Her terror turned into anger, and Rebecca had to clench her jaw. The entire situation was a powder keg, and she'd just lit the fuse. And she wasn't sure who was going to explode first.

Marie's mouth dropped open as she seemed to be putting everything together for the first time. "You killed them? You said the witch's curse killed them because they betrayed the coven!" She glanced down at the knife pressed against her throat. "You said we needed to meet this evening, but there's only the two of us. You wanted to kill me too!"

With a sudden surge of strength, Marie rammed her

elbow into Abigail's stomach, then headbutted her right in the nose as she bent over to catch her breath. Blood sprayed everywhere, and the knife clattered to the hard dirt floor as Abigail reached for her bloody face.

She still had a grip on Marie's hair, but the girl didn't seem to notice or mind, as she rounded on her would-be killer. "You bitch! I never should've trusted you!" Just as Abigail moved her hand away from her face to attack, Marie's fist came up and connected squarely with her cheek.

"Viviane!" Rebecca shouted, moving toward the tangled pair.

Abigail rocketed back, her head bouncing off the wall only to reconnect with Marie's elbow. And she didn't stop there. The pissed-off redhead proceeded to swing blindly. Her fists and feet pummeled Abigail from all angles.

Together, Rebecca and Viviane pulled Marie off Abigail, whose face was now streaked with blood and tears. Marie continued to kick and scream, her grief and rage spilling out uncontrollably as Rebecca finally managed to catch both arms and pull the girl away from her former friend with Viviane moving in.

"Boss?" Hoyt's voice was filled with worry.

Viviane grabbed Abigail by the arm and flipped her over onto her stomach, snapping handcuffs around her wrists. "Suspect is down. Victim is secured."

"Good. 'Cause we're blind as bats, thanks to these assholes shining their lights right into our eyes."

Marie's adrenaline must have run out at that point, because she collapsed in Rebecca's arms. She slowed her fall and lowered them both to the ground, wrapping an arm around the girl for comfort.

"I trusted her." Marie wailed as she held onto Rebecca's arm like a lifeline. "And she tried to kill me."

Rebecca's heart dropped at those words. She knew all too

well what betrayal felt like. Sitting on the cold ground, she shifted her free arm, brushing Marie's tangled hair away from her face. "I know, honey. I'm so sorry. I know."

Her sleeve was suddenly soaked with hot tears as Marie, a teenage girl who'd nearly lost everything, curled up in her arms and cried her heart out.

Viviane hauled Abigail upright, pausing to look down at Rebecca, silently offering her strength.

Booking Abigail Miller and dealing with the media outside could wait. Cradling the sobbing girl, Rebecca knew the most important job she had was to comfort her. The sting of treachery and deception hung heavy in the air.

The girl would never know how deeply Rebecca shared her pain or how badly she wished she could have prevented it.

40

Rebecca approached the two state police officers standing sentinel at the nondescript door, deep in the bowels of town hall. Their uniforms looked crisp and bright against the drab walls of the makeshift jail. Both women had showed up earlier, paperwork in hand, ready to transport their prisoner to a more secure jail, where she'd wait for her day in court.

Rebecca passed over the paperwork, releasing Abigail Miller to the state police. "Give me a few minutes, before you take her?"

"Of course." The shorter, dark-haired trooper's face betrayed a hint of curiosity.

"Don't worry, I'll update the recordings before I send them over." Rebecca opened the door, its hinges groaning in protest, and stepped into the dimly lit room.

Abigail, not yet dressed in the faded orange jumpsuit and white slip-on shoes she'd receive once she was booked at the jail, sat slouched over the single table, a picture of indifference.

She raised her head to see who'd entered and dropped it back down after making brief eye contact with Rebecca.

Her nose was still swollen, and she sported two black eyes. Marie had done a hell of a job. If Abigail had ever bothered to get to know her friends, she would've learned Marie had three older siblings, and all four of them went to the same MMA dojo to spar together, despite the six-year age difference.

Rebecca pulled out the metal chair across from Abigail and sat down, the sound echoing off the concrete walls.

"Your friends," Rebecca was loathe to use the word, since it was clear Abigail had no concept of friendship, "Carrie and Marie told us everything after your arrest. How you started the coven. How you demanded they follow your every word and stay quiet about the meetings you held. How you required them to pretend they barely knew each other in public. Now two are dead and one is guilty of murder. How does it feel, Abigail, to ruin three lives?"

Abigail's lips curved into a semblance of a smile as her eyes remained cold and detached. "Carrie dug her own grave. And Whitney's too." She snickered at her own sick joke. "I'm not responsible for her choices."

Rebecca felt a twinge of frustration at the girl's callousness. She had rarely discussed therapy with anyone, but she wasn't ashamed of it. Darian, Bailey, and her assistant Margo Witt had been to therapists too. And she'd bonded with Serenity McCreedy over that topic as well. The young woman before her could certainly benefit from a mental health professional. Or three.

Searching for a crack in Abigail's armor, Rebecca pressed on. "There's something I can't figure out. Why? Why the need to control and manipulate your friends like pawns? Why did your group even need a leader?"

"Without a leader, there's no point to forming a group." Abigail's voice took on an edge. "Friends should serve a purpose. Everything is transactional, isn't it?" A sigh broke out of her mouth that sounded too old and jaded for someone her age. "You go to your old auntie's house because she's about to die and you want to make sure you're in the will. So you make her feel loved."

Rebecca badly wanted to ask questions but held her tongue.

Abigail shrugged. "Then the old bag dies, and you take her money, and you use it so other people will treat you nice and make you feel loved. Transactional. Nobody really cares about each other, only what they can gain from the relationship." She shifted slightly in her chair. "Well, I didn't have money to buy love and obedience, so I had to use power. And you don't have power unless you have control. And you can't control people unless they're afraid of you."

"That's why you used the story of the old witch. The kids who grew up here already feared her. You just co-opted her legend to make yourself feared as well." It made a terrible kind of sense, if you were monster enough to apply that logic to living, feeling beings.

"Exactly." Abigail pushed herself up, looking a bit less bored now that Rebecca was catching on. "I'm not like my mother. She believes in the myth of 'true love' and 'finding her soulmate.' And all she ever got was left behind. I know love isn't worth the money it costs her to pretend. Fear and respect last longer anyway."

Rebecca searched Abigail's face as she absorbed the bleak worldview the young woman harbored, a life painted in stark tones of power and submission. Abigail's philosophy, a perversion of human connection, seemed woven into her very being. It was unsettling how a person could be so marred by another's search for happiness and love.

"Well, the good news is that where you're going, there's not a lot of need for money. And there's always going to be someone more powerful who wants what you have." Rebecca stood. "You should fit right in."

"Sounds great. I'll have to start at the bottom again and work my way up. But really, what's jail except a group that you can't get out of without dying?" Abigail grinned, and because of the dark bruises straddling her nose, she looked sinister.

Rebecca felt the air grow colder, the reality before her crystallizing with unsettling clarity.

This girl was a sociopath, devoid of empathy.

She could pour out all the truths about human kindness and compassion, but it would be like offering moral instruction to a statue.

Rebecca's thoughts wandered to Ryker, as they'd been doing. Though he'd betrayed her, she felt sorry for him, having learned how he'd been raised by monsters. Abuse was putting it lightly. But his actions in the end might've saved her life, and Rebecca couldn't help but still love him. Her favorite memory of them was still the first one, when she was just a little girl.

A boy with stick-thin arms had run up to her on the beach and asked if she wanted to play seaweed tag. For that month, they'd been the best of friends. And for several years after that too.

Looking back, she'd wondered where he'd gone or why he hadn't been around when she came back in her teenage years. Now she knew. But thinking about his smile, the sound of his laughter, and the way he looked at her like she was the most fascinating person he'd ever met…

With him dead now, she would never learn how much of that was real, but she missed that about him anyway.

"Everything has a price. Even love." Abigail gave her a knowing look, as if reading Rebecca's turbulent mind.

Rebecca shook her head. It didn't take a witch casting a

spell on her to know about her troubled past or her wayward and tragic love life. She was certain it had been the talk of town, once it came out that Ryker had been the son of the Yacht Club rulers.

There was nothing more to gain here. It was time to leave Abigail's twisted world behind.

Without another word, she got up and left the table.

Opening the door, she stepped out into the hallway. "She's all yours, ladies."

Her responsibilities taken care of, Rebecca walked past the troopers and headed out to where her SUV was waiting in the parking lot. The gold lettering down the side looked more brown than shiny metallic today, with winter's cloud cover settled over the island.

Rebecca climbed into the driver's seat and rested her forehead on the steering wheel.

Transactional relationships. Abigail and her mother weren't the only ones who believed in those. If she'd ever gotten the full truth out of Ryker, she was certain he would've admitted to it. Hell, the man had gotten a dog and pretended to care for it just to get close to her.

Trent Locke, Darian Hudson, and Greg Abner had only followed her because she was the interim sheriff. Meg Darby had only started talking to her for the same reason. She had power and authority in this tiny community. That was what had led most people to get to know her.

Even Hoyt…

She lifted her head and pondered that.

Hoyt had thrown a lot of responsibility at her feet, and that responsibility had come with a lot of authority over him as well. Perhaps he hadn't wanted to take that burden on himself, but he hadn't forced her into taking it, even if he did call her "Boss" all the time.

And Viviane…

She'd been a friend since their first meeting. Her first houseguest after moving here. Viviane had even brought over beer and chips and salsa, just to have an excuse to sit and get to know her. That had been before Wallace's death, back when Rebecca was still working as a temporary deputy.

She needed to stop letting Abigail's poison seep into her own worldview.

Rebecca took out her phone and called Hoyt.

"Hey, Boss, what's up? You need me to come back in?" She knew he was wary about another case dragging him back to the job. Still, his voice held a note of camaraderie. And hope.

"Nothing much, Hoyt." She knew that using his first name would make it clear this was a social call and not professional. "I have some paperwork I need to finish. But I was wondering if you'd mind if I swung by for a beer tonight?" She started the engine to get the heat going. "Humphrey's been getting restless, and I thought a doggy playdate could be just what he needs."

"Yeah, Rebecca. We'd love to have Humphrey over. You, too, of course." Hoyt's reply had his natural hint of humor peeking through his fatigue. "We've still got leftovers if you're hungry. Even though the boys have been out of the house for a while and didn't make it to town this year, we still make the same amount of food every Thanksgiving. So there's plenty if you want a plate."

There was a faint sound of Angie talking in the background.

"Angie says she'll put some of those hoity-toity coffee beer things in the fridge."

"Appreciate it, Hoyt. Angie's cooking is always worth the trip." A smile stretched her lips as she imagined the warmth of their kitchen, the savory aroma of Thanksgiving still lingering. And Angie had been thoughtful enough to stock her favorite beer, even though Rebecca knew neither of them drank it.

"See you in a couple of hours, then. I'll let Boomer know she's going to have company."

They both said their goodbyes, and Rebecca hung up before putting the SUV into drive.

The community might have its shadows, but it also had its havens—places where trust and friendship weren't a currency but a gift freely given. And as the sheriff, Rebecca was both a guardian of peace and a recipient of the bonds that held this island together. Shadow Island was a good place to call home.

41

Hoyt sat on his porch, a thick blanket draped over his lap to ward off the chill while he nursed a beer, its bitter taste doing little to distract him from the horrors that haunted his thoughts.

The past few days had been a nightmare, and today continued the trend. Their gruesome grand total at the cemetery had ultimately reached thirty-four bodies, when all the excavating had been completed. Blyberg's diligent crew had discovered four more bodies buried in shallow graves in the landscaped beds of the cemetery. Some of the victims had been identified, but most remained nameless, their stories still untold.

Of those who identified, most of them had ties to the Yacht Club. Several of the victims displayed the hallmark signs of a Stokely kill. Traces of drugs had been recovered from some of the bodies that still had tissue and hair, and a chilling five bodies had gunshot holes in their skulls.

"Angie's right," he muttered to himself, taking another swig of beer. "It isn't my fault...but I can't help feeling responsible."

He felt a sense of duty to Rebecca, to be there for her as she navigated these treacherous waters. His heart ached as he mourned the loss of both Greg and Alden, two men who'd stood by his side through thick and thin. And then there was Darian…

How could he have forgotten about him?

The realization shook him. His guilt wasn't just about the Yacht Club. It was about being the last man standing from a generation that had allowed such atrocities to happen under their watch. While Trent blamed himself, as well, Hoyt no longer agreed with that. The Yacht Club had gotten their tentacles into the younger deputy and turned him into an unwitting spy. The more he thought about it, the more Trent seemed like another innocent victim who'd been used.

It had started the night Alden died, gotten worse when Hoyt had been the only one left without a major injury after getting ambushed on Little Quell Island, and then reared its ugly head again when Greg had been shot while Hoyt was steering the boat chasing down one of the Yacht Club's hired killers.

When Boomer popped her head up from her resting spot on his blanket-covered feet, Hoyt realized Rebecca had arrived. The back door creaked open, and she stepped out into the cool night air, her face etched with exhaustion and sorrow.

Humphrey tumbled out next, chased by Angie's laughter.

Boomer rose up, her majestic tail swishing back and forth like a flag. She trotted over, and Humphrey calmed down enough to give her a few sniffs before leaping off the back porch to search for a stick for them to fight over.

Hoyt handed Rebecca a beer, and she accepted it with a nod of thanks.

"I told you he was restless."

Hoyt chuckled. "Aw, he's a young pup still. Chock-full of

the zoomies. Besides, it's been a hell of a week. He knows it too."

Rebecca nodded and sank down into the seat next to him. A seat once occupied by his best friend, Alden Wallace, after long days at work. They sat in silence for a moment, the weight of their shared burden pressing down on them like the darkness that enveloped their tiny island paradise.

The night stretched on around them, punctuated only by the distant cries of seagulls and the gentle lapping of waves against the shore. It was a stark contrast to the chaos that had consumed their lives in recent days—a reminder that even in moments of despair, there was still beauty to be found.

And judging by the excited barking happening along the dune line, there were also plenty of sticks to be found.

"Sorry." Hoyt spoke suddenly and without much thought.

"About what?" Rebecca looked at him, puzzled.

"Letting things on the island get so bad." He took a deep breath, his chest tightening with the weight of his confession. "Abner, Hudson, Wallace…this is all on me."

Rebecca shook her head and snorted. "None of those deaths are on you. If anything, they're all on me. Also, you had no way of knowing how bad things would get. Neither did they. If it wasn't for Abigail Miller, we still wouldn't know about those victims."

He sighed, running a hand through his hair. She was right, and that was even more depressing. "How'd the last interview with her go?"

"I'm no psychologist, but that girl is a total sociopath. Two girls are dead. Two girls are going to prison for a long time. Another is probably traumatized for life. And Abigail did it all just to feel like she had some kind of power in her life because she doesn't believe 'love is real.'" Her gaze drifted to the dogs racing back and forth in the unlit yard.

"Tragedy all the way around." Hoyt nodded but hesitated before speaking again. "I've been thinking about retirement."

"Have you got a date in mind yet?" She inhaled deeply and took a sip of her coffee-flavored beer. "I'd hate to lose you, but you've worked long and hard. You deserve to retire and spend more time doing nothing but this."

"Not yet. I have to see this through to the end. The bodies, the reporters, everything. I can't rest until this place is the peaceful paradise it's supposed to be."

Rebecca laughed, a hint of warmth breaking through the somber night. "Well, then, just let me know, and I'll schedule your retirement party…in ten thousand years once all crime has been eradicated."

Hoyt snorted. It did seem like an impossible task right now. But last Thanksgiving, he hadn't even believed the Yacht Club was a real organization to be taken down. Then they'd become the bogeymen of the island, and everyone thought they were untouchable. Now they were all in prison or in hell where they belonged.

Maybe it wouldn't take nearly as long as he feared. "I'll hold you to that. And allow you to pick up the tab too."

"Deal." Rebecca laughed and raised her beer.

As the two clinked bottles, Hoyt already felt a twinge of relief. If anyone could control Shadow's fate by straightening out the island and keeping it safe, it was Rebecca. And he was damn glad she'd made this little patch of sand her home.

42

Morning sunlight streamed through the gauzy curtains of Rebecca's kitchen, casting a warm glow over the polished stone countertops as she sipped her black coffee. The caffeine buzz hummed pleasantly in her veins, a welcome companion to the endorphins from her jog along the beach.

Humphrey was sprawled on the couch, his chest rising and falling rhythmically as he napped. Rebecca had plopped down next to him with her coffee.

She logged on to her computer and opened the portal for her eight o'clock telehealth session with her therapist. After she stared at the image of an empty couch in a virtual waiting room for a while, a ping sounded, and the face of her therapist filled the screen, a bright smile lighting her features.

"Good morning, Rebecca. How are things going?"

"Hey, Terri. I'm well."

Humphrey nuzzled her side, and his large snout made the therapist laugh.

"What would you like to talk about first? I know we had

to end the last session while you were still talking about Ryker. Do you want to pick up there?"

And with that, Rebecca unburdened herself. Everything about Ryker's betrayal came flooding out. She hadn't even realized it had been that close to the surface. She'd been over all the small deceptions, and she knew she should hate him for what he did. But she couldn't. Her love for him, even now, was as strong as ever.

Rebecca was often surprised during her therapy sessions at how just talking to someone brought clarity to her feelings. Understanding why she felt a certain way—and more importantly that it was perfectly normal—had helped her process more trauma in the past few years than most people had to deal with in an entire life.

It's part of the job.

Losing her parents, the destruction of romantic relationships, burying her colleagues and friends. It all took a toll. Thankfully, Terri had been a rock. A voice of reason and a nonjudgmental sounding board. Rebecca always felt lighter after her sessions, and she wished her schedule allowed her to meet with her therapist more often.

As the fifty-minute session came to an end, Rebecca closed out of the portal and stretched. Humphrey shifted his weight to press more firmly into her leg, as if to convey he didn't want her to get up.

The ringtone of her phone sliced through the momentary silence, and Rebecca reached for it with a sigh, not bothering to check the caller ID. "This is West." It had been a quiet weekend, but it was Monday morning again, and those always seemed to spell trouble.

"Rebecca, it's Meg Darby. I just wanted to thank you again for closing that case with the girls so quickly. You've got quite the knack for untangling these messes." Genuine gratitude underscored by weariness laced Meg's voice.

"Thanks, Meg." Rebecca perked up, surprised and relieved to be getting a phone call from a friend and not a call to show up at a crime scene this early in the morning. "How are you feeling?"

"I'm doing okay. Getting stronger every day. Dale's been fussing over me like a mother hen, so I'm happy to escape his good intentions by spending a few hours at town hall when I can."

"Oh, Meg, I'm so glad to hear that. You gave us one hell of a scare."

"Well, you can put your worries aside about me. I'm gonna be just fine." Meg cleared her throat, and Rebecca sensed a change in mood through the phone line. "Listen, I've been fielding calls all morning from folks around the island." An edge of frustration slithered into her tone.

"About the case?" Rebecca straightened, her brows knitting together.

"Sort of. It's those damn articles. I don't put any stock into what they're saying, and I doubt many here do either."

"Articles? What are you talking about?" Rebecca's hand tightened around her mug.

"Have you not read them?" Meg sounded genuinely surprised. "Do a web search for your name. You'll see what I mean."

"Give me a second." Rebecca set her cup down with a clunk and pulled her laptop from the coffee table. Her fingers flew across the keys, pulling up a search engine. She typed her name and hit enter, her heart rate ticking upward with each result that loaded onto the screen.

"Oh, boy..." Rebecca muttered as headlines screamed "Local Hero or Hidden Villain? Ex-FBI Agent's Dark Ties to Yacht Club" back at her. Each article painted her as a conspirator, alleging she'd orchestrated events from shadowy corners, even suggesting her departure from the FBI was due to illicit connections with organized crime.

"Jeez, I knew they'd be pissed after the way I yelled at them, but this is just slander." Anger boiled in her gut as she continued to skim the results. "But why are people coming to you with this crap? Why not me?"

"Most are just looking for confirmation, wondering if there's truth to the madness. They know I'll give it to them straight." Meg sighed. "As for why they're not hounding you…maybe it's just my position as the chair of the Select Board and retired dispatcher for the sheriff's office. People trust me."

"Your position…" Rebecca echoed, skepticism clouding her tone. She herself was a figure of authority, too, and yet they steered clear. Doubt gnawed at her. Was their trust in her waning so quickly? Because of a few salacious headlines? The articles themselves didn't even cite any sources.

"Rebecca, the journalists might've moved on to the next big story, but you know how this place works. This isn't necessarily over." Meg's voice softened with empathy. "People love to gossip, and right now, you're prime pickings."

"Thanks. I appreciate you setting things right where you can." Rebecca's words were tainted with resignation. "I just can't believe anyone would believe this trash."

"Of course I'm going to set them right. Like I've been saying all morning, those bastards are just mad you didn't give them interviews. And that's why they're trying to drag your name."

"I gave them interviews last time they came out and hounded me during a case." Rebecca tried to think back to how long ago that had been but couldn't remember. "They weren't even asking me anything new. You'd think if they worked in the news, they'd be able to at least come up with different questions."

Meg laughed. "Why bother when they can just make shit up? Anyway, hun, I just wanted to make sure you knew about this mess. And to remind you I've got your back."

"Thanks. I appreciate it. Truly."

After exchanging quick goodbyes, Rebecca hung up the phone, her gaze drifting to the sleeping form of Humphrey. He snored softly, oblivious to the turmoil that brewed beyond the walls of their sanctuary. She wished she could join him in his blissful ignorance, but possible defamation and slander lawsuits ruined any chance of it.

The serious allegations threatened to unravel the trust she'd nurtured within this community. As she considered the implications, the weight of the badge on her chest felt heavier than ever.

In a small, remote community like this, rumors spread like wildfire. And reputations were as fragile as sea glass. Rebecca knew the battle ahead would be about more than just clearing her name. It would be a fight to maintain the delicate balance of trust and order she'd worked so hard to establish.

Rebecca slumped into the plush cushions of the couch, exhaling a sigh as she settled next to Humphrey. The chocolate lab stirred briefly, lifting his head to glance at her with sleepy milk chocolate eyes before flopping back down. She clucked her tongue softly as her fingers scrolled through the litany of absurd headlines on her tablet. Each one was more preposterous than the last, a colorful mosaic of lies and exaggeration.

"Former FBI Agent Turns Rogue," one read, while another screamed, "Island's Hero or Hidden Villain?"

Rebecca shook her head, her lips curling into a wry smile. These journalists had no idea who they were dealing with. But if they were going to make her a villain, couldn't they have done something cooler? Like making her out to be a

Bond-type villain and not just "a narcissist drunk on her own power after being dispatched from the FBI."

Which didn't even make sense. Wouldn't being dispatched from the FBI have put a damper on her own power? Who wrote these headlines?

Her ringtone jerked her out of any brief amusement. She swiped the screen with a practiced thumb, bringing it to her ear. "Hey, Meg, did you see this one about me holding court every week because I'm obsessed with the sound of my own voice?"

"Uh, Boss, it's not Meg, it's Elliot." His tone was relaxed but professional.

"Elliot. Sorry about that. What's going on?" She straightened a little.

"Got a dead body at I Scream You Scream ice cream parlor. Looks like poison."

"A poisoning? Did someone die from eating ice cream?" Rebecca leaned forward, resting her forearms on her knees.

"Well, yes and no." The sound of papers shuffling indicated Elliot was reviewing the report. "It was called in as a medical emergency first. Ambulance crew tried, but…" He trailed off, the implication clear.

"Explain." She rose from the couch, Humphrey watching her with a puzzled expression, as if sensing the shift in the air.

"EMTs are trained to recognize certain things, you know? They think they know what killed him because of the symptoms." Elliot's voice lowered, and Rebecca could picture his light-brown eyes narrowing in concentration.

"Symptoms? What kind?" The list of possibilities ran through her mind like a Rolodex spinning out of control.

"He died from ingesting fentanyl. They think the fentanyl was *in* the ice cream."

The End
To Be Continued...

Thank you for reading.
All of the Shadow Island books can be found on Amazon.

ACKNOWLEDGMENTS

How does one adequately express gratitude to all those who have transformed a shared dream into a stunning reality? Let us attempt to do just that.

First and foremost, our families deserve our deepest thanks. Their unwavering support and encouragement have been our bedrock, allowing us the time and energy to translate our collective imagination into the words that fill these pages. Their belief in our vision has been a constant source of strength and inspiration.

As coauthors, our journey has been uniquely collaborative and rewarding. Now, with Mary also embracing the additional role of publisher, our adventure has taken on an exciting new dimension. This transition from solely writing to also publishing has been both a challenge and a joy, opening doors to share our work more directly with you, our readers.

We are immensely grateful to the entire team at Mary Stone Publishing — a group who believed in our potential from the very beginning. Their commitment extends beyond editing our words; it encompasses the tireless efforts of designers, marketers, and support staff, all dedicated to bringing our stories to life. Their expertise, creativity, and passion have been vital in capturing the essence of our tales and sharing them with the world.

However, our greatest appreciation is reserved for you, our beloved readers. You took a chance on our book, generously sharing your most precious asset—your time. It is our fervent hope that the pages of this book have rewarded that generosity, offering you a journey worth taking and memories that linger.

With all our love and heartfelt appreciation,

Mary & Lori

ABOUT THE AUTHOR

Nestled in the serene Blue Ridge Mountains of East Tennessee, Mary Stone crafts her stories surrounded by the natural beauty that inspires her. What was once a home filled with the lively energy of her sons has now become a peaceful writer's retreat, shared with cherished pets and the vivid characters of her imagination.

As her sons grew and welcomed wonderful daughters-in-law into the family, Mary's life entered a quieter phase, rich with opportunities for deep creative focus. In this tranquil environment, she weaves tales of courage, resilience, and intrigue, each story a testament to her evolving journey as a writer.

From childhood fears of shadowy figures under the bed to a profound understanding of humanity's real-life villains, Mary's style has been shaped by the realization that the most complex antagonists often hide in plain sight. Her writing is characterized by strong, multifaceted heroines who defy traditional roles, standing as equals among their peers in a world of suspense and danger.

Mary's career has blossomed from being a solitary author to establishing her own publishing house—a significant milestone that marks her growth in the literary world. This expansion is not just a personal achievement but a reflection of her commitment to bring thrilling and thought-provoking stories to a wider audience. As an author and publisher, Mary continues to challenge the conventions of the thriller genre, inviting readers into gripping tales filled with serial killers, astute FBI agents, and intrepid heroines who confront peril with unflinching bravery.

Each new story from Mary's pen—or her publishing house—is a pledge to captivate, thrill, and inspire, continuing the legacy of the imaginative little girl who once found wonder and mystery in the shadows.

Discover more about Mary Stone on her website.
www.authormarystone.com

Lori Rhodes

As a tiny girl, from the moment Lori Rhodes first dipped her toe into the surf on a barrier island of Virginia, she was in love. When she grew up and learned all the deep, dark secrets and horrible acts people could commit against each other, she couldn't stop the stories from coming out of the other end of her pen. Somehow, her magical island and the darkness got mixed together and ended up in her first novel. Now, she spends her days making sure the guests at her beach rental cottages are happy, and her nights dreaming up the characters who love her island as much as she does.

Connect with Mary online

facebook.com/authormarystone

x.com/MaryStoneAuthor

goodreads.com/AuthorMaryStone

bookbub.com/profile/3378576590

pinterest.com/MaryStoneAuthor

instagram.com/marystoneauthor

Made in the USA
Middletown, DE
12 August 2024

59009596R00159